The Twenty-Year Pact
By Larissa Johns

I0586001

THE TWENTY-YEAR PACT

First edition. April 4, 2022.

Written by Larissa Johns.

Dedicated to my ten nieces and nephews, whose names are hidden throughout the story. Thank you for being you!

Chapter 1: 2019

Love had never come easily for Freya Collins, or at least not until Jim Tyler came along. She'd met him six years earlier and had fallen for him, hard. It was basically love at first sight, something she had been far too practical to ever consider before meeting him. But Jim had changed everything, and she had assumed they would be together forever.

Until now.

"Jim," she screamed, tears forming in her eyes almost before she could process the sight in front of her. "What the hell are you doing?"

It was a ridiculous question. There were only so many reasons her boyfriend would be naked in their bed, atop a younger blonde woman, and none of them seemed particularly compatible with a continuing happy relationship.

"Freya!" Jim at least had the decency to look horrified as he got off the bed. "I... This isn't what it looks like."

A harsh laugh escaped her mouth. "No, I'm sure this is your accountant and you're getting your taxes done, right?"

The mystery blonde leapt out of bed then, grabbing at the dress which she'd discarded earlier on the floor. She slipped it over her head and wordlessly made her way to the door, not even bothering to pick up her bra and knickers. Freya stared at them on the floor. The underwear was, of course, matching, and much nicer than anything Freya owned. Typical mistress. She idly wondered if the other woman wore this stuff all the time, or if she'd made a special effort because she knew she was going to see Jim. Her boyfriend. Freya's boyfriend.

Freya fixed her steeliest gaze on Jim. People had always told her how withering her stare could be when she truly wanted it to, and there was true fire behind it now. "Get out."

"Frey –"

"Get. Out."

There was no point in arguing with her, and Jim knew it. He left, reminding Freya of a dog slinking out with his tail between his legs. Even though she was the one who had ordered him out, Freya was slightly stunned at how quickly a relationship could just... dissolve.

She sank to the floor, all the strength and fire she had directed towards Jim leaving her as she began to sob.

TWO HOURS LATER, FREYA was on her couch with her two best friends. Alex and Hannah were always the first people she called on in an emergency, and as always, they had dropped everything and come straight over.

"So," Alex said. "I think we can now safely tell you that we always thought Jim was a dick."

Freya sighed heavily. "That's not as helpful as you think it is."

"No, she's right," Hannah said cheerfully. "We never thought he was good enough for you. I mean, I never thought he'd *cheat* on you – partly because you were too good for him.

He should have appreciated that instead of shagging someone new."

"You could have told me this a few years ago," Freya grumbled, but she knew it wouldn't have done any good. When she'd been loved up with Jim, even her best friends' words of warning wouldn't have convinced her otherwise. *They just don't know him the way I do,* she would have argued. *They don't see the real Jim.*

Well, she'd seen the real Jim now, and it wasn't good.

"Please," Alex snorted, clearly coming to the same conclusion. "Then you'd just have kicked us to the kerb and kept him."

"Never," Freya protested. She knew she wouldn't have been receptive to Alex or Hannah telling her what they really thought of Jim before today, but she would never have ditched her oldest friends over it, either.

"What's the plan?" Hannah asked. "Will you keep the place?"

"We didn't really get into all of that. I was too busy throwing him unceremoniously out of my house."

"Go, Freya!" Hannah said, leaning in for a high five.

"I don't even want to talk to him again, but I guess I'll have to," Freya sighed. "We can make our arrangements and he can get the hell out of my life."

"Empowering."

"It doesn't *feel* particularly empowering. I just... I don't know. I never thought I'd be single again." Freya tried not to sound as self-pitying as she felt. She'd never really had an issue with being single, but being with Jim had given her such a feeling of security, she hadn't imagined she would ever wind up here again.

"I know, right? We're all thirty-seven and unhappily single," Alex said. "Does it get any more pathetic than that?"

"Probably not," Hannah replied casually, popping a handful of M&Ms in her mouth. "Well, at least until we're thirty-eight and all unhappily single. Or..." she shuddered. "...*Forty* and all unhappily single."

"At least you're thinking positive."

"We need that pact we set up in high school," Freya said, laughing through her tears. "Remember that?"

Alex frowned in confusion, then the penny dropped. "Oh. The Twenty-Year Pact?"

"Yeah. You know, we made that twenty years ago this year. We're due to be married by now. That's what we need," Hannah laughed. "Arranged marriages. If only we were still in touch with the boys, all our problems would be over."

Chapter 2: 1999

"Freya!" Hannah said in a loud stage whisper, beckoning her friend. "Come here!"

Freya sighed as she got up from her bench seat in the library, where she usually spent most lunchtimes. The bench seats were a new instalment the previous year, and she'd been excited by the opportunity to have a comfortable, private spot to read by herself. The only problem was that everyone now knew she could be found there. It was tough to find alone time when everyone around you was so bloody social.

"Hey, Han," Freya said as she approached her friend. "What's up?"

It was their second break on a Friday, and Hannah often had some suggestion of something to do before they made their way home after school. They attended school in Fortitude Valley, an inner-city school, which meant they all needed to get public transport home. The other two lived relatively close to the city, but Freya's bus ride home was over forty minutes. Hannah never really understood that all Freya wanted to do after school was get home so she could relax. Freya sometimes wondered if Hannah was even capable of relaxing. She always seemed to be on the go.

Sure enough, "Let's go into the city after school," Hannah said now, opening the door to lead them out of the library and onto the sunny steps outside. "I want to see a movie."

Freya suppressed a groan. "No, thanks, Han. I really just want to get home today. I have a new –"

"Don't be boring," Hannah answered, her typical response whenever someone didn't want to go along with one of her many schemes. "Everyone's in. Nick's coming, of course," she said, naming her boyfriend of three months. "And Alex. And Sam. And *Ethan*," she added meaningfully, wriggling her eyebrows up and down.

Freya rolled her eyes. Nick wasn't Hannah's first boyfriend, but he was the most serious one yet. Hannah had been boy crazy for years now, but it had only got worse, rather than better, now that her gaze was focussed entirely on Nick rather than being shared between all the boys in their grade. He was the first guy she'd really fallen for. They'd been friends for years, which seemed to help make things more serious for Hannah. They'd met back in Year 8, when they shared Science class together. Freya could still remember Hannah gushing about her crush on the cute brown-haired, brown-eyed boy in her class. When Freya met him she had taken an instant liking to him, too, but in a purely platonic way. He had introduced them to his best mates, Sam and Ethan, and the six of them had remained friends since. It had always felt like a split group – the three girls and the three guys – but now that Nick and Hannah were together, there was nothing split about it. Hannah and Nick were joint at the hip, so the rest of the group seemed to be spending all their waking moments together, too. Freya liked them all, but sometimes she wished she could go back to the times when it was just the three of them. She always felt a little shyer in a big group, and she liked the way she was able to open up more with her two closest girlfriends. She would never say anything to Hannah, though. Freya felt like if she tried to take a step back from the group of six Hannah would take a step back from her, instead.

It wasn't that Hannah wasn't a good friend, she was just... obsessed. She couldn't stop talking about Nick, he went everywhere she went, and Alex and Freya had heard far more than they would have liked about their personal life. Hannah and Nick had had sex for the first time on their one-month anniversary, and Hannah had discovered a whole new world. She was the only one of the three girls to have lost her virginity, and she seemed hellbent on making it her mission to get her friends across that line, too.

"I'm not interested in Ethan," Freya said, patiently, for what felt like the hundredth time.

Hannah laughed. "So you keep saying. But before we got together Nick kept insisting he wasn't interested in me, either, and look at us now."

"I don't care what Nick said! I'm telling you the truth. I'm *not* interested in Ethan."

Freya was, in fact, telling her friend the truth. She liked Ethan, but not as anything more than a friend. Sure, he was cute enough, in a geeky sort of way, with his brown hair, freckles and skinny frame. And he was a nice guy, and funny. But the truth was, she had little interest in any boy. She didn't think she was a lesbian, or anything like that. She simply didn't feel like dating anyone. Her older sister Iris had met her first boyfriend in university, and they'd been together for three years now.

Freya didn't really see the point of dating anyone in high school. It wasn't as if those things ever worked out, anyway. What was the point of putting all your energy into dating someone if it wasn't going to last?

AS ALWAYS, HANNAH GOT her own way and soon the six friends were taking the fifteen-minute walk from the Valley to the city, chatting amiably on their way. Hannah's enthusiasm was infectious, and even Freya had started to look forward to the movie outing. She had called her parents from Alex's phone before they left to tell them she'd be late. Quite a few of the Year 12 students had their own phones now, but Freya's parents were a holdout. It didn't really matter too much, since she could always use a friend's phone when she needed to get on to her parents, and she'd never really loved talking on the phone anyway.

"Thank God it's the weekend!" Hannah exalted as they approached the cinemas. Nick was walking with his arm draped around her, and she grinned at her friends. "And the finish line is in sight," she added.

Freya felt her stomach drop. She knew Hannah was referring to the end of the school year, which had been one of her favourite topics of conversation since late the previous year. Freya knew she should be excited for graduation, like everyone else, but she couldn't imagine life without the routine of school. Unlike most of her friends, Freya actually enjoyed school, and she had applied to study education at university. Alex was planning to study psychology, while Hannah was planning to take a year off to "find herself". Every so often Alex asked her what she was planning to do during her year of discovery, but Hannah just laughed it off and said, "As little as possible!"

Freya couldn't imagine it. If anyone had an excuse to be blasé about the future it was Alex, with her wealthy family, but she had a strong work ethic and was completely motivated for her future career. Unlike Freya, she even seemed *excited* about leaving school and going to Uni. Didn't Hannah want to start studying or working like the rest of them did? Freya honestly wasn't sure if her friend didn't care about her future, or if she just had no idea what she wanted to do with her life and was covering it up by pretending not to be interested.

They arrived at the cinemas with no plan of what to see, like they usually did. Calling the movie line seemed more tedious than just turning up and seeing what was on, so unless they were at Alex's house and could read her dad's newspaper, taking a chance was the way they went about it. There was almost always *something* they could see, and on the off chance there wasn't, they would go for milkshakes at the café next door.

"There's not much on," Sam said, frowning at the list of titles.

"Oh, I want to see that one!" Alex said, pointing.

"*The Pact*?" Ethan asked, frowning dubiously. "That sounds... romantic."

"It isn't! Well, it kind of is, but it's a comedy. It's about a couple who makes a marriage pact when they're young."

"Hmmm," Sam said doubtfully, but Nick shrugged.

"There's not much else on. Come on, let's go."

They all bought their tickets and popcorn, then headed into the cinema.

"Come sit here, Freya," Ethan said cheerfully, patting the chair beside him.

Freya forced a smile. She'd always enjoyed Ethan's company, and when they were fourteen and fifteen they'd actually had a lot in common, chatting about their mutual interest in science-fiction books and their love of animals. He'd even lent her some of his comics, something she'd never thought she'd be interested in, and she'd been surprised by how much she enjoyed them. Over the last year or so, though, his feelings had obviously become something more, and now there was an uncomfortable vibe between them – or at least it felt that way to Freya. She hoped he would just get over his crush and they wouldn't have to talk it through or anything. She had no idea how to let a guy down gently, and she knew for sure she didn't want to go out with him.

Freya sat down beside him, unsure how to get out of it. Besides, she could at least sit next to him in a movie. It wasn't like he was going to try anything in front of all their friends. Hannah and Nick were snuggling together in their seats, of course, and Sam and Alex were chatting away cheerfully as well. Freya wished it could be as easy for her as it was for her friends.

"What have you been up to lately?" Ethan asked when they were both seated. "I feel like I haven't seen so much of you."

Well, that wasn't true. The six of them had had lunch together every day for the past month. She wondered if he meant that he hadn't seen much of her alone, which *was* true. Last year they'd been in the same French class, but this year they didn't have any classes together, so they only saw each other as part of the bigger group. Freya was quite happy with that arrangement. Ethan was never pushy, but he was also never as subtle about his feelings as he probably thought he was. He was always finding excuses to sit near her, and he had arranged a few weekend catch-ups for the group. When she told stories in their group, his eye contact was pretty intense. If Freya was interested in dating, she might have been thrilled by his attention, but it just made her feel awkward.

To her relief, the trailers started before they could get into a proper conversation. Freya settled back into her seat and waited for the movie to start.

"THAT'S WHAT WE SHOULD do!" Alex exclaimed two hours later, as they walked out of the movie.

"What's what we should do?" Ethan asked, looking around in confusion.

"We should make marriage pacts."

Freya started to laugh, but then realised her friend was serious. "You're joking, right? We're only seventeen."

Alex rolled her eyes. "Not pacts for *now*. Pacts for later. For like, twenty years from now."

Hannah raised her eyebrows doubtfully. "As if we're going to be single in twenty years."

"Then what's the harm in creating a pact?" Alex replied. She looked around at the group of them. "I was thinking about it during the movie. We're all friends, right? And we're three girls and three guys, so it's perfect."

Hannah reached protectively for her boyfriend. "You're *not* marrying Nick."

"Oh, I wouldn't dream of it," Alex laughed. "You can have Nick, obviously."

"We'll already be married by then, anyway." Hannah smiled lovingly at her boyfriend. "*Obviously*."

Nick gave a nervous laugh.

"Okay, so you two are married off. So then Freya and I get to choose between these two handsome gentlemen."

"I'll take Freya," Ethan said quickly, and Freya started to blush. She heard Hannah snort out a laugh behind her. "I bet you will," Hannah muttered under her breath.

"Alright," Alex said, turning to Sam. "That leaves you and me, baby."

Sam laughed. Neither he nor Alex had ever shown the faintest interest in the other beyond an easy friendship, but his cheeks were tinged with pink now. "Sure," he said awkwardly. "Why not? But only if we're both single in twenty years."

Chapter 3: 2019

Hannah Nicholson had never been short of confidence – or male attention, for that matter. Her frame was on the curvy side, but in that sexy, voluptuous way, even back in high school. She was a D cup by the time she was in the tenth grade, which earned her the boys' attention. Her flirtatious nature kept them keen. Nick was the twelfth guy she'd kissed at the school, but he had been her first serious boyfriend.

Now, at thirty-seven, Hannah was the same girl she'd always been, at least on the outside. She still had the same sparkling green eyes, caramel coloured hair and her million-dollar smile. If you asked people to describe her, she knew they might say things like *loud, brash, confident* or *the life of the party*.

On the inside, she felt like everything had changed.

Looking back on her high school days, it felt as if she might as well be watching a movie. It didn't feel like those experiences had really happened to her. She couldn't explain it. She remembered the intensity of her relationship with Nick, naturally, and she remembered how much she had giggled with her girlfriends: Freya and Alex, of course, but also the larger group of them, the group that came together for parties or school dances. They weren't her closest confidantes, but they were always there for her.

What she didn't remember was *appreciating* it all.

Her grandma had always said "Youth is wasted on the young". Hannah had hated the expression when she was growing up. Youth wasn't wasted on the young; youth would be wasted on the old! They'd just spend their days in their armchairs, watching life passing them by, complaining about everything. No, you had to be young to truly live your best life.

Now, though, she understood what her grandmother had meant. If she was given her youth back again, she would really make the most of it. She knew it sounded shallow, but she'd love the opportunity to be so popular again. She still had her fair share of friends, of course, but she didn't have the sheer amount of people her own age around her like she did when she was a teenager. Her work as a personal trainer wasn't exactly solitary, but she spent a lot more time with clients than with colleagues. A lot of her co-workers were younger, anyway, and they didn't seem to have all that much in common. Hannah knew most of the people who were around her regularly would call her a friend simply because of her outgoing personality, but she didn't feel like they saw the real her. Freya and Alex did, but they were both so different to her. She thought their differences made the friendship work – opposites attract, after all – but she knew the other two had a lot more in common than she did with either of them. The three of them were all equally tight, but she still couldn't help but feel left out when Alex and Freya started talking about some of the intellectual things they found fascinating.

Her love life wasn't what she'd expected as a teenager, either. She'd slept with a hundred men – and a woman or two – since Nick, but none of them compared. Not physically, of course; she'd had some pretty fantastic sex in the intervening years, and while it had always been good with Nick, their mutual inexperience had definitely showed. But never again did she feel the same irresistible *pull* towards a guy. Never again had a partner filled her thoughts the way Nick had when she was a teenager. She sometimes wondered why that was. Would it be possible for anyone to do so? Had she just not met the right man since, or was it impossible for any romance to be as powerful as your first?

"Hannah," a male voice said beside her. She turned, startled, and saw Angus, her co-worker at the gym. "Are you okay?"

"Yeah," she said, brushing a stray hair out of her eye. "Why?"

Angus gestured towards the machines. "You're blocking me. I asked you if you could move."

"Oh! Sorry." She moved out of the way as requested, smiling apologetically at Angus' client. It was the end of Hannah's lunch break and she needed to get back to work. She had no business just standing there, starting into space like an idiot and reminiscing about the high school days.

Her own client arrived a minute later, and Hannah busied herself with working her way through their routine. She'd stumbled her way through a few jobs after she finished school, but hadn't really found anything she loved until her mid-twenties. She lived at the gym anyway, and she'd struck up a friendship with Jessica, one of the personal trainers. After a particularly rigorous gym session Jessica had mentioned that she thought Hannah would make a great trainer herself. It had never been something she'd considered, but she'd thrown herself into her course, and then the job itself, with gusto. It was the perfect fit for her personality. She was bubbly and she could talk to anybody. Her enthusiasm for life motivated the people around her, which got better results from her clients as they tackled their gym work. No two days were ever the same, which meant she didn't get bored.

Only Hannah knew that when she got home she collapsed on the couch, exhausted. Only Hannah knew that it wasn't the physical demands of her job that caused her such fatigue, but the requirement to be 'on' all the time. Only Hannah knew that inside the confident, energetic body there lived a quieter, more serious person. Sometimes she wished there was someone around her who could see the real her.

Chapter 4: 2019

Alex Reynolds was disciplined. It was the most apt word to describe her. She managed her life with a strict routine. Three mornings a week – Tuesdays, Thursdays and Saturdays – she got up early and went for a jog before work. Monday nights she did a cook up for the week ahead. On the last Tuesday of each month, she had her book club. Wednesday nights, she used her body scrub and face mask and kept the TV off, instead reading or catching up on emails. Thursday nights, she had family dinner with her parents and siblings, as well as their partners and children. Fridays brought Indian takeaway and a movie at home.

Of course, she wasn't completely inflexible. Every so often she had reason to go out, which would shift her routine. Freya and Hannah coaxed her out every so often, and much more rarely, she would go out on a date. For the most part, though, she stuck to her routine. Her friends thought the strictness of her life was dull, but Alex truly enjoyed knowing what each day was going to bring. She liked the structure. She knew she was a fun person to be around; her idea of fun just looked a little different to some other people's.

The one thing that hadn't fitted into her timeline was her love life. At Uni, she had it all planned out. She would meet the right man in her twenties (by twenty-eight at the latest), and marry him around her thirtieth birthday – a little before or a little after was fine; she could be flexible here. She was fairly ambivalent on the idea of having children, so that would be up to her partner, but if he did want to have kids, they would have two of them, with the second born before her thirty-fifth birthday.

It was all neatly planned.

The only thing she hadn't accounted for was that she would have to find a man who was not only willing to go along with her plan, but whom she also deemed suitable to fill that role in her life.

So far, she hadn't.

She was actually reasonably contented being single. She hadn't been in a relationship since she and James had broken up three years earlier, and she'd only had a couple of dates since. For a while there Alex had thought James was the one, but it wasn't meant to be. He thought she was too rigid; she thought he needed to grow up. He was only two years younger than her, but sometimes it seemed like a lifetime.

James had hated her routines.

Her friends had teased her about that, too, when enough time had passed after the break-up for them to be able to joke about it. They acted like his disdain for her routines was the only reason they'd split. "How much does Alexandra Reynolds love her routines?" Hannah had asked, and Freya had replied, "More than her boyfriend!" They had fallen about laughing.

Alex hadn't laughed.

The truth was, she *would* have given up her routines for the right man. Of course she would have.

But the right man wouldn't have wanted her to.

FROM VIRTUALLY THE moment she started high school, Alex had known that she wanted to go into psychology when she graduated. Her cousin Blake was a psychologist, which was probably what had prompted the decision, but she couldn't remember ever making the choice to do it. It had seemed as natural as waking up each morning.

Perhaps because it had all seemed so pre-destined, it was all the more disappointing to Alex when she had only lasted a couple of years in private practice. Maybe she was too empathetic, or maybe she just wasn't cut out for the work. She couldn't handle it. In her mid-twenties she'd had some kind of quarter-life crisis, and in an uncharacteristic move she'd quit her job without really thinking it through. After a stressful month of unemployment, she had found a job as a telephone counsellor at Kids in Crisis, an anonymous helpline, and she'd never looked back. She loved helping the kids over the phone, and the fact that they were anonymous and usually one-time callers meant that she didn't get emotionally invested in the same way as she had with her face-to-face clients. Kids in Crisis didn't pay the kind of money she could have earned in private practice, but it was a lot less stress, and a lot more exciting. For her, anyway. She knew some of her colleagues burnt out, unable to face the fact that they didn't know what the caller on the other end was going to say, or how extreme their problem was going to be. Some couldn't face not knowing the end result, the way you would with a physical client. But to Alex, that was a benefit. It gave her the distance she needed to provide information and move on with her day.

Another benefit was that the work itself didn't seem that hard to Alex. At first she had wondered if she was doing it wrong; if the fact that it seemed relatively easy to her meant that she wasn't doing a good enough job. Eventually she had realised that she was just doing exactly what she was supposed to be doing with her life, and it felt easy because she was where she was supposed to be.

Today, though, was more stressful than most. The phone wouldn't stop ringing, her shift replacement was late, and they were already short staffed that week. She just wanted to get out of there and head home to make dinner and relax, but she couldn't leave until Holly, her replacement, turned up. Alex sighed heavily, stretching her neck from side to side in an effort to relieve the tension in her shoulders.

It was times like this when she wished she had someone to go home to. Alex knew she was lucky; she was perfectly happy in all the ways that really mattered. But the bad days seemed worse when you couldn't go home and vent to a sympathetic partner. It seemed like everything would be a little bit easier if she could get a foot rub from someone. At least she had her dog, Baxter, to greet her at the door every night.

She should be used to it by now, really, after three years of the single life. Hannah flitted from relationship to relationship, and Freya had been with Jim for so long. Alex had always seen herself as the odd one out, the one who just couldn't find the right man. But now, for the first time she could remember, they all seemed to be in the same boat. Freya's relationship had imploded while Hannah hadn't even been on a date in two months, which was a record for her. Alex was obviously upset about Freya being so heartbroken by Jim, but she had to admit it was nice not to be the only single one for once.

It was strange that none of them had ever married. Of course, Freya and Jim had essentially been married for a few years now, but Alex was glad they had never made the commitment official. Even though they lived together, the break-up would be more straightforward this way. Alex had thought she might marry James for a while there, and they'd even had a few discussions about getting engaged. But deep down, she had known there was something missing. The idea of making a lifelong commitment with someone you weren't sure about was terrifying, but was anyone ever really sure? Or were other people just more daring than Alex was? She knew Freya would have said yes to Jim if he'd ever asked, but he had never been worthy of Freya, even before they knew he was a cheater. As for Hannah, she didn't seem to feel the need to settle into any kind of serious relationship, let alone to marry someone. Sometimes Alex was envious of that. It had to be easier to negotiate the single life if you were as happy with it as Hannah obviously was.

She couldn't stop thinking about the pact that Freya had brought up. It had been Alex's idea in the first place, back when they were teenagers. She'd been joking, to an extent. She'd seen the movie and got carried away. She probably never would have suggested the pact if she'd thought it would really happen, and she *knew* Freya, with her famed disinterest in the opposite sex back in their school days, never would have agreed to it if she'd taken it as anything more than a joke. Besides, even if there had been a part – a small part – of Alex that had taken it seriously, the way things had ended up with the three guys didn't exactly open things up to the possibility of endless love.

As they'd grown up, she'd thought less and less of the pact, but maybe the fact that they were all now single, twenty years later, meant something. Maybe it was a sign of some kind. After all, what were the chances that they would all end up single at the exact time the pact was meant to come to fruition? She wondered if the three men were single, too. Surely not! The odds were certainly against it. It was pointless to even think about it.

"Sorry! I'm here!" Holly burst in, breathless, pulling Alex out of her thoughts. "The bus was late, and it's raining out there, so it was all a bit crazy. But I'm here now!"

"Oh," Alex said, trying not to look as flustered as she felt. "That's okay. I was just about to head off." She packed up her things and left as soon as she could, not wanting to make any more conversation than she had to.

On her walk to the Southbank train station, rain sleeting down on her, Alex returned to her thoughts. When she was on the train and out of the weather, she pulled her phone out. On impulse, she messaged Hannah and Freya in their group chat.

Alex: I know it's late notice, but anyone free for dinner tonight?

Hannah: Ooh, look at Ms Reynolds being all spontaneous!! I'm in!

Freya: Can you guys come to me? I'm still miserable and I look like a pile of shit.

Alex: I'm sure you don't, but we can definitely come to you. Anything for our bestie in her hour of need.

Freya: My hour of need may yet turn into a week of need. A month of need. Potentially a decade of need. Bestie needs chocolate.

Hannah: Alex can bring chocolate, I'll bring the wine. Sounds needed.

Freya: Also, don't expect my house to be tidy.

Alex smiled fondly as she read that. Freya always warned them that her house was untidy, only for them to walk in and find it neat and organised.

Alex: Sure, sure. Are we getting dinner along with this chocolate and wine?

Freya: We can get takeaway. Sounds like we have it all covered. See you soon!

Chapter 5: 1999

Nick was famous for his parties, and Hannah was particularly excited for this one. It would be the first since they'd become an item. She saw it as her golden opportunity to make her debut as Nick's girlfriend, officially. Everyone in their grade knew they were together, but Hannah figured it couldn't hurt to let everyone see it for themselves. She wasn't talking about public displays of affection or anything immature like that, of course. Nick and Hannah were far too settled to need to do anything like that. No, she was going to appoint herself the official co-host of the party. When the other Year 12 girls saw her swanning around, offering plates of chips to guests like she owned the place, there would be no doubt in their minds about how serious the relationship was.

It wasn't as though Hannah was insecure. It just didn't hurt to make sure everyone knew the score. After all, Nick was hot with a capital H. It was only natural that some of the other girls would have their eyes on him, so she needed to make sure they knew not to try anything.

She had another plan for the evening, though. As well as elevating her social status, Hannah had serious plans to work on the developing relationships between Sam and Alex and

Ethan and Freya. After all, they'd made *marriage pacts* only a week ago! Her two girlfriends didn't seem to have too much genuine interest in the boys just yet, but they would get there. How perfect would it be if the three couples really did end up together? They could be friends forever, the six of them having dinner parties once a week. Going away on beach holidays together each Christmas. They could even have babies at the same time and raise them like cousins! It would be amazing. It was certainly more than Hannah had ever had, growing up. She was close enough to her mum, but Dora Nicholson was a hard-working single mother who was also trying to have her own love life, so she wasn't around as much as Hannah would have liked. Hannah wasn't particularly close to her older brother Isaac, and she had no cousins. It wasn't exactly the kind of family life you watched sitcoms about. The thought of a big, extended family around her – even if it was made up of friends rather than actual family – was hard to resist.

It was uncharacteristic of Alex to suggest the marriage pact, but it was a good sign, as far as Hannah was concerned. It showed that her friend had at least some interest in boys and getting married someday.

When the day of the party rolled around, Hannah had her plan well in hand. She would keep finding excuses for the guys to talk to the girls, to strike up conversations and get to know each other a little better. Then, after they'd had some quiet alone time, she would suggest a group game of spin the bottle, casually designed to get her friends kissing their potential love interests. It was possibly a bit on the immature side – they were in Year 12, after all – but she could play it off like it was just a bit of a laugh, even though she was deadly serious about it. Who knew the effect the game could have on her friends? Maybe they would find true love, and it would all be thanks to Hannah.

It was a smaller party as far as Nick's get togethers went, with only about thirty people there, all from school. With nearly three hundred people in the year level, Hannah didn't know them all well, but she smiled and made everyone feel welcome, doing her bit as the good host.

When Ethan and Sam walked in together, Hannah wasted no time in racing over to them. "Hi, guys!" she called, shooting them her most winning smile. "How are you going? Do you want a drink or anything?"

"Let us come in first," Ethan laughed, looking around. "Where's Nick?"

Hannah waved her arm vaguely through the air, as though Nick's appearance at his own party couldn't have been less important. "He's around here somewhere. I'm co-hosting," she added, self-importantly. Of course, Nick hadn't actually used the term 'co-hosting' as such, but she knew he wouldn't mind.

She dashed off to get them their requested drinks. On her way back she ran into Alex, who had just walked in. "Oh, Sam! Alex is here," she called out in a singsong voice as she handed him his drink. She felt a smug satisfaction at seeing Sam blush slightly.

Sam and Alex had sort of got each other's names by default in the marriage pact, but it was actually perfect. They were both blonde, pale and blue-eyed, so they looked good together, but they were well-suited in other ways, too. Alex was the academic girl, the 'band geek' of the group. She had always reminded Hannah of a swan as she glided her way through life, tall and skinny and graceful, her hair always up in a high bun. Alex was a lot of fun in her own way, but she was also on the quieter side, organised and structured. She knew where she was going in life and she had the work ethic and ambition to get there. She was the perfectionist, the youngest of four in a wealthy family, and failure wasn't an option. Sometimes Hannah wondered how her own, often scatterbrained nature fitted into Alex's life, but their friendship had always worked for them.

Sam, too, was a quieter soul, happier to listen to other people than to be the centre of attention. Ethan, on the other hand, was the class clown, always ready to make conversation with anyone. Freya sat somewhere between Hannah and Alex on the introversion scale. She had her more demure side, but once you got her talking you couldn't stop her chatting away and giggling. Ethan could bring out her fun side, while she could bring down his tendency to need to show off. It was meant to be.

Hannah and Nick, of course, were both athletic, popular, and – could she say it about herself? – charming. If you looked through a catalogue of all the people at school, it was pretty likely you would pick out Hannah and Nick as the other's perfect partner. Hannah wasn't full of herself, but she was confident enough to know they were two of the better-looking people in the grade, too. She just *cared* more about her appearance than some of the other girls, who thought a simple ponytail was good enough to turn up to school with.

Yes, Hannah thought to herself with a feeling of satisfaction, they were three matches made in heaven. The boys seemed ready to be persuaded of that fact, too. She just had to convince her girlfriends.

Chapter 6: 2019

"So how have you been, Freya?" Alex asked when the three women were settled on Freya's lounge. The house wasn't quite in its normal state of near-perfection, but it was close enough, considering just over a fortnight had passed since Freya had had her heart broken. Alex sometimes wondered if Freya actually soothed her problems by cleaning. If so, it was a tactic Alex wished she could adopt. She certainly wasn't untidy on a typical day, but when things were falling apart like they were for Freya, the house fell apart, too.

"I'm okay. I'm adjusting," Freya said. "I actually think I'm more upset by the loss of a relationship than by the loss of Jim himself. You know? Like, I knew who I was when I was with him. Now that I'm single, I'm not sure."

"I can't relate," Alex laughed, having had more than enough time over the past three years to adjust to being single. "I kind of feel now like I wouldn't know who I was if I *was* happy with someone."

"I get that. But I've been with Jim for six years. Six! I think a part of me knew I could have a better relationship, but it was kind of easier to stay with him, you know?"

Alex's heart broke for her friend, who had always been smart, kind and funny. It was terrible to picture her settling for someone who was less than she deserved. Alex had always known that Jim wasn't good enough for Freya, but she'd never realised a part of Freya had known it as well. Somehow, that made it seem so much worse.

"There are worse things than being single," Hannah said sympathetically. "Being with the wrong person is definitely worse."

"I wish I could be more like you," Freya told her. "You always seem so happy with your own company. I'm not sure I can be like that."

Hannah shrugged. "I mean, it's not always easy. But what's the alternative? It's not like I can conjure the perfect guy for me out of thin air, so I might as well not be miserable all the time."

"It's like I said," Alex said, her mind going back to the pact again. "We need arranged marriages."

Freya thought for a moment. "I mean..." she said, a little hesitantly. "There's always social media. We could see what the boys are up to."

"You're not serious?" Alex asked doubtfully. "For starters, you only broke up with Jim about three minutes ago."

Freya shrugged. "Why not? I don't owe Jim anything, and it's not like I'm getting married tomorrow or something. I'm allowed meet up with some old friends. You can't tell me you guys have never Facebook stalked any of them."

They were silent as they all considered the truth of those words. Hannah had regularly told them she considered herself a world-class social media stalker; even using a fake name wasn't enough to hide from her. She simply tracked down mutual friends and acquaintances, a long trail, until she found the person she was after. Alex had spent longer than she liked to admit lingering over the boys' profile pictures, particularly Sam's. His public images didn't show much; not even a current photo of him. He had an avatar as his profile pic and his cover photo was the Taj Mahal. She couldn't see much else of him. Not that it mattered, of course. She was a successful, independent woman. She wasn't *seriously* going to go back and marry some virtual stranger, just because of a pact she'd made twenty years earlier.

A WEEK LATER, HANNAH was scrolling through her phone absentmindedly. It was something she did more often than she'd like to admit after coming home from a busy day at work. She wasn't a reader like Freya, and she didn't have a routine to dictate her week like Alex did, *thank God*. She loved staying fit, but she got enough of that before and during work. By the time she got home, all Hannah really wanted to do was collapse in front of the TV. When she did so, the phone often came out. Sometimes it got to the point that the TV felt like unnecessary background noise while she scrolled.

Without letting herself think too much about what she was doing, she opened the Facebook app and looked up Nick's name. His privacy settings were good, but she could see his profile pictures. There were some older photos of him with a pretty woman with jet-black hair, but his latest profile picture, which he'd had for a year, was him alone, grinning at the camera with his arms wrapped around a Labrador. The photo was taken at a distance – definitely no professionally filtered profile shots for Nick – and he looked undeniably good, with his brown hair and gorgeous smile. He had some sexy stubble now, which only added to his appeal. He was clearly fit, too, as much as you could tell through his red shirt and jeans.

She hadn't looked at his profile in years, so this was a new photo to her. Hannah stared at it, not entirely sure how she felt about seeing the guy who had meant so much to her back in the day. Fortitude High didn't do reunions, so Hannah had never even entertained the idea that she might see him again. Now, suddenly, she was surprised to realise that she wanted to.

Hannah took a deep breath as she opened her message group with Freya and Alex.

Hannah: I say we go for it. Let's see if we can track down the boys and make a plan to meet up.

She waited, uncharacteristically nervous to see what they would say, but Alex's reply came through quickly.

Alex: I'm in! It'll be good to see the guys, if nothing else. We were all such good friends back in the day. It could be our own little mini high school reunion.

Freya: I don't know...

Hannah: Oh, come on! If nothing else, the sex with Nick was great. Maybe we can have another romp for old time's sake...

Freya: Not entirely sure how that helps ME...

Freya: Besides, I've JUST become single again. Not sure I really want to be rushing into anything with anyone.

Hannah shook her head impatiently as she read the message. Freya was being overly cautious again.

Hannah: It's not like you really have to marry Ethan. Maybe you'll get under him and get over Jim?

Freya: Is there only one thing on your mind?

Hannah: On good days!

Alex: Honestly, Frey, don't feel you have to meet up with him BUT I do think it could do you good. It's not like Asshole Jim's wasting any time!! Worst case scenario, you're not remotely interested or you're not ready or whatever, and then you just have a nice afternoon catching up with an old friend. E was always so lovely.

Freya: Yeah, yeah, okay. Whatever you guys think.

Hannah grinned triumphantly. She messaged them again, taking care not to sound like she'd been staring at Nick's photo for the last twenty minutes.

Hannah: I'll organise it. I'll track Nick down on Facebook and send him a private message. He can get in touch with the others, I'm sure.

Hannah worked on her message to Nick for longer than she liked to admit, even to herself. Eventually she went with something that she hoped sounded breezy and nonchalant. "Hey, stranger! I happened upon your profile so thought I'd say hi. I'm still friends with Freya and Alex and we thought it might be fun to catch up, the six of us, again? Just like old times. What do you think?"

She held her breath as she pressed send, her heart thumping in her chest. It was unlike Hannah to be so nervous about approaching a guy, but then, Nick wasn't just any guy.

He didn't reply until the next day, and the wait was nearly interminable.

"Hey, Han – talk about your blast from the past! It was good to hear from you. I'm not in touch with Sam or Ethan anymore, but I've had a quick look and I can see their profiles, so I'll send them a message. Let you know when I hear back!"

She smiled, reading over the message several times. He certainly sounded like the same old Nick. She knew he would have changed a lot in the last two decades, just like the rest of them had, but for now he felt comfortingly familiar.

HANNAH: Nick replied! He's not in touch with the other two anymore, but he's going to contact them so hopefully they see the message and let us know ASAP. This just might end up happening, after all!!

Alex read her friend's message, feeling vaguely disappointed to hear the three guys weren't still in touch. It was silly, but if they were still good friends it would feel like not so much had changed since high school. Sometimes the fact that it had been twenty years since they graduated still shocked her. Seeing Freya and Hannah so regularly made it easier to dismiss those changes; when you saw each other every week, you didn't notice the signs of ageing or the small signs of people maturing in their personality. She wasn't sure she was ready to confront the sight of their three old friends twenty years after seeing them.

Still, it was out of her hands now. It only took a couple of days before Nick messaged Hannah back to say that Sam and Ethan had responded to him and were happy to meet up. Hannah wasted no time in making plans for a face-to-face meeting.

In one week, the six old friends would see each other again.

Chapter 7: 2019

The day of their meeting with the three men Hannah, Freya and Alex drove in together, with Alex behind the wheel, as usual. It was a safety in numbers thing. None of them wanted to be the first to get there, and to have to face an awkward silence with a man they hadn't known since he was a boy.

The guys obviously hadn't made the same choice, though, which became obvious when the first of them arrived. Nick. He looked around blankly at first, then saw the three of them and lifted his hand in a wave.

For the first time in her life, Hannah felt what she could honestly describe as her heart skipping a beat. She had thought she was prepared to see her old boyfriend again after all these years, but she was wrong. It was surreal. The sight of him took her breath away. He was still gorgeous, even more so than he looked in his profile picture. His eyes still crinkled in the same friendly way they had when he was seventeen. He had aged, obviously, but not as much as she had expected. If anything, he looked better now, in the infuriating way some men did with age. It was hard to believe twenty years had passed. Seeing him, Hannah felt like a seventeen-year-old girl again. She wondered if it was just nostalgia that was responsible for the butterflies in her stomach, or Nick himself. It would have been so easy to run into his arms, to kiss him the way she had back then.

Until she saw him, she didn't really take the twenty-year pact seriously. Oh, sure, they could meet up with the guys again, and see what happened, but she was hardly going to marry her high school boyfriend simply because she'd been so sure of their relationship when they were teenagers. She had gone along as a lark more than anything else, with the possibility of getting some action with Nick not far from her mind.

Now, though, something more serious didn't seem like such a stretch. She and Nick had always had undeniable chemistry, and at the heart of that, a lot of affection for one another. Was it really so impossible to think that they could recreate it now?

"Nick!" Freya cried as he came over, seemingly more at ease than Hannah for once – which made sense, given she didn't have the same history with the man that Hannah did. "It's good to see you!" She stood up to give him an embrace. Hannah was surprised at how comfortable Freya seemed. She had always been so quiet and introverted, while Hannah had been the whirlwind.

Hannah still considered herself a fun, bubbly person, but she'd calmed down from the girl she was at school. Freya, on the other hand, was still quiet and enjoyed her own company, but she had come out of her shell and become more confident as an adult. It was almost like they had met in the middle. Of the three of them, it was Alex who most resembled her high school self. Hannah wondered sometimes if that was because Alex had already been so mature back in school. She was still serious and intellectual, but sociable nonetheless. As a teenager she had possessed a calm, self-assured quality, and she still had that now. She wasn't worried what others thought of her. Alex had always been comfortable in her own skin. It was something Hannah had always envied about her. She herself had always come across as so confident, but the truth was she second guessed herself all the time.

Nick hugged Alex next, and then it was Hannah's turn. The exes took each other in for a minute before Nick wrapped his arms around her. "Hey, Han," he said softly.

Hannah closed her eyes, breathing him in. It was as if no time had passed at all. He felt so familiar, but his touch didn't feel the same as it had when she was a teenager. It was probably just the fact that so much time had passed, she told herself. Once she got him alone, they would be feeling the old magic in no time.

The reunions with Sam and Ethan, a few minutes later, weren't as fraught with tension. Ethan, in particular, seemed casual and totally at ease with the three women he hadn't seen since they were teenagers. Sam was a little more reserved, but still friendly and approachable. The women hugged the other two men, and Nick shook their hands. Hannah couldn't believe how little they had all changed, physically. Maybe more than physically. Sam had always been the quietest of the three guys, and Ethan always the most outgoing, so they hadn't changed in that way. She half-wondered if Ethan was going to start babbling about comic books over lunch.

The six sat down at a table together, seemingly none of them wanting to be the first to talk. The silence that settled over them was more than a little awkward. Hannah found herself wishing for the easy camaraderie they'd all had when they were teenagers, when they would talk for hours without much of a pause for breath. She wondered if they could ever reclaim that now that so much time had passed. What had they talked about back then?

Suddenly Alex squealed as a bug flew at her face, circling around her long blonde hair, which she'd worn out for once. She waved her hands frantically in front of her face, which caused the desired effect of the bug flying off.

"Where did it go?" Alex gasped, patting down her hair, still not convinced she was free of the bug.

"There!" Freya cried, pointing.

They all followed her finger, staring in disbelief directly at Nick's crotch, where the bug was now resting.

"What?" Nick asked, baffled.

"It looks like a Christmas beetle," Ethan mused, staring at his old friend's shorts.

"That's not really what I'm concerned about! Nick! Stand up!" Hannah cried, standing herself, as if to show him what to do.

"What? What is it?"

"Just stand up!" Freya and Hannah yelled together.

Nick stood up and Alex, acting on impulse, leaned forward with her napkin. "Move your legs apart!" she cried, waving the napkin directly at his crotch where the beetle, against all odds, was still perched peacefully.

The rest of the group dissolved into hysterical laughter as Alex waved the napkin harder between Nick's legs until finally, mercifully, the bug took off.

"Bloody hell," Nick said, sitting down again.

"That was disturbing," Freya said, trying to get control of her giggles.

There was a pause as they all started to settle down. Then Ethan said, suddenly, "I hope there's no CCTV here."

That broke them up again, Alex wiping tears of laughter from her eyes.

The ice was well and truly broken, and once they'd settled down, the conversation took a more serious turn. "You guys are still in touch?" Alex asked, looking at Sam and Ethan.

They nodded. "We are, but we hadn't seen Nick for... what would it be, mate? Over fifteen years, easily," Ethan said.

"Why did you guys lose touch?" Hannah ventured. She wasn't sure if she should be asking or if it would open up some old wound, but the three men just shrugged.

"No reason, really," Nick said breezily. "You know how these things just happen. I was always busy with work, so the guys saw each other a few times without me and before you knew it, it was harder to fit back in than it was to just... drift away." He nodded at them. "I'm more surprised you three are still so tight."

The three women looked at each other. "We did start to drift apart a little, too, after we graduated," Hannah said. "We were all doing our own things, and we didn't have school in common anymore. These two *lived* for Uni, and I was going from job to job, trying to figure out what the hell I wanted to do. I thought our friendship might have been done for a while there, but then Alex invited us to her beach house."

The three women smiled, remembering. The invitation had come out of the blue. It had been six months since their last catch up. After seeing each other every day at school, keeping the friendship alive when they didn't have a natural reason to see each other seemed difficult. But then, not long before their twenty-first birthdays, had come the beach house stay. They had spent the weekend drinking, dancing and laughing together. They had reconnected and they hadn't looked back. Alex had always said that inviting them away that weekend had been the best decision she had ever made. Who knew what would have happened to them if not for that weekend of bonding? Hannah was grateful they didn't have to find out. She couldn't imagine her life without Alex and Freya.

"IT WORKED OUT WELL that we all live in Brisbane still," Nick said. "I moved to Sydney for work for a while, but I came back a couple of years ago. So... good timing, I guess."

"Well, I don't live here, technically," Sam offered. "I'm in Ipswich. But yeah, close enough." Ipswich was only half an hour from Brisbane.

Freya nodded. "It is lucky. I'm happy we decided to do this."

"So, tell us about yourselves." Alex directed her statement to the men. "It's been twenty years, after all. It's like we need to all introduce ourselves again."

The men all looked at each other, and then Nick spoke up. "Well, I'm in marketing, like I'd always planned," he said with a slightly self-conscious laugh. "I'm single and I live alone."

"And you like long walks on the beach," Ethan joked.

"I'm in sales," Sam added. "Typical quiet office job that everyone always expected me to do." He shrugged. "It pays the bills, and I don't mind the work."

"And you, Ethan?" Freya asked. "Anything about you a surprise?"

"I'm an accountant," he said. "I think that would probably surprise people."

Freya nodded. She didn't know what job she would have expected for Ethan, but accounting wasn't it. He had always had such a great sense of humour, and accountants had such a reputation for being stuffy and boring. She tried to think back to high school, to remember if he'd spoken then about what he wanted to do when he left school. She didn't think he had, or maybe she just hadn't been paying enough attention.

"So, speaking of surprises," Nick said, "I didn't expect to hear from you." There was a pause, and then he said "Is it... Did you contact us for the reason I think you contacted us?"

Freya suddenly felt ridiculous. When she'd been chatting to the girls, the idea of contacting the boys had seemed reasonable, even natural. But looking at them now, she just felt stupid. What sort of grown women contacted men they hadn't seen in almost two decades because of some old marriage pact? Besides, these men were all gorgeous and successful. What were the odds that they hadn't been snapped up already? None of them had mentioned a wife, but that didn't mean they didn't have one. And even if by some miracle they were all single, they weren't exactly about to fall to one knee and propose to these virtual strangers.

"Well... yeah," Hannah said, sounding as uncomfortable as Freya suddenly felt. "We got to talking about the fact that we're all single now, and someone mentioned the Twenty-Year Pact."

Ethan laughed suddenly, and they looked at him. "I told him that," he said, pointing at Sam. "He didn't believe it, but I said I was willing to bet that was why you guys suddenly got in touch."

"I know it sounds dumb," Alex said, her cheeks starting to redden. It was clear the other two women both felt as self-conscious about it as Freya did.

"It's not dumb," Ethan replied. "I get it. I'm not with anyone, either. It's crossed my mind before."

"It has?" Freya asked, staring at him. She was, after all, the one he'd been 'matched' with in the pact. The idea that she had crossed his mind, even in a fairly abstract way, was somehow appealing to her. She remembered how little interest she'd had in the brown-haired boy as a teenager, and she felt like slapping her younger self. Ethan was gorgeous, and he seemed genuinely sweet. Why had she thought he wasn't good enough? It wasn't just him, though, really. She hadn't been interested in any boys at school. She hadn't even developed her first proper crush until her second year of Uni, one of the guys in her lecture who had turned out to be largely irrelevant to her life. Her first 'real' boyfriend had come a few months after that. She was a late bloomer, but it had worked for her, for a while at least. She'd had a few semi-serious boyfriends and then she'd met Jim, who she had thought would be the last one. Looking at Ethan now, a part of her wished she hadn't been so damned serious at school. Why couldn't she just have kissed him drunkenly at a party, let him feel her up after school, gone on a date with him like everyone else was doing? Who knows where it might have led? She could have married him straight out of Uni. She could have a house with him, and three kids and a dog.

She wasn't even sure that that life was what she wanted. But it would have been nice to have had the option.

Chapter 8: 1999

"Hey, I have a fun idea," Hannah said in a deliberately light tone.

They were two hours and at least a few drinks each into the party. Hannah had tried to time it perfectly – they needed to have had enough drinks to have loosened their inhibitions, but not so many that they'd forget the whole thing had ever happened the following day. She had already been responsible for a few of their classmates getting together; perfect matches who totally failed to see how good they were together until Hannah came along. She didn't get nearly enough credit for being a master hook up initiator, honestly.

"More drinks?" Nick laughed, raising his beer in the air.

Hannah swatted his hand down playfully. "No! I thought we could play spin the bottle," she announced loudly, trying to sound just a little drunker than she really was. That made it easier to pass the idea off as silly fun, rather than something she was serious about.

Nick laughed again. "You're joking, right?"

"It'll be fun!" she protested. "Come on, let's go for it." She shot Nick a meaningful look. "Maybe you'll land on me."

"Or maybe you'll land on a girl," Nick mused thoughtfully. "Yeah, okay. Let's do it!"

"Great!" Hannah pulled out an empty bottle of beer that she'd put aside earlier. "Come on, guys!"

She got a few people in the circle, and virtually pushed Alex and Freya in as well. Freya, in particular, was protesting. Alex had had a boyfriend the previous year, but Hannah knew that Freya had never kissed a boy before. She felt a twinge of guilt at convincing her to join in on the game, but she pushed it to the side. Freya would thank her when she was in a happy relationship with Ethan. She just needed the motivation. Besides, seventeen and never been kissed? It was lame, Hannah told herself. Freya had a whole new world waiting for her to discover and once she did, she would never look back.

Of course, there were no guarantees that Freya or Ethan would actually land on each other but if her friend had to kiss a few frogs before finding her prince, well, that was entirely out of Hannah's control.

Finally, she had the game together. There were seven girls and five guys sitting in a circle, which was an even enough number for Hannah's liking, and the fact that the game wasn't huge worked in her favour. It increased the odds that Freya and Ethan, or Sam and Alex would have their kiss. Yes, she really couldn't have planned it any better.

"I'll spin first," Hannah chirped, grabbing the bottle. She spun it around and landed on Connor, one of Nick's friends whom she barely knew. She shot Nick a guilty look before crawling forward and kissing Connor, quickly. Rules were rules, after all.

"Your turn," she said, passing the bottle to Ethan, who was on the left of her.

Ethan spun and they all watched as it landed on Nick.

"No way," the two said in one voice. "I'm *not* kissing a guy," Ethan added. "I didn't sign up for this."

"We didn't make any rules about that," Hannah replied. "But, sure, you can spin again." She didn't really want to see Nick kissing anyone else, least of all a guy! And besides, Ethan spinning again doubled his chances of landing on Freya.

Ethan spun again and this time he landed on Emily, a cute redhead. Hannah rolled her eyes as Ethan and Emily leaned forward for their kiss. Then she sighed as the kiss deepened.

"Okay!" she said eventually, clapping her hands together. "I think that's enough." She knew she sounded like a matronly teacher, but she needed to break this up before things got out of hand. "Pass the bottle."

Ethan sighed, pulling away from the kiss and handing the bottle to his left.

The rest of the game was similarly unsuccessful. Freya took off before it was her turn, and Alex and Sam didn't land on each other once. The only plus side was that Nick landed on Alex when he spun. While Hannah didn't want to see him kissing anyone other than herself, at least Alex was harmless. Fiona, one of the bubbly girls from Hannah's dance group, was there as well, twirling her chestnut hair around her finger and giggling in Nick's direction. Hannah was sure Nick wouldn't have had any interest in Fiona anyway, but there was no point in tempting fate.

When the game finally broke up Hannah resumed her co-host duties, taking drinks around the party and offering plates of nibbles. It was on her second trip around the living room that she saw them. Ethan and Emily, pressed against each other in the corner, making out like their lives depended on it.

Hannah groaned out loud, exasperated. She'd managed to make a love match, alright. It just wasn't the one she had planned.

Chapter 9: 2019

"Why did we pick twenty years, anyway?" Sam pondered now, as they munched on bruschetta together. "Why didn't we say when we were thirty-five, or when we were forty or something?"

"I think it was a twenty-year pact in that movie we watched," Alex replied. "Besides, forty seemed *so old* back then. We never would have done that."

"It doesn't seem so old now," Ethan murmured, and Hannah agreed.

"I know, right? I still feel the same as I did ten years ago," she said. "Forty used to feel... I don't know, daunting or something. Like this thing that was looming over me. Now it's just another age."

Freya didn't feel the same way. She had always planned on having kids someday. She knew Alex was on the fence about children, and Hannah had openly expressed her lack of interest in motherhood on more than one occasion. Freya wished she didn't care. It had to make things easier. The further into her thirties she got, the more abstract a notion having kids seemed. How could she possibly have children when she couldn't even find someone to do it with? She had before considered going it alone, but she just couldn't go through with it. When she pictured her own childhood she thought of her parents and their loving relationship; the fun adventures they had all had together, the two girls always accompanied by their mum and dad. She couldn't bring children into the world without someone to share it all with.

And so she waited, but the longer she waited, the harder it became.

"I THOUGHT IT MIGHT be an idea if we all went off and had a bit of a chat," Alex said after they'd chatted a little longer. "You know. The three 'couples.'" She used hand quotes and tried to make her voice sound light, but she felt embarrassed as she said it.

Sam looked at Ethan and laughed, a little shakily. "Well, we can do that, but there's one thing I should probably mention about myself," Sam said. "I'm, uh. I'm already in a relationship."

Alex nodded, feeling a little deflated, but unsurprised. The odds of all six of them being single at the same time were unlikely. She couldn't deny she was a little disappointed that it was 'her' partner who was coupled up. It was kind of ironic, given that the pact had been her idea in the first place, but what could you do?

"That's okay," she said. "We can just have a chat as friends – if you think your girlfriend would be okay with that, that is."

Ethan laughed.

Sam ignored him. "I'm in a relationship," he continued, "with a man named Richie."

"Oh!" Alex felt her cheeks turning red. "Oh, sorry, I didn't realise. Well, Richie probably would be okay with us chatting, then," she added, laughing a little to hide her embarrassment.

Sam nodded. "For sure. It would be great to have a chat," he said earnestly. He nodded his head towards the other four, who were already deep in conversation. "And we can leave those lovebirds to it," he added under his breath.

Alex smiled as they stood up, the first two to do so. Despite her initial disappointment, a small part of her felt relieved as well. At least this took the pressure off, and she still wasn't sure that love and marriage were really in her future. After three years of the single life, maybe she'd become too set in her independent ways to want to date again. It was so much less complicated this way.

"So do you really think there might be something there?" she asked Sam now, gesturing back towards the others.

He shrugged. "It's hard to say. I mean, it's been twenty years! It's a hell of a long time. And I haven't seen Nick in so long, I have no idea what he's even like anymore. I'm not sure they can get that feeling back. But Ethan..." He paused, seemingly trying to find the words for what he wanted to say. "I wouldn't go as far as to say he's never gotten over Freya, or anything dramatic like that. But he's mentioned her from time to time. I think it's safe to say there could be a part of him that never forgot about her."

Alex smiled at that. She hadn't expected Sam to be quite so positive. It was no kind of guarantee that things were going to work out between Freya and Ethan, but it was nice to hear some positive words. How amazing would it be if things actually did proceed between them! Freya deserved a little luck in the love department, after wasting all that time with Jim.

"I wanted to say something else," Sam blurted out suddenly, and Alex's heartrate quickened. She knew what his words were going to be about, and she suddenly couldn't make eye contact with him anymore. They walked alongside the Brisbane River, an awkward silence settling between them.

"I'm sorry," Sam said. "For..." His voice trailed off.

"I know," she said. Twenty years later, she could be generous enough not to make him say it.

He smiled. "I guess I was hoping you'd say, 'what for?' I was hoping you might have forgotten all about it by now. I didn't really think you would have, though." He looked ashamed, and it made him look more like the schoolboy he had been back then. "There's no excuse for it. What I did was awful. But I guess I want you to understand. I was a shy young guy and I was just realising... things about myself that I wasn't really ready to realise."

Alex nodded. "It's okay. Really. It was a long time ago, and I know I gave you hell about it at the time, but we've all moved on since then." It was her favourite thing about getting older, actually. People always said not to sweat the small stuff, but when you were young it was just an expression. When you were older, it was true. There was no point getting hung up over the little things in life. Something that had felt so huge at seventeen was inconsequential – almost laughable! – at thirty-seven.

"Plus," Alex continued, "I think I understand it more now that I know you're gay." She realised as she said it that he hadn't actually used the term 'gay' himself, so he could have been bisexual or something. He nodded, though, so he obviously wasn't bothered by the term. Alex went on. "I know obviously the marriage plot thing isn't going to work out so well for us, but I feel like we could definitely be friends again."

"I'd like that." Sam smiled as he gestured in the direction they'd walked off from, where they'd left the other four. "Besides, we might need to be friends if we're bridesmaid and groomsman at two weddings..."

The two laughed together as they walked.

Chapter 10: 1999

In the weeks following the party, Ethan and Emily became a fully-fledged couple. Freya swore that it didn't bother her in the slightest, but everyone else seemed upset by it. Hannah, of course, was lamenting the loss of her planned relationship between Ethan and Freya, while Alex had said she was mostly disturbed at the fact that it meant Emily was suddenly hanging around with the six of them. She'd always been a little on the anti-social side, so suddenly spending so much time with a girl they didn't know well was a factor she hadn't counted on. Sam and Nick didn't seem bothered by Emily as such, but they did make a couple of grumbling comments about how Ethan wasn't around as much anymore.

"So, you and Emily," Hannah ventured to Ethan one day when they found themselves uncharacteristically alone.

"Yeah, me and Emily," Ethan grinned. "She's great, isn't she?"

Hannah made a non-committal noise. "I suppose. I thought you were all hung up on Freya, though."

Ethan tried to laugh, but it sounded awkward. "I'm not hung up on Freya! Who said I was?"

Hannah said nothing in response, but raised her eyebrows at him pointedly.

"Well, I guess I was a bit interested," he said finally. "Freya's cute, and she's nice and all, but... I mean, I can't wait around for her forever."

It was the closest he'd ever come to admitting his feelings out loud, and Hannah's heart went out to him. It was true that her attempts at matchmaking had started because she loved the idea of the six of them all being friends forever, rather than out of real concern for the emotions involved, but now... She hadn't realised quite how serious Ethan was about Freya. He didn't have to say it. It was written all over his vulnerable face.

"Ethan would ditch Emily in a second for you, you know," she told Freya later, when the three of them were walking to English class. It was the only class they all had together, so they enjoyed the chance to catch up.

Alex nodded her agreement, while Freya shook her head, frowning. "I don't think so," she protested. "He's really happy with Emily."

"Only because he thinks he can't have you!"

"Well, he can't. I'm not interested, remember? I'm glad he's found Em. She seems really sweet. Maybe *they'll* get married and you can go to *their* wedding." This part was said with a teasing smile. It didn't take a genius to realise Hannah's plan with the spin the bottle game, and Alex and Freya had both been on to her from the start. They had teased her about her plan on and off since the party.

Hannah sighed heavily as they arrived at their classroom. "I just think you're being a little stubborn."

"And I think you're being a little obsessed," Freya countered. "There's more to life than boys, you know."

"Not *much* more."

"Well, there should be! I have plenty to focus on without having to worry about guys. Maybe someday I'll be as interested as you are, but for now I'm just not."

"Well, that's good," Hannah grumbled, "since you've obviously lost your chance with Ethan."

Freya shrugged. "That's fine. Nursing a crush isn't good for anyone. I'm glad he's moved on."

"Whatever," Hannah sighed. "I'm just trying to do the right thing by you two. One day you'll change your minds, and it'll be too late."

Chapter 11: 2019

"I can't believe it's been so long," Nick said when he and Hannah were finally alone. Freya and Ethan walked off in the opposite direction to Sam and Alex, while Nick and Hannah stayed at their table.

Hannah smiled over at him. "I can't believe how little you've changed. Honestly," she said. "You're obviously not seventeen anymore, but you're still... the same. I feel like I've changed more than you have."

"Nah, you still seem the same to me."

Hannah mulled that over. "I guess I am. I mean, I feel... calmer now. I don't know how else to put it," she said with a little laugh. "I'm still really energetic and everything, but you do change in your thirties, don't you?"

"I think so," Nick replied. "You kind of slow down, I think. Not physically, I mean, we're not ninety! But I think... yeah. I think 'calmer' sums it up. It's like life isn't in so much of a hurry anymore."

Was that all they needed? Hannah wondered. Would they be the perfect pair, now? Maybe timing had been their only problem. Their break-up back in school had been tough, and unexpected, but not particularly nasty or dramatic. They'd just been *young*. Maybe they both just needed to grow up, to get out into the world and see some sights, experience different people and different situations. Had she gone through everything she'd gone through in her life, all the career changes and different partners, just to end up with the boy she'd loved in high school? There was something romantic about it, in one way, but also something sort of unsettling. She wasn't sure if it was a romantic twist of fate or if it just seemed somehow desperate. She couldn't imagine making two decades of progress, only to end up back where she'd started. But then, maybe that was a good thing, like Nick had been there waiting for her all along.

She tried to think of something else to say.

"Do you like your job?" It felt so weird to be making small talk with Nick. Nick!

He shrugged. "Mostly. I mean, there are definitely days I'd rather stay in bed, of course. But I like it. It's always different and challenging."

"It must be amazing, doing exactly what you've always wanted to do." Hannah thought about her own lack of ambition at high school. She'd always envied Nick's direction.

"It's amazing and it's hard, sometimes. I feel like I should be filled with excitement every day, or something. Most of the time it's just like any other job. I watch the clock like everyone else. It's not what I pictured in high school, that's for sure."

"Nothing ever is."

Their relationship might be further proof of that, Hannah thought. She couldn't shake the feeling that things didn't feel the same between them, but she tried to push it out of her head. Had she expected to see him and suddenly feel like no time had passed? It was only natural that they would need some time to warm up to each other again.

After a moment of amiable silence, she said, "So tell me about Sydney. What was it like living there? It must have been exciting."

"Oh, it was okay. I enjoyed it, but it was really hard to make friends."

She nodded. "Everyone says that about Sydney. I've always loved going there on holidays, but I'm not sure I'd want to live there. You moved there for work?"

"Um." He ran a hand through his hair, and she remembered the gesture from when they were teenagers. "Actually, I did get a really good job down there, but I moved for a woman, actually."

"A woman?" It shouldn't have been surprising. It wasn't as though she'd expected he'd remained chaste since they'd last seen each other. Still, it was the first mention he'd made of a partner, and she was momentarily taken aback. Briefly, she wondered if it was possible that he was still with her. He hadn't mentioned a relationship the way Sam had, but he hadn't outright said he was single, either.

"Yeah. Sarah. She was... my wife."

"Oh!" Now she was more than taken aback. It had never occurred to her that he might have been married, although statistically, it probably should have, of course.

"Yeah. I was married for five years. We split nearly three years ago, and I haven't really seen her much since it was all finalised. We didn't have kids or anything, so it was a clean break, or as much as it ever can be. I moved back here when we divorced." He looked away for a minute, lost in thought. "It's a bit strange, you know. Being married to someone and then having them just be... someone from your past. Don't get me wrong, I don't regret the divorce or anything."

"Do you regret the marriage?" she ventured.

Nick looked like he was really thinking this over, rather than just giving the expected response, which Hannah appreciated. "No," he said. "I loved her, and we had a nice life together. We just grew apart, really. We weren't right for each other anymore. I'm mostly sad that I lost what could have been a good friend out of it." He paused. "I think that's part of why I was so open to meeting up with you five again. Between moving cities and losing friends in the divorce, I guess I've been feeling a little bit lonely. It never hurts to have some new friends. Well, old friends."

Hannah smiled, touched at his honesty. It was strange to think of Nick having a whole different life that she knew nothing about, but it was also kind of nice, in a way. It showed that he wasn't afraid of commitment, but that he also didn't feel the need to cling onto something that wasn't working. She tried to picture Nick on his wedding day, but failed. To her, he was still the seventeen-year-old with the cheeky grin. He probably always would be.

Chapter 12: 2019

Freya and Ethan spent their first minute together in silence. "So, how have you been?" he finally asked, in a voice more serious than she was accustomed to from him.

"Oh, you know," Freya said, before realising that he didn't know at all. They hadn't seen each other for two decades, and sometimes it felt as though her life had only really started after high school. "Well, I work at Fortitude High." They had talked about the guys' jobs when they were together, but she realised now that they hadn't got into what the women were doing with their lives.

"Really? That's crazy!" he enthused. "It must be strange, being back at the old school every day."

"It is, a bit," she laughed. "I see the kids in their uniforms, and I just picture us. Plus, they all look so little! We always felt like we were so grown up, but I guess we weren't."

"Oh, I don't know. I think you were born mature," he replied. "And what else is new in your life? You're single, I take it? Do you have a roommate or anything? A dog?"

"No. I'm actually only recently single, so when my partner moved out, I decided I could handle the rent by myself." She wanted to gloss over the topic of Jim as quickly as possible. "No pets, either. Alex is the one with the dog and the mortgage."

"Sam and I used to live together," Ethan said then. At the startled look on her face, he laughed and added "As roommates, I mean. We got a place right after we finished Uni and we lived together for five years. Then I moved in with a girl, which obviously didn't last, and he met Richie not too long after that."

"You guys are still really close." It was an observation rather than a question, and Ethan nodded.

"Yeah. At school I was closer to Nick at first, but when he started dating Hannah, he sort of withdrew a bit. I became closer to Sam, and we've stayed that way."

She wondered how old Sam was when he'd come out, and if it had caused any changes in their friendship, but she decided not to get into anything so personal just yet. Ethan had never expressed any bigoted views, and he and Sam certainly seemed tighter than ever.

"Do you have a roommate now?"

He shook his head. "Same as you, I decided I could do it alone, and I didn't really want to have a roommate I didn't know. It just felt exhausting."

Freya had felt the same way when Jim left. The idea of having someone else move into her space – of having to get to know someone well enough to actually share her living space with them – was too tiring. She much preferred the idea of having the place to herself.

"What do you do for fun?" he asked. "You were always a big reader."

It was only then that it struck her that this really was like a first date. She had expected their alone time to be an extension of the chatter they had had as a group of six, but it was more like he was really trying to get to know her, the way you might with someone you had just met. She thought of when they were teenagers together, and how Hannah had always insisted that Ethan was really into her. She had always laughed it off, but deep down she had known it was true. She wondered if he was still interested now. More to the point, was she?

"I still am. Actually, I'm a librarian," she added, realising his assumption was probably that she was a teacher. "It's a bit of a dying career these days, unfortunately, but I think I'm pretty stable at Fortitude High. And I love being able to share the joy of books with the students. I read a lot of young adult books for my work, but I also do a lot of reading for myself."

"And when you're not reading?"

"Um, I go out to dinners with the girls pretty often. Alex and Hannah, I mean," she added, clarifying. "And we have some work social events, and..." She paused, thinking. Until recently she had gone to Jim's bowling nights, and they had had monthly dinners with his group of mates. She hadn't realised that she'd let her own personality and interests slip. It was getting hard to think of things that she truly enjoyed doing, which was an incredibly depressing fact to realise. "Oh, and I love the theatre," she added, feeling oddly triumphant at having come up with something else. "What about you?"

"Same sorts of things. I catch up with my mates, we'll have a beer at the pub together, and I'm in a soccer team. The usual, I guess."

They kept walking along slowly and chatting, filling each other in on their lives now and sharing anecdotes from their teenaged years. It had been a long time since Freya had enjoyed getting to know someone this much.

She tried to match this man in front of her up to the energetic, funny boy she'd known twenty years ago. In some ways he hadn't changed at all, but in others he was a whole new person. More attractive, more charming, more introspective. Smarter, kinder.

Or maybe it was just that she was seeing him in a new way.

Chapter 13: 1999

A lex walked into her home and hung her school bag up on the hook by the door. All four of the siblings' school bags used to hang there, but now she was the only one left at school. She had watched Tyson's schoolbag leave the rack first, then Curtis', and finally Katherine's. Her sister was two years older than her, so she should have been used to seeing her lonely bag there by now, but it felt symbolic of something larger. Her siblings were growing up and leaving her behind. Watching Tyson move out with his girlfriend Isabelle had been strange, and then seeing Curtis move in with friends had been even stranger. Katherine was the only one still left at home. Alex was a mature, driven seventeen-year-old, but she couldn't help but wonder sometimes if she would ever stop feeling like the baby of the family.

"Hello?" she called out. "Anyone home?"

"Here," a lazy voice shouted out. It was Katherine. Alex walked in to find her sister draped on one of the armchairs in their family room, one leg hooked over the side of the chair.

Alex rolled her eyes. "Busy day?"

Katherine and Alex were as different as two sisters could be. Maybe because she felt like she was always playing a game of catch-up, Alex had never stopped trying to be number one.

The second she arrived at Fortitude High she made it her mission to join the band, the debate club and the volleyball team, just to see which were the right fits for her. She had dropped debate fairly quickly but kept up volleyball and her main love, band. Now she was in Year 12 she had joined the school magazine team and the formal planning committee. She didn't even care whether she attended her formal, which was coming up in August, but since she knew Hannah wasn't going to let her get out of it, she might as well have a hand in planning it.

Katherine, on the other hand, had coasted through school, caring more about her social life than her grades. In some ways, she reminded Alex of Hannah, which at least meant Alex could speak her language, even if Katherine couldn't always speak hers. After school she had struggled over what to do, before eventually starting a job with a nanny company. It wasn't Katherine's life ambition, but it paid the bills and it filled her days. Katherine was happy with that, particularly since it freed her up to spend most of her time with her boyfriend. Alex couldn't imagine that. It was one thing to struggle with your identity and to have some issues deciding what you wanted to do for the rest of your life, but it was entirely another to fill your days with something you didn't even want to do. Their parents had instilled a strong work ethic in their four children, so it wasn't that Katherine was lazy, as such. She just wasn't driven the way the other three were.

"As a matter of fact, *Alexandra*," Katherine replied sardonically, "it has been quite busy. I quit."

"You... what? You're joking, right?"

Alex's parents had money – partially inherited from their parents, and partially earnt through their own successful computer company. Alex thought it was the least interesting thing about herself, but a lot of her classmates couldn't get over it. They weren't the types to have a full-time maid or anything, but they were more than comfortable, and the four kids had grown up taking annual overseas holidays. They had all been gifted a car on their seventeenth birthdays. Their parents insisted on supporting them until they were out of university (or at a similar age, in Katherine's case, since she chose not to take on further study) but then, they were on their own. Alex liked it that way. She didn't want to be some trust-fund baby, gliding through life on her parents' money. She knew Tyson, who was an engineer, was fine, but Curtis, the twenty-four-year-old teacher, was struggling to adapt to his lower income. When the time came, Alex would just have to work that much harder to ensure she didn't struggle.

"I quit," Katherine repeated in a serious tone, before breaking out into a grin. "...because I got another job."

"What? Oh, Katherine, that's awesome! I didn't even know you were looking! Another nannying job?"

"No, I've got a job as a party planner! Well, I'm an assistant at this stage, but I'm sure that's only a matter of time."

"Oh, wow! That's amazing. Congratulations!"

Alex tried, somewhat unsuccessfully, to hide her surprise. She'd had no idea her sister had any further ambitions, but now that she'd said it, party planning was the perfect fit for Katherine. She was extroverted and popular in a way Alex could never hope to be. Alex was genuinely happy for her, and hoped her sister had found her passion.

Despite her happiness, she felt a pang. She was certain psychology was right for her, but what if it wasn't? What if she did all her hard work and didn't end up where she wanted to be?

It was lovely, being a part of her family. She was close to her parents and she usually got along well with her siblings, also. She knew she was lucky to have the life they had, complete with a pool and spa, tennis court and so many extravagant holidays.

Sometimes, though, she felt envious when she looked at Freya and Hannah's families. They had loving families, too, but they were entirely different to Alex's. She knew Hannah sometimes thought her own family was too small, and Freya sometimes envied everything Alex's family had, but their families just seemed so... uncomplicated to Alex.

Alex loved her parents, and her brothers and sister. But sometimes she wondered what they would think of her if she ended up failing. She wondered what she would think of herself.

Chapter 14: 2019

When the six of them came back together after their separate 'couples time', Hannah was quick to suggest a regular catch-up.

"We should start a group chat," she enthused, pulling out her phone and getting the guys' details. "It would be great to do this again."

Freya wasted no time in agreeing. She would love to say it was because she wanted to reconnect with old friends, but the truth wasn't quite so simple. She had loved her one-on-one time with Ethan and wanted to recreate it, but she couldn't imagine asking him out, or him doing the same to her. Meeting up as a group was much easier.

The others were quick to agree, too. Alex and Sam obviously had no romantic potential to gain from it, but they had clearly enjoyed spending time together. Freya hoped they could be friends, since there wasn't the opportunity for anything more.

The two groups of three parted ways, with the girls hopping in Alex's car and heading back to her place to debrief. The mood between the three was slightly awkward at the start of the car trip, uncharacteristically so. It wasn't like them to struggle to find anything to talk about, but none seemed to want to be the first to bring up the topic of the three men.

It was Freya who finally broke the silence. "Alex, are you disappointed about Sam?"

Alex paused for a moment, clearly thinking the question over. "Not really. I mean, a little. It would have been amazing to be able to just meet him and have feelings for him and know we were all set! But I was never going to actually marry a guy based on a silly pact, so I guess the odds of us having feelings for each other weren't in my favour. Especially since I'm not, you know. A man."

"It's such a shame, though," Hannah burst in. "Can't you just picture it now? It would be the perfect Alexandra Reynolds set up. Face masks on Wednesday, Indian on Friday, marry the guy you made a marital pact with twenty years ago on Saturday."

Alex rolled her eyes as her two friends cracked up. "I guess life didn't have the same sort of plan that I did," she said. "What about you, Freya? Is the boy Freya Collins rejected at high school the man Freya Collins needs now?"

"Ummmm..." Freya said, and the two others whipped around to look at her, Alex forgetting momentarily to keep her eyes on the road.

"No way! You're *not* actually into him?!" Hannah exclaimed. Freya wasn't surprised by her friends' shock. She was very different now to the girl who had had no interest in dating, but her break up from Jim was still fairly recent, and Freya had never been the type to rebound as quickly as Hannah did. Besides, she had been so dismissive of Ethan back in high school.

"Look, I wouldn't say that," Freya laughed self-consciously. "He's a really nice guy, and obviously he's attractive. But we had, like, a ten-minute conversation by ourselves. You can't tell anything from that."

"Tell that to the speed dating industry," Hannah muttered.

"Seriously, Frey, it would be amazing if something happened," Alex said. "I'm happy for you."

"Nothing's happening yet."

"I know, but at least you have potential there. And of course, saving the best for last. How was Fortitude High's most fabulous couple, twenty years later?"

Hannah sighed deeply, although Freya wasn't sure if she was stalling for thinking time or just being dramatic. "I really don't know. It was amazing seeing him again, and there were definitely some butterflies, but I don't know how much of that was just the fact that it was Nick. You never forget your first love, you know? I don't think I'd have felt the same pull towards him if I just met him today." She paused. "I would have thought he was hot, obviously."

"Well, you do have eyes," Freya laughed.

"Yeah, but I don't know if it's anything deeper than that. Like you said, it's hard to tell much from a quick conversation. I guess I just wait and see what happens next time?"

At that, Alex pulled up at her house and the three women piled out, greeting Alex's dog Baxter enthusiastically as they walked in. Once Alex, ever the attentive host, had them set up with drinks, she sat down beside them on the couch and continued the conversation.

"I do feel like Sam could be a good friend again, though."

"So you've forgiven him?"

"Yeah, of course. It's ancient history. And I mean, it was pretty mortifying to a seventeen-year-old, but it doesn't seem like such a big deal now."

"I guess we'll have to see them again to really know if there's any potential," Hannah said pragmatically. "I might just send a quick message to the group thread to say thanks for meeting up." Pulling out her phone, she did exactly that.

It only took a few minutes for the replies to start coming in.

Sam: Thanks for organising it! It was fun to catch up, looking forward to doing it again sometime.

Ethan: So good to have time to chat xx

Hannah and Alex squealed out loud as they saw the text. "XX!" Hannah exclaimed. "He's *so* into you!"

Freya tried to protest, but her heart wasn't in it. She was grinning from ear to ear as she read over the message.

Nick: Yeah, what they said! Thanks for organising, looking forward to next time ☺

"That all sounds pretty positive," Freya said, trying to calm the feeling of excitement that was growing in her belly.

"I guess the key is not to get carried away," Alex cautioned.

Hannah laughed. "Easy for *you* to say, when you know your man is a no-go."

"Anyway, enough of this," Freya said sternly. "We have better things to talk about than boys. We can try to pretend, but we're really *not* seventeen anymore."

The others nodded, and then they all looked at each other in silence.

"Or maybe we don't," Hannah joked.

"Yes, we do! Tell me about your work."

"My work is boring," Hannah said petulantly. "Back to boys."

"Even you don't believe that. Seriously, tell me."

Hannah sighed, but gave in quickly. She launched into a story about a client of hers who had come in overweight and out of shape, and was now gearing up for her first body building competition. "That's awesome!" Freya said. "You made that happen."

"I didn't *make* that happen, she did," Hannah argued, but the pride was obvious in her eyes. "I just gave her a push. She says she never would have thought she'd be able to do it if I hadn't convinced her."

"See? That's amazing! And Alex, what about that cute little nephew of yours?"

Alex smiled as she filled them in on her nephew Kyle, her sister's new baby. He was only three months old and she tried to see him as often as possible. Over the years, Katherine had turned her party planning job into her own business, and now she had four employees who were running it all while she was on maternity leave. Alex and Katherine had become closer as they'd aged, with Alex acting as the Maid of Honour at her wedding, and soon to be appointed as little Kyle's godmother. She told her friends that while she had no immediate pressing desire to have children of her own, she was happily wrapped around her nephew's finger. She had older nephews as well, her brother's children, but she had always loved babies.

"You're acting like our own personal feminist warrior," Alex laughed when she'd finished talking. "What about you? What's going on in your life, aside from your oh-so-dreamy high school boy?"

Freya grimaced. "Well for starters, I think we can definitely stop calling him *that*," she laughed. "Especially considering my day job. Speaking of which, it's been really rough lately. These kids these days seem to have... I don't know, bigger problems than we did? Or less coping skills? I'm not sure. Not that I hear that much about it in the library, but I can see when they're upset."

Hannah winced. "That's tough. Honestly, I think we were just lucky we had each other. It helped us get through those tough times."

Freya went on in an attempt to lighten the mood. "In better news, though, I finally got that grant to redo the reading corner." She smiled proudly, remembering how much she had loved the library renovation that had happened when she herself had attended Fortitude High. It seemed insane that it was due for another refurbishment, but then, it seemed insane that two decades had passed since they were at high school.

Chapter 15: 1999

"Have you heard?" Hannah asked urgently at lunch one Monday.

"Heard what?" Freya sighed. She had stayed up late the night before studying for her History test, which meant that today she was tired, cranky, and entirely not in the mood for her friend's dramatics.

"Emily and Ethan. Apparently they..." she looked around, as if checking no one was listening. "...*had sex,*" she finished, her tone grave.

Alex and Hannah both studied Freya's face, which she tried to keep neutral. The truth was, she had really never been interested in Ethan, but hearing that he'd slept with someone else was oddly jarring.

It shouldn't have been. Over a month had passed since the party, and Ethan and Emily were still together and seemed completely smitten with each other. It was probably only natural that they would start sleeping together, but still, the news somehow took her by surprise.

"Oh."

"Oh?" Hannah repeated. "That's all you have to say? How do you feel about it? Are you dying of jealousy?"

Freya shrugged. "Ethan's sex life is none of my business. How do you know, anyway?"

"I have a telescope aimed at his bedroom window." At the looks on her friends' faces, Hannah laughed. "How do you *think* I know? He told Nick and Nick told me."

"Nothing would surprise me with you," Alex muttered.

"His first time?" Freya asked, attempting to keep her voice casual.

Hannah nodded. "Yeah. Not hers, though, apparently. He was all nervous about being with a more experienced girl."

"Wow, you... really do know it all, don't you? Are you *sure* you don't have a telescope?"

"Just keeping tabs. Are you really okay about this? Because I'm sure you could still pry him away. Or you know, even if he's hers for now, there's always next year. High school relationships never last."

"What about y–"

"Nicholas and I will be the exception."

"Naturally," Alex laughed.

"Well, no. I'm not interested," Freya said patiently. "I'm perfectly happy for Ethan and Emily. I hope they get married and have babies."

She really wasn't bothered by it, she told herself firmly. Jealousy was a normal, human emotion. You could still feel it even when you really didn't care for someone.

Chapter 16: 2019

"Do you remember how you used to use banana shampoo?" Nick asked Hannah.

The other two women burst out laughing while Hannah cringed. "Oh, God, don't remind me," she laughed. "I used it *all the time*. For three years or something."

"Hey, don't knock the banana shampoo," Nick protested. "It was your thing. I used to smell it when I sat behind you in Maths in Year 9."

"You used to smell my hair? That's creepy."

"Not deliberately! Just, you know. The banana smell was kind of potent."

They all laughed again. Their second meeting was going much more smoothly than the first, so far. The six of them had been chatting about their lives when suddenly, they'd started reminiscing about their high school days.

Hannah put her hands up. "My only defence is, it was the nineties."

"That's all the defence you need," Alex said. "It's my answer to everything. Unflattering old photo? It was the nineties. Unearthing my butterfly clips in an old box at Mum and Dad's? It was the nineties."

"It's a good excuse," Ethan added. "Not as good as the eighties, but still. The nineties definitely had their own feel, didn't they?"

"I didn't think so at the time!" Freya exclaimed. "That's what's so crazy. Suddenly everyone's all nostalgic for the nineties – even me! But I remember in the nineties I used to love listening to old eighties music and I thought how much more fun it all was back then."

"Oh, that's right. Weren't you a huge Eurythmics fan back in the day?"

"Oh my God. You remember that? I don't even know how I got into them, but I still love them," Freya laughed. "I was the only seventeen-year-old in 1999 who had all the Eurythmics CDs."

"Man, kids these days don't even *have* CDs."

"They probably don't even know what they are!"

"Well, *I* was all about the nineties music," Hannah interjected. "Remember my Green Day shrine on the wall?"

"I remember *you* loving boy bands." Freya directed this comment at Alex.

"I did not!" Alex exclaimed, and the other five all laughed, disbelief on their faces.

"Don't lie to us!" Hannah said. "We were there. We remember! I'm a little disappointed in us, to be honest, Freya, that we haven't reminded her of this every month for the past twenty years."

"Ugh, fine. I had a *small* thing for a boy band or two," Alex sighed. "It's hardly a crime, is it? Like we said – it was the nineties. *Everyone* loved boy bands."

"Not a crime at all," Sam said. "It just never seemed very… Alex-like of you."

Alex frowned, but the other five were all nodding sagely. "That's exactly it," Freya said. "Not very Alex-like."

"I don't even want to know what that means, but it definitely feels like an insult."

"It means it felt like you should have been locked away in your room listening to classical music or something," Hannah explained.

"Right, so definitely an insult, then."

"We all had our *things*. Freya and her reading," Hannah said, managing to make 'reading' sound like a terrible insult. "Ethan and his comics."

"Hey, I was just ahead of my time," Ethan protested. "Geek culture is so mainstream now. It's *cool* to be a geek. Hell, the highest grossing movies are always comic book adaptations! Everyone knows the names of these characters that used to be obscure. It's downright unfair."

"Unfair?"

"Yeah. If I was a teenager now, all the girls would love me."

They continued their trip down memory lane for a few minutes more, and then Hannah looked around at the group. "Right," she said decisively. "Should we go off in pairs again to have a chat?"

For the first time that day, a slight awkwardness settled over the group. Alex broke the silence by nodding. "Sure," she said. "Ready, Samuel?"

"Ready, Alexandra."

The six friends stood up and went their separate ways.

"SO, TELL ME ABOUT YOU and Emily."

Ethan looked startled for a moment, then laughed. "God, I haven't thought about Emily in so long. What do you want to know?"

Freya felt silly all of a sudden. Ethan and Emily had still been together when they finished high school. She had wondered from time to time, despite herself, whether they had lasted, whether they'd ended up married and lived happily ever after. Although she really hadn't been bothered when they'd first got together, she remembered the pang she felt when she found out that he'd slept with her. That they were serious. That had been the first time she'd really felt any kind of jealousy. It hadn't lasted long, and she hadn't really wanted to be with him. She just hadn't wanted to picture him with anyone else. It was mostly down to Hannah's constant input, she had always told herself, rather than any actual feelings towards Ethan. Besides, as much as she hated to admit it – even to herself – Ethan's attention towards her back in high school had been flattering. She had felt the absence when his gaze was directed to someone else.

"I guess... how long did you stay together? Why did you break up? That kind of thing."

"Oh, that. Well, I went on to Uni, as you know, and Emily was just working at a dress shop, not really sure of what she wanted to do. Anyway, a couple of years after school finished she applied for this job as a personal stylist in Melbourne, and she got it. I guess I was a bit shitty that she hadn't talked to me about it before she applied. She said she never thought she'd get it, but that was Em, you know? She never really wanted to have the difficult discussions. So we talked about what it would mean for us. I've really never liked Melbourne much, and I couldn't see myself living there. She loved the idea of making it her home – Melbourne was her favourite city. Neither of us wanted something long distance, so we ended it."

"Wow." Despite herself, Freya felt a small stab of jealousy that they'd lasted for two years after school finished. It was ridiculous, given that she and Ethan had stopped being friends before school even finished. Besides, it wasn't as if she had any right to be jealous of his dating history. Hell, she herself had been living with her partner not so long ago!

"And what about you? I know you weren't so keen on dating in high school," he said lightly. Neither of them had mentioned his obvious feelings for her at school, and she was happy not to do so. She didn't want to make things awkward for him – or for herself, for that matter. "Anything I should know about your love life?"

She shrugged. "Like I said, I lived with Jim for a while. He was my last relationship."

"When did that end?"

Freya grimaced. "More recently than I want to admit, to be honest. I'm completely over him, though."

Ethan shrugged. "It's none of my business, really. I was just curious."

There was a long pause between them, and then she said, "What if it is your business?"

"What do you mean?" Ethan studied the ground.

"Well, I don't place too much stock in this silly pact," she laughed, trying to act serene when her heart was racing a million miles an hour. She'd never made the first move with a guy before, and she hadn't planned to today either, but she couldn't deny the way she felt around him. It was still only early days, but she had to know where they stood. "But I guess I'm... seeing you in a way I never did before. I'm not saying we should get married, but maybe we could go out or something? What do you think?"

The silence felt interminable this time. Then Ethan shook his head, letting out a long breath. "I'm sorry, Frey."

She nodded and stared down at her feet, feeling her face get hot. She never should have said anything. Ethan was a gorgeous, kind, funny, single man in his thirties. He probably had a million women chasing after him. Her self-esteem had never been sky-high when it came to the opposite sex. What on earth had possessed her to make the first move?

"It's not you," he went on. "Well, in a way I suppose it is. But... it's just that I spent two years in high school completely in love with you. I'm just not sure I want to get in that head-space again."

She nodded, feeling oddly on the verge of tears. Ethan was nothing more than a little crush, if he even qualified as that. So why did she feel like she was about to dissolve in front of him? It was probably just humiliation. No one liked to be rejected. She should have asked him out over text or something. Or better yet, not at all.

"I get it," she said finally, forcing a smile. "Forget all about it. I know I didn't really give you the time of day in high school."

"It's not like you led me on," he laughed awkwardly. "You made it pretty clear that you weren't interested. I guess I was just too stuck on you to really see it."

Freya nodded, clearing her throat. "I guess it's about time we get back to the others."

They walked back in silence.

Chapter 17: 2019

While Freya and Ethan were having their heart-to-heart, Hannah was starting to wonder what the hell her problem was. How was it possible that the boy she'd had such amazing chemistry with had become a man she felt nothing for?

She'd had such high hopes when they had met up the first time. Nick was still gorgeous, and sweet, and charming, and all of the things he'd been in high school. She'd still felt the nervous flutters in her stomach at the sight of him. She'd mistaken it for feeling like maybe, maybe, there could be something there.

But now, the second time she was catching up with him, it was unmistakeable. Maybe it was the conversation they'd had about the nineties, which got her thinking about how much time had passed. Maybe it was just seeing him again without the shock and butterflies of their first meeting in twenty years. Whatever it was, she had to face facts. As much as she still liked Nick, it was only friendship she felt, nothing more.

They hadn't discussed it as such, but the feeling seemed to be mutual. Their conversation was easy and light-hearted, but he wasn't exactly trying to make the moves on her, either. They talked the whole time they were together, but they were busy discussing movies they'd seen and the best and worst parts of their jobs, rather than their long-term plans or anything that might have come up if there was something more promising on the horizon.

"Should we head back?" Hannah asked eventually. Part of her didn't want to stop chatting to Nick, but she knew the others would be waiting. She also knew that if she felt something more for him, the thought of their friends waiting for them never would have been enough to tear her away.

Nick nodded, and the two walked back.

When they arrived back with the others, Hannah's senses immediately alerted her that something was wrong. Alex and Sam seemed fairly normal, but there was a tension in the air that she could only assume came from the other 'couple' in the room. Freya looked like she was on the verge of tears.

"Well, I'm afraid I'll have to cut this party short," Ethan said somewhat awkwardly, standing up as soon as he saw Nick and Hannah returning. "Thanks guys, this was fun. I'll... see you next time?" It came out, unmistakeably, as a question.

The group of five all said their goodbyes, and the two other men headed out soon after.

The women stuck around at the restaurant after the men had left. Hannah wasted no time in asking the question she was dying to know the answer to. "What happened there?"

Freya took a deep breath. "I... I told Ethan I was interested in him, and he rejected me. Nicely," she added hastily. "But still. A rejection is a rejection, right?"

"Oh, Freya," Alex sighed. "I'm so sorry. It's not easy to put yourself out there!"

Hannah nodded in agreement. She knew how bad Freya must have felt when Ethan didn't reciprocate her feelings. It had to be all the worse happening so soon after her split from Jim. Even if her feelings for Ethan were nothing serious yet, at the very least it would have bruised her ego.

"I really thought it would happen for you guys," Hannah said, her voice filled with regret.

Freya made an obvious attempt to hold it together, but she burst into tears. Mortified, she wiped them away, but her friends each put a consoling arm around her and that set her off even further. "I hate crying in public," she sobbed.

"I know, I know," Alex cooed. "But you're hurt, and you're allowed to cry. He's not good enough for you."

"He is, though!" Freya burst out. "He is, and I can't even be angry at him. He's right. I knew how much he liked me in high school and I barely even deigned to glance his way."

"You can't force yourself to feel something you don't," Hannah argued. "You just weren't into dating when you were in school. He's just being stubborn." Her high school self had been so frustrated with Freya's seriousness, and her refusal to show any interest in the opposite sex, but now she felt nothing but sympathy for her friend. Okay, so Freya had hurt Ethan's pride when he was a teenager. The fact that he couldn't get over that now, twenty years later, was nothing short of ridiculous.

"And you and Nick?" Freya asked later, when her tears had subsided. "What's happening there?"

Hannah shook her head. "Just friends for us, too. He didn't do anything wrong. The chemistry just seems off somehow. I can't explain it." She gave a deep, dramatic sigh. "Like banana shampoo, maybe some things are just better off being kept in the nineties."

"So, this has been a highly successful experiment, then," Freya laughed dryly. "One in a same-sex relationship, one who I actually fell for who wants nothing to do with me, and fizzling, not sizzling, from the Fortitude High Wonder Couple."

Hannah sighed, thinking back to her lofty hopes back in high school of their future love and marriages. It was a romantic notion, but clearly, it was one she had to let go of. Real life didn't work that way.

Chapter 18: 2019

A week later Alex was sitting in a staff meeting, trying to concentrate. She had been running herself ragged lately and she was struggling not to yawn, sitting there at the table in the conference room. Between her exercise schedule, her normal weekly routine and her increased social life, it seemed like she was rarely home. She had enjoyed the outings with the guys as a change of pace, but maybe it wasn't such a bad thing that life was going back to normal. She was craving some more of her old routine.

Her ears pricked up at something her boss, Andrew, said. "Recent data shows our key demographic is eleven- and twelve-year-old callers," he said. "So we're going to target our marketing attempts at that age group, to try to get more people to call in."

"I think we need to do the opposite," Alex blurted out, regretting it immediately when all eyes in the room swung her way. Although they were staff meetings where everyone was welcome to contribute, most of the time it was the group passively listening to what Andrew said until they were allowed to get back to their *real* work. In everyone else's eyes, Alex knew, she had just needlessly extended the meeting.

"How do you mean, Alexandra?" Andrew asked, his tone somehow welcoming and wary all at once.

"My friend works at a high school and sees a lot of kids with various problems," Alex said, thinking back on Freya's words from a few weeks earlier. "We all know that older teenagers face things like self-harm and unwanted pregnancies. It got me thinking, why aren't those older kids calling us for help? It's not as though their problems go away – in fact, we all know they tend to get bigger." She paused, half-expecting to be cut off, but the room was silent. "Maybe we need to start a new division for teens? Or to market to them better or something? I don't know if it's the name 'kids' or what, but it doesn't seem to be working for older kids. I just don't want them feeling like they have nowhere to turn. We all know what that can lead to."

There was a thoughtful pause, and then her boss said, "You're right." He held up his hands as Alex's eyes began to gleam with excitement. "Don't get ahead of yourself, I'm not saying anything will happen yet. But it's worth looking into. Good thinking, Alexandra."

"Oh, that's amazing," she gushed, trying to stay professional. "I can help out with all the research. Like, maybe they'd rather message someone than actually talk on the phone? I can talk to my nephews and see what they'd be happiest with," she added, referring to her brother's two kids, who were fifteen and sixteen.

Andrew nodded, the wariness back in his eyes. "As I said, don't get ahead of yourself. I'll have a talk to the team and get back to you," he added, referring to the higher-ups at Kids in Crisis.

Alex smiled to herself as the meeting resumed. She knew she should take Andrew's advice and not get carried away, but it was so nice to feel this excited about her work again.

TO EVERYONE'S SURPRISE, it was Sam who kept their newly rediscovered friendship alive.

After being wounded by their romantic failings, Hannah and Freya hadn't planned to message the group again. Alex told them she had been interested in seeing her new friend Sam again, but she didn't feel comfortable arranging a one-on-one catch up. But Sam messaged the group, suggesting they all catch up for dinner the following week. "We still haven't had a proper catch up with all six of us," he pointed out in his message. "We all keep going off in pairs. What do you say? I'd love to hear more about what you've all been up to! Well, except Ethan. I know more than enough about his life."

Freya smiled at his attempt at light heartedness. He'd clearly been filled in on Ethan's rejection of her, as all good friends would be, but it was sweet that he still thought they all could be friends. She wasn't eager to see Ethan again after her embarrassing attempt to come on to him the week before, but it wasn't as though they were still in high school. There was no reason she couldn't see them all as friends, even if she and Ethan weren't going to be anything more. Besides, he'd managed to be friends with her in school even though he'd wanted more. The least she could do was return the favour now.

"Sure," she wrote back, feeling a sense of satisfaction at her own maturity. "I'm free Sunday lunchtime if everyone else is?"

The plan was set, and when Sunday rolled around, Freya was surprised to find herself feeling nervously excited. Of course it would be nice to see everyone again, but she had expected to be so filled with dread at seeing Ethan that she'd barely be able to get herself out the door. On the contrary, she was looking forward to seeing him, too.

She wondered briefly whether it was because she felt so comfortable with her old friend... or whether it was because her feelings for him were still there.

Freya sighed, not wanting to think any further about it. After all, Ethan had rejected her, after she'd essentially done the same to him back in high school. Clearly, timing was not on their side, and that was okay. She hadn't even been single long enough to care, she reminded herself sternly as she drove to the lunch venue. Some time alone would be good for her.

Getting more comfortable every time they saw the boys, Freya, Hannah and Alex had opted to drive themselves to the restaurant this time. It was a cute, charming little Greek place in West End that Freya had only been to once before. Ethan had suggested it, saying the location was central enough for those on both the north and south sides of town.

Freya arrived first, so grabbed a table and sat down, staring at her phone. She'd never really been attached to her phone the way some people were, but looking at it when she was waiting for people in public was as much a shield as a time waster. Having her phone in front of her helped to give people the sign that she wanted to be left alone, whereas sitting staring into space and daydreaming, the way she preferred, was somehow seen as an invitation for chat. Her sister Iris had lectured her about it in the past, in the way that only older sisters could. "Why are you hiding out from the world?" she'd asked, pre-Jim. "How are you ever going to meet anyone if you don't put yourself out there?" Then Freya had met Jim, and she'd got her sister off her back. Permanently, she'd thought, but apparently not.

Freya sometimes felt like she could actually murder Jim for what he'd done to her. She knew most people after a break-up said they were happy the relationship had happened, because it had given them the opportunity to grow, blah-blah-blah. This was not the case for Freya. She wished she'd never met him. She'd been perfectly fine being single, before meeting Jim. It had been nearly two years since her prior relationship and she had convinced herself that she was happy to be alone forever. But then Jim had come along and swept her off her feet, and suddenly, without him, she was struggling in a way she never had before.

She and Jim had only spoken a few times since the break-up, and even then it was only logistics. Moving his stuff out of the unit, and so on. Freya knew she was lucky the split was so easy. They weren't married, they didn't have kids, they'd never even adopted the cat they'd talked about. She should have realised all along that they were all talk.

At the same point, at least if they'd had a more concrete commitment then there would have been more of a sense of closure. It was so strange to share so much of your life with someone, only to have them simply disappear from it. It was as though the entire relationship had been some kind of fever dream.

Freya forced herself to snap out of her thoughts. She felt dangerously on the verge of tears, sitting there at the tiny

Mediterranean restaurant. She needed to pull herself together before the others arrived. She just hoped Ethan wasn't the first.

Fortunately Alex got there first, and Freya smiled with relief as she got up to hug her friend. "Are you okay?" Alex asked curiously. It wasn't unheard of for the women to hug in greeting, but they saw each other so often that they didn't usually bother except on special occasions. Freya just smiled, not wanting to get into the reason why she had felt the sudden need for comfort. "Just happy to see you," she said simply.

The two were flipping through the menu and chatting about their week when Nick turned up. In stark contrast to the teenaged girls who had barely had a conversation with Nick that Hannah wasn't involved in, the conversation between the three of them now was easy. Getting older might have had its drawbacks, but there were advantages to it, too, Freya thought.

Ethan was the last to arrive, which was noticeable since he was normally so punctual. Freya couldn't help but wonder if he had deliberately turned up later so as not to risk being alone with her. It was understandable, if so, since she hadn't wanted to be alone with him either... but still, it would sting a little. She pushed the thought out of her mind. After all, no one had forced Ethan to come to the get-together. He had obviously been happy enough to see her again, despite everything that had happened.

As promised, the group of six stuck together this time, rather than splintering off into their 'couples'. Given that the couples idea was essentially dead in the water anyway, it seemed the more sensible thing to do, and the conversation between the six of them flowed easily.

Freya found herself feeling pleased with the way their friendship group was going. Things with Ethan were much less awkward than she'd expected, and she knew she'd be happy to keep catching up as a group. She might not have found true love through their little marital pact, but you could never have enough good friends. Besides, there was something special about the people you met in high school.

Chapter 19: 2019

Ten days after the staff meeting where Alex had proposed her idea about a teens' crisis line, her boss called her into her office. Alex felt a tickle of nervous excitement. She was fairly sure the unplanned meeting was going to be about her idea, one way or the other. But would Andrew shoot her down entirely, or give her the go ahead?

Fortunately, he didn't beat around the bush.

"We've decided to start the new teen division you suggested," he said, and her stomach gave a somersault of excitement. Andrew went on. "It will be a smaller division, but I think it's important for the older kids to have somewhere they feel they can turn. Anyway, it will be an official subdivision of Kids in Crisis. We're going to call it Teens in Turmoil."

"TIT?" Alex asked sceptically. At the look on his face, she smiled and went quiet. There was no point in pushing her luck.

"Since it was your idea and you've offered to help run the research, we'd like you to head the division."

"Me?" It came out as a squeak.

"Yes. It will be a small team, though," he warned. "We'll just have two phone operators – one day and one night – to help you out to start with, and then we'll see where it goes from there. You'll need to essentially act as the social media manager, researcher, data analyst *and* help out with the phones as needed. Obviously, if it grows substantially then we'll look at expanding the team. If you do want to take this on, you'll have to be prepared to be extremely busy for a while."

Alex nodded, feeling overwhelmed. It would be a huge responsibility, but she felt truly excited about her work for the first time in a while. She had always enjoyed a challenge, and this was shaping up to be a great one.

"Of course," Andrew went on, "I say phone operators for want of a better term. I agree that teenagers don't really talk on the phone anymore, so I think some kind of instant messaging system will be the best option, like you suggested, although they can still phone if they want to. The IT department can run the technical side of things for you, but for most of the day-to-day operations, you'll be on your own."

"Do I get a budget?" she asked, trying to get things sorted in her head.

"You'll have a small budget to assist with marketing, naturally. Aside from that, it will just be your wage and that of the other phone operators."

Alex smiled and thanked her boss before walking away, her mind whirring. She would have to be careful with her marketing budget to ensure she got the word out there. She wanted Teens in Turmoil to be a huge success.

THE SAME DAY THAT ALEX was enjoying her success, Freya was having a decidedly less positive time.

She went straight home from work and got into the shower, breathing in deeply as the hot water hit her back. It had been another fairly stressful day, but coming home always made her feel good. She couldn't help but wonder when the work that she'd always enjoyed had started making her feel so tired.

When she was dry she slipped on her favourite silky nightie with a matching robe over the top, and got ready to settle in for a quiet night. She was surprised by the sound of a knock on the door. She didn't often have unannounced visitors, especially on a Monday night. She went to the door, tightening her robe around her as she did so. The nightie was perfectly respectable, but it still felt a little embarrassing to be caught in her pyjamas at just after 5pm.

"Jim!" She stared in shock at the man in her hallway.

Jim glanced down at her body, then looked away, running a hand awkwardly through his hair. "Hey, Frey. Sorry, I guess I should have called first."

"I also feel like you've lost the right to call me 'Frey,'" she said, her tone curt. "That kind of familiarity went out the window when you hooked up with what's-her-name, wouldn't you agree? What *is* her name, anyway?"

"Beth," he said in a low voice, looking at his feet.

"Ah, Beth. Are you happy together?" She tried to sound blasé, but the truth was, she didn't really want to know. She didn't want him to be happy with Beth, but she didn't want him to have thrown their entire relationship away for a short-lived fling, either.

As much as she tried to play it cool, she was hurting. Seeing Jim in front of her made the whole situation far too real, and it was only then that she realised how she had avoided facing it. She had thrown herself into her work, and more recently, into socialising with the guys from high school. She hadn't realised quite how much of a coping mechanism the distraction had been. Now that Jim was here, standing larger-than-life in her doorway, it was hard to pretend he had never mattered to her. She wished she could.

"We're not together." He ran his hand through his hair again. She had always thought that gesture was kind of cute, but now, it was infuriating. Everything he did was infuriating. "I... can I come in?"

Freya thought about slamming the door in his face but, sighing, stepped back and let him in. She was angry, yes, but she was hurt and confused, as well. She wished there was only pure rage. Besides, she couldn't deny feeling curious about what he was here to say.

She led him to the couch, wondering if she should offer him something to drink. This was what her six-year relation-ship had come to? Wondering if she should offer him a glass of water, like he was a woman in her mother's sewing circle or something?

"The place looks good," Jim said, looking around the apart-ment that used to be his. Freya was pleased that he had at least had the decency to move out without her having to ask him to, rather than trying to convince her she should be the one to move. She loved living there. Maybe one day she would move further out of the city, but for now, she was content to stay there, in the modern apartment with its amazing view.

There was silence for a moment when they sat on the couch, and Freya had to forcibly stop herself from filling it. Jim had come to her, after all. He had to be here for a reason. She wasn't going to sit here and make small talk to make him feel more comfortable.

"Freya, I'm taking a leap. I know you probably don't want to hear it... it's just... I made a huge mistake," he said finally, looking at his hands. "I threw away the best relationship I've ever had. I don't want to be with anybody but you."

You should have thought of that before you climbed on top of Beth, Freya thought, but she kept silent.

"I was wondering... I know I don't deserve another chance, but if you take me back, Freya, I'll spend the rest of my life making it up to you."

She stared at him, unable to form any words in response. This was beyond anything she'd ever expected. She'd hoped he might realise he'd made a mistake, but to actually come back, begging for another chance? Freya knew she should feel victorious, amused at his misery. But she didn't. She felt somehow sad, almost empty.

"You were always too good for me," Jim went on in a rush, possibly sensing her shock. "I don't know why I did it. She was just paying so much attention to me, and I fell for it. I made a stupid mistake. I'd never do anything like that again. We could get married. We could have kids. The whole deal."

Freya's brain seemed to be going at a hundred miles an hour. She opened her mouth to speak, but no words came out. Here was Jim, begging for another chance. He'd hurt her, true. But they'd had so many good times together. Since the split she'd zeroed in on the negatives of their relationship, possibly because it was easier than thinking about the positives after he'd hurt her. But here he was, saying he'd made a mistake. Saying she was too good for him. She thought about Ethan, and his rejection of her. She thought of Alex and Hannah, two beautiful, successful women who were having the same limited luck dating in their thirties as she was.

She was smart enough and confident enough to know you were never supposed to settle for something, just to avoid being alone. But life without Jim was no picnic, either. He seemed so remorseful about what he'd done. And would she ever find anyone who loved her as much as he did? Did the saying "better the devil you know" have some truth to it, after all?

Sure, people said you shouldn't settle, but the people who said that were probably all married. Not everyone knew how rough life could get for older single people out there in the world. She did know, and she didn't relish living that life forever.

She didn't relish a life with Jim forever, either. But she was uncertain enough not to want to slam the door in his face, at the very least.

"I need some time," she said finally, and Jim's face lit up.

"Of course," he said quickly. Clearly, even a request for time was more than he had expected. She wondered if it was more than he deserved.

WHEN JIM LEFT, FREYA paced around her apartment, thinking back to the early days of their relationship.

Their first date had been pretty standard stuff, Saturday morning brunch. She had liked him straight away, but wasn't sure there was that much potential there. Still, her sister had been on her case about the fact that so few of her first dates led to second dates, so she had decided to go out with him again when he asked.

As usual, Iris was right. The second date was where Jim really shone.

He picked her up from her house. It sounded lame, but she'd never actually been picked up for a first or second date before, instead always meeting the guy somewhere. That had been enough to impress her, even without anything else.

He'd driven her to the inner-city suburb of Saint Lucia, leaving his car by the river. She hadn't had a clue where they were going. Then he had walked her, hand-in-hand, to the river, where there was a City Cat stop. Despite having lived in Brisbane her whole life, Frey had never travelled by City Cat before. She'd thought of the riverboats as a cute transportation option for tourists, getting people from here to there in a leisurely way. Freya always needed to get places in a hurry. She didn't have the time to dawdle along the river. She caught the bus to work in the Valley, and she drove everywhere else. But somehow, that night, it was perfectly romantic.

They had taken the riverboat to Southbank, where he took her to a charming family-run Turkish restaurant. The conversation sparkled, and she felt like she'd known him forever. As if dinner wasn't enough, he'd taken her to a rooftop bar afterwards, where they'd had expensive cocktails and clinked their glasses together from their seats overlooking the city. Dates, for Freya, had usually consisted of a simple dinner and maybe a kiss goodnight. This felt like something out of a romantic movie.

At the end of the night, she hadn't wanted to say goodbye to him. She couldn't wait until he messaged to arrange a third date, and then a fourth. By their first anniversary they had rented their place together and they were talking seriously about being together forever.

Around the time of their two-year anniversary, they'd taken a trip to England together. His family was English, although Jim himself had moved to Australia when he was four so had a very limited English accent. They had stayed with his aunts and uncles, which had given them the opportunity to live and eat like locals while sightseeing like tourists. That four-week trip remained one of the highlights of Freya's life. Even after they'd split, she couldn't look back at their holiday with anything other than fondness.

Freya had always wanted to get married, but it had never been on Jim's agenda. She'd convinced herself she was fine with it. Of course the true fairy-tale for her would have involved marriage, but she would rather be with Jim, whatever that looked like.

And now, Jim was willing to offer her everything she'd wanted. Everything Ethan wouldn't give her. She just wasn't sure if she wanted it from Jim anymore.

Freya sighed. She was confusing herself, going around and around in circles like this. She needed to talk it over with her friends.

HANNAH AND ALEX WERE predictably outraged when they heard about Jim's plea to come back into her life.

"You've got to be kidding me!" Hannah exclaimed, her eyes flashing furiously. "After what he did to you! And it's not like he ever deserved you in the first place, anyway." Alex was nodding along in angry agreement.

Freya remained silent, thinking of how Hannah's words unknowingly echoed Jim's own. It seemed the only person who didn't think Freya was too good for Jim was Freya herself.

"You're *not* considering this?" the always perceptive Alex asked, obviously picking up on Freya's silence.

Freya sighed. "I don't know! I mean, I'm still angry at him for what he did, but is one mistake worth throwing six happy years away for?"

"Yes!" her two friends chorused emphatically.

"Besides, it's not just one mistake," Alex went on. "Think about what your relationship was like, even before he cheated on you."

"That's all I've been doing all d–"

"No, *seriously* think! Don't look with rose coloured glasses. Because here's what I see." Alex paused. Freya wasn't sure whether she was thinking carefully about her next words, or if she just wanted to give them added gravity.

"The Freya who was with Jim was always at his beck and call. You wouldn't stay out late if he didn't want you to. You always checked in with him before doing anything, even just going for a quick drink after work. Which would be *fine* if he'd shown you the same courtesy once in a while, but he never did. The Freya who was with Jim was always quieter when he was around, and that's not a good sign. It was like you didn't want to say the wrong thing around him. Plus, the Freya who was with Jim was happy to give up her dreams of marriage and kids, just to be with him."

That stopped any protest that might have escaped Freya's lips.

She knew Alex was right. Freya had tried to deny how much she wanted marriage and children, even to herself. She had told herself that she was content enough with Jim for it not to matter. But it always had. She had tried to never let on to her friends, but obviously Alex, at least, had caught on. She should have known there was no fooling her.

"He's saying he'll give me all that now," she said finally.

Alex shook her head furiously. "Too little, too late. Do you really want someone who only wants to marry you – to have *children* with you – so he can get you back?"

Freya sighed, trying to put her feelings into words. The lump in her throat didn't help. "It's not like I'll get marriage and kids anytime soon with anyone else, though. I might not even be able to *have* kids anymore. I'm not exactly a spring chicken."

"People your age get pregnant all the time," Hannah protested.

"Besides," Alex added seriously, "do you really want to do all of that with Jim?"

Freya sighed. Deep down, she knew her friends were right. As hard as it could get sometimes, being single, she owed herself more than settling for Jim. She knew that if Ethan had accepted her advances, she would never even have considered getting back with Jim over him. The fact that Ethan didn't want her didn't mean she had to go back to her ex. She was an independent person. If she never found someone else, well, she would be just fine.

She just wished she felt happier about it all.

Chapter 20: 2019

June ended up being the busiest time at work for the three women. For Freya it meant the end of the first school semester was approaching, which led to students spending more time in the library, trying to make up for the study they should have been doing all along. Alex was working overtime to try to achieve as much as she could to prepare for the launch of the Teens in Turmoil programme, which had become her greatest passion. As for Hannah, the personal training business had traditionally been at its slowest during the winter months, so for the past two years she had been pushing a "get your summer body in winter!" campaign with special deals and an eight-week fitness challenge. It had paid off, and now June was one of her busiest times.

Their long work hours meant that six weeks had lapsed since they had last seen the guys. It was Alex who suggested they organise a catch up again, knowing from previous experience how easy it would be to let the friendship slide if they left it too long between get-togethers.

To their surprise, Nick suggested holding the get together at his place. "I have a big deck, and it might be more comfortable than a restaurant?" he suggested. Naturally, Hannah took to the women's private chat group in response, saying "I remember Nick's BIG DECK well!"

In the bigger chat group, the six of them arranged what they would all bring and made a date for the following Saturday at lunchtime.

HANNAH WAS THE FIRST to arrive for once. Armed with a pesto pasta salad, she let herself up to Nick's apartment and looked around, stunned.

He wasn't joking about the big deck, but the whole apartment was much larger than she'd have expected, especially in West End, which wasn't cheap. How much did marketing managers make, anyway? Hannah wondered, looking around. It was also artfully furnished. The walls and tiles were cream, providing a nice neutral palette. He had black leather lounges and just a few touches of his personality around the place, such as some framed art pieces. It looked like it had been professionally decorated.

"This place is great," she enthused to Nick as she placed the pasta salad down on his kitchen bench. "Two bedrooms?"

Nick nodded. "Yeah, it's pretty roomy, hey? And the location's great," he added, gesturing out towards the deck which overlooked West End, with its trendy café and boutiques. "Prices in Sydney went up a fair bit after we bought there, so I came home with a pretty good deposit for this place."

"Good job," she said, sidestepping any mention of his ex-wife. "It's really nice."

"The only downside is you can't have dogs here."

"Oh, you're a dog lover?" Hannah wondered if that was something she'd known and forgotten. Nick's family had owned a dog, an Alsatian named Connie, when they were dating, but she hadn't realised it was a priority for him. She suddenly flashed back to the photo of him hugging the Labrador when she'd Facebook stalked him. She nearly asked whose dog that was, but stopped herself. No need to make herself look too creepy.

Nick shrugged. "I mean, sometimes it would be nice to have something to come home to."

Hannah nodded, trying not to let anything show on her expression. She was mostly happy living alone, but sometimes she felt the same way as Nick. Coming home alone, night after night, wasn't always the easiest life.

"Anyway, have a seat," he added. "Can I get you a drink?"

Hannah settled herself on the couch while Nick fixed them each a sparkling water. She thought of the teenaged boy who'd lived off soft drinks and energy drinks, and wondered what he would think of this health-conscious man.

To her surprise, when Nick came to sit down he settled right beside her, rather than taking one of the other armchairs. He leaned back casually with his hand on the back of the couch. She knew he was just making himself comfortable, but it also felt like he was putting his arm around her. Hannah thought back to their previous meeting, and how she had dismissed them as having no chemistry anymore. She wondered now if that was accurate. Was it possible she had given up too easily?

"Nick..." she said, unsure where she was going with her sentence. In the end, it didn't matter. The two of them made eye contact for a moment and then, with a familiarity that surprised her, they both leaned in for a kiss. As their lips touched, Hannah momentarily felt seventeen again.

She didn't know what might have happened next if not for the knock on the door. Nick leapt up as though he had been caught doing something wrong, which in a way, he had. He made for the door and let Ethan in, who was followed in quick succession by Alex. The other two each turned up within the next ten minutes, and the whole group was together again.

Hannah's heart was still racing as she made small talk with her friends. She wondered if anything showed on her face, but neither of her girlfriends gave her the meaningful look that she knew would have been directed her way had they caught on. Besides, what was the big deal? She had kissed her old boyfriend. They were both single, consenting adults. They hadn't done anything wrong.

After a few minutes, Hannah excused herself for the bathroom. She didn't actually need the toilet, but she did need some time alone to process her thoughts. She sat down on the edge of the toilet lid, her head in her hands, trying to figure out how she felt about the whole thing.

The kiss had felt... warm. Safe. Familiar. All of those good things.

But it hadn't felt *right*.

It felt like returning to your childhood home as an adult. It felt comforting, but you knew it wasn't your home anymore.

Hannah couldn't deny that she felt drawn to Nick, but not because she wanted to be with him. The thought of him took her back to a simpler time, when she was so sure of the future. As she got older, everything seemed to get more complicated.

Was it a crime to feel a little nostalgic? But that was all it was, nostalgia, like watching your favourite old sitcom when times got tough.

Nick was a great guy, but he was no longer the one for her.

She hoped he felt the same way about her, or things might have just become very complicated.

LATER THAT EVENING, Hannah deliberately stuck around after the others left. Freya gave her a quizzical look as she went to leave. "Are you heading down, too?" she asked, gesturing towards the elevator.

"Um... no, I think I'm going to help Nick tidy up here."

Hannah wasn't typically the type to stick around and tidy, but if Freya suspected anything, she didn't let it show. Lifting her hand in a wave, she disappeared out the door.

"So," Hannah said, the moment they were alone.

Nick laughed. "So. Not so much here to help me tidy up, then?"

"I mean, I can do that too, but I thought we should probably talk."

"Yeah, I agree. Come have a seat," he said, and went and sat on the couch again. This time he sat first, so Hannah helped herself to one of the separate armchairs. After what had happened last time they got on the couch, she didn't want to take any chances.

"Ah," he said. "I guess that tells me everything I need to know."

"It was a good kiss," she said honestly. "I mean, I think we've always had pretty good chemistry."

"Yeah, I remember that too..."

They both smiled, Hannah reminiscing about how they couldn't keep their hands off each other back in the day. The combination of their famous chemistry and normal teenage hormones had been unbeatable. But now, it felt like they were talking about two different people.

"But..."

"But it's not right. Not anymore," Nick finished for her. "I've been thinking the same thing. The kiss took me by surprise, I've got to say! But I honestly think we just needed to test the waters," he added. "See if there was anything there. And now we know for sure."

Hannah let out a breath, relieved. "Okay, good. I'm glad we're on the same page. I was worried things just got a lot more complicated."

"I'll always love you," he said openly, "but not in the way I used to. I think that part of our lives has gone now. Friends?"

Hannah smiled over at him, feeling lighter already. "We'll always be friends."

Chapter 21: 2019

Only two weeks after Hannah and Nick's kiss, the group met up again. This time they went to a bar, which Freya was reluctant about at first. The bar scene had never really been for her. As it turned out, they had a great time. The music was loud enough to add to the atmosphere, but not so loud they had to scream to be heard. The drinks were flowing, and Freya was surprised to find herself having the time of her life.

In fact, she couldn't remember the last time she'd had this much fun. How had they let the guys out of their lives for so long? Since the split with Jim her life had consisted of work and her limited social circle. Now, she felt ten years younger than she had before they'd made contact with the guys. Even though the marriage pact hadn't worked out, she was glad it had led to this.

Hannah grabbed her now, pulling her out on the dance floor and Freya followed, laughing. She normally wasn't much of a dancer, but she felt like it tonight. She wanted to be the sort of young, free person who would go and whirl around on the dance floor without thinking twice.

Soon Ethan had followed them out there and the three of them whirled around together in giddy circles. The others watched from the bar, looking amused. Freya knew there was no point trying to get Alex out to join them, but Ethan went back to coerce Sam. Freya could see Nick shaking his head – he wasn't going to be convinced, either.

Sam joined them and the four of them danced together, laughing and spinning. Suddenly, a slow song came on. Sam grinned at Hannah, then took her in his arms. She smiled back at him as they danced together.

Ethan shrugged at Freya, looking self-conscious, and she smiled back. It seemed a little too close for comfort to dance with Ethan so soon after she'd expressed her feelings for him, but it would be all the more awkward to go and sit out, like she was trying to make a point or something. She shrugged back at him and stepped closer.

Ethan put his hands on her sides, the two of them swaying together. Freya felt colour rising to her cheeks. For God's sake, it was just dancing! And yes, she had been embarrassed when Ethan hadn't returned her feelings, but she wasn't a child anymore. She could deal with this. For now, it was nice to dance with an old friend, she told herself firmly. That was all this was.

The song felt like it went on forever. Freya was quietly thrilled when it finished and she could make her way off the dance floor without drawing attention to herself. "I think I'm all danced out," she laughed, trying to sound light-hearted. "I'm going to go have a water break."

"Yeah, me too."

The two of them signalled to Hannah and Sam, who were still dancing, and went back to the bar where Alex and Nick were making awkward small talk.

"You guys looked like you were having fun out there," Alex said.

"Oh, we were!" Freya said, possibly too quickly. "You know how I love to dance." She caught the dubious look Alex threw her, but didn't acknowledge it. Alex, thankfully, was tactful enough not to point out that Freya decidedly did *not* love dancing on a typical night out.

"Alex was just telling me about her work," Nick said. "I think Teens in Turmoil is such a great idea."

"You should do some marketing for her," Ethan suggested.

Nick looked at Alex thoughtfully. "I mean, I could."

Alex looked pleased, but said, "I don't have a huge budget, I'm afraid. It's just a new part of the business, so I've been tasked with doing most of the work myself to get it off the ground."

Nick shrugged. "It doesn't sound like a huge job, so I'm more than willing to give you mates' rates," he said, reaching into his wallet. "Take my card and shoot me an email at my work address if you want to talk about it."

"Okay, I will. Thanks, Nick!"

"How *is* your business going?" Freya asked him. "Moving up from Sydney must have been a bit of a setback."

"Not as much as you'd think, actually. It's a smaller market, obviously, but that also means there's less competitors out there. Plus, Brisbane's home, so I already had a few contacts here. It seems to be doing pretty well."

"That's great," Freya said sincerely. She could see his work meant a lot to him.

"What about you? Would you ever work somewhere else?" Nick asked her.

Freya thought it over. "I don't know. I love working at Fortitude High and I've made a good name for myself, but sometimes I feel a little... stunted, I guess? I mean, I went to school there and now I work there. But the idea of starting somewhere new kind of scares me."

"Scary can be good," Ethan pointed out.

"True, but it can also just be... scary. I've always been pretty happy in my comfort zone."

Hannah and Sam came back then, giggling. Sam was breathing heavily but Hannah, used to being active on a daily basis, seemed largely unaffected by her time on the dance floor. "That was fun," she exclaimed. "I need another cocktail. Anyone?"

Nick shook his head. "I should be going, actually. I've got an early breakfast with Mum tomorrow."

"Aww!" the three women exclaimed in unison, and Nick laughed.

"Yeah, I'm an amazing son, I know, I know. It was good to see you all!"

"Actually, I'm going to head off with you," Sam said, and held up a hand as they started to protest. "I know, but I need to head soon too, and at least this way we can split the cost of the Uber."

"Boring," Hannah sulked, but she didn't seem too distressed as she lined up to get her cocktail.

The four remaining friends laughed together for another hour before Alex pulled out her phone to check the time, stifling a yawn. "I might have to go, too," she said.

"What's *your* excuse?" Hannah demanded.

"I'm old and exhausted."

"I'm going to stay a bit longer," Ethan said. "Freya, you're not going yet, are you?"

"Um... no, I'll stay," Freya said, hardly daring to hope. Did Ethan just want to stay out to avoid going home to a quiet house, or did he actually want to spend more time with her? She realised Alex was wondering the same thing when her friend grabbed Hannah.

"Hey, Han, why don't you come with me?" Alex asked, her hand on Hannah's wrist.

"Seriously? The night's still y–" Freya could see Alex's grip tighten on Hannah's arm and their friend suddenly seemed to catch on. "Oh, yeah. I guess I should have an early one. I've been overdoing it lately!" Hannah laughed, too loudly. "We'll leave you guys to it, then?"

Freya rolled her eyes as her girlfriends left. Sober Hannah had never exactly been known for her tact, but Drunk Hannah was something else entirely!

Left alone with Ethan, Freya tried to calm her thoughts. Somehow, being alone with Ethan at the bar was even more uncomfortable than dancing with him had been. Well, *uncomfortable* wasn't exactly the word. Both moments had filled her body with a heat she didn't want to think about. Ethan had made it pretty clear that he was only interested in her as a friend. She didn't want to get carried away.

"Do you want a drink?" she asked finally, trying to break the silence that had fallen over them since they'd been left alone.

Ethan shook his head. He was staring at her, something unreadable in his eyes.

"What is it?" she asked finally, quietly. She didn't want to make things stranger than they already were between the two of them, but she couldn't stand there with him staring at her, either. It was a little too close for comfort. One way or another, she had to know what he was thinking.

"It's just..." he paused, sighing. It seemed like he was as lost for words as she was. "It's just that I think I was lying to myself."

Now it seemed like there was little mistaking his words. She supposed he could have meant anything, but it seemed pretty clear that he might feel the same way she did. "How so?" she asked, hoping she didn't sound as anxious as she felt.

Ethan gave a short laugh. "I think you know how," he said, and then he took a step closer to her.

Freya stared up at him, wordlessly. Then she reached up and wrapped her arm around his neck, pulling him in for a kiss.

She didn't know what she would do if he pulled back, if she really had misunderstood what he was saying. But she didn't need to worry. He kissed her back, deep and intense. It was exactly the way she'd been picturing.

"Wait," she gasped after a while, pulling back. Her body was screaming at her to keep going, but she needed to know. "I just don't want this to be... I mean, I *really* like you, Ethan. Is this just a physical thing? Or is there maybe something more?"

To her surprise, Ethan laughed. Her heart hammered in her chest as she waited for his response.

"Freya," he said seriously, putting his hand gently on her cheek. "One thing you never have to worry about is how I feel about you."

It was as though all the noise in the crowded bar had disappeared. It seemed like they were the only two people left in the world. The feelings that surged through her then were so intense, it was hard not to burst into tears. She had never before had a man look at her the way Ethan was now, or admit to his feelings so openly. In her past relationships she had always been the one who wanted to talk about feelings, who seemed more into the relationship than the guy was. This was all new to her. Ethan truly was a prize.

They leaned back in again, their kisses growing even deeper and more urgent this time. She couldn't imagine that she'd gone all this time without being close to Ethan in this way. It felt so right, as though they should have been together all along. Maybe they should have been.

"Let's get out of here," she whispered in his ear, and he nodded wordlessly.

Ethan's place was only fifteen minutes from the city so when they jumped into a cab together, he gave his address. Freya's heart was pounding. Was she really going to go back to Ethan's place five minutes after they'd kissed for the first time? What was she thinking? This wasn't what calm, sensible Freya Collins did.

She didn't care.

When they got back to Ethan's place, they wasted little time in starting to kiss again. It had been an exercise in self-control to keep her hands off him in the cab ride home. He led her into the bedroom and they fell into bed together, their hands and lips never leaving the other's body.

Freya had never slept with anyone on the first date before, and this couldn't even be classified as a date. This was unheard of for her. But this was *Ethan*, who she'd known for so long. She'd never felt safer. She'd never wanted to be with anyone more. As Ethan's hands unbuttoned her jeans, she pressed her hips up into his body, urging him on.

Being with Ethan felt new and exciting and somehow familiar, all at once. The sex was amazing, but it wasn't just that. It was the feeling that finally, finally, she was with the right partner.

Chapter 22: 2019

When Freya woke up in Ethan's bed, the sheets tousled and suddenly all too aware of her nudity, she had felt momentarily embarrassed, as though she'd been caught doing something she shouldn't. But then she'd remembered the feeling of Ethan's hands all over her body and she'd been filled with pleasure. So much so, in fact, that she soon initiated round two at six o'clock in the morning.

They'd fallen back asleep after that, his arms wrapped around hers. When she'd woken up again at nine, he was gone, and she'd panicked for a moment before remembering that it was his apartment. Wherever he'd gone, it wasn't as though he'd disappeared forever. And sure enough he came back moments later, holding a glass of orange juice and a plate full of danishes.

"Did you make them?" she asked, surprised.

He laughed. "Thanks for the faith in me, but no. There's a bakery downstairs," he said, pulling his shirt off and sliding back into bed with her.

Freya reached over and ran her hand up the side of his jeans. "You're still a little overdressed," she said, and he unbuttoned his jeans and pulled them off without needing any further invitation.

Ethan grinned at her, suddenly looking more like his cheeky teenaged self. "Man, if seventeen-year-old Ethan could see us now..."

"It's a crazy old world, isn't it?" Freya asked. "Here I am, naked in bed with Ethan Moore, casually eating a cheese danish."

"Crazy, but good. Here, try the raspberry." He held his danish out to her and she leaned over and took a bite.

"So good! I can see why you live here."

"Yeah, I'm paying way too much for the place, but I just can't give up the bakery. I'm on a first-name basis there."

"This isn't where you lived with Sam, is it?"

"Nah, we gave that place up a while ago. It's always been just me here."

"It's a nice place." Not that she'd had much time to admire it as they'd raced towards the bedroom, she thought, having to fight the urge to burst out laughing at nothing in particular.

"Yeah, I'm happy here."

The two fell into a companionable silence then, eating their danishes side by side. It was only then that it occurred to Freya that she might be overstaying her welcome. "Did you have any plans for today?"

Ethan shook his head. "I thought I might be a bit hungover, so I didn't make any plans. I was going to do some housework, but that was about it. And I mean, now I have a naked girl in my bed, so housework can definitely wait."

"And the hangover?"

"Doesn't feel too bad at all," he said, giving her a quick kiss.

"Happy to stay in bed a little while longer, then?" Freya asked. "I'm cold, and I'd hate to get up too soon."

"I'll warm you up," Ethan said, and she squealed with laughter as he reached over and lay the bulk of his body on top of hers. He gazed down at her and they were soon kissing again, just as passionately as they had the night before.

It was hard to remember a better day.

Chapter 23: 2019

Freya, Hannah and Alex wouldn't normally have seen each other so soon, but when Ethan finally drove Freya home just after midday, she messaged her friends immediately.

"Come to my place," she wrote, a directive rather than a request. "I'll buy hot chocs. See you in an hour?"

The two replies came in quickly, one after the other. Yes, both women were free and would be around at her place soon.

Freya smiled as she walked down to the nearby café to buy some hot chocolates. It was only when she got there that she realised how starving she was. She might have eaten her weight in danishes, but she and Ethan had worked up quite the appetite! She bought a spinach roll on a whim, munching on it as she walked back to her place, imaging her friends' reaction to her news.

Alex arrived first, but Freya was determined not to say anything until Hannah was there too. "Hot chocolate?" she asked, holding out the drink.

Alex eyed her suspiciously. "What's going on?" The sudden demand for her friends to come over wasn't typical for Freya on a Sunday afternoon, especially after seeing each other the night before.

Freya shrugged. "I just felt like hanging out with my girls. How are you feeling after last night?"

"Fine. I didn't drink too much, and I actually had a sleep in this morning."

Freya hid a smile, knowing that Alex counted 7.30 as a sleep in.

Hannah burst through the open front door a few minutes later, looking a little dishevelled.

"And how did *you* pull up after last night?" Freya laughed, looking at her.

"I feel like shit," Hannah said bluntly, flopping down on Freya's couch. "I'm too old to drink."

Her two friends laughed. Hannah made this proclamation on a fairly regular basis, and just as regularly she had a big night again. "But I'm here, so you're welcome," Hannah went on. "I didn't need a sleep-in."

"It's after one."

"Yeah, like I said. I got out of bed for you. What's up?"

"Oh, nothing," Freya said coyly, enjoying dragging this out.

"Freya!" her two friends chorused in unison.

"Oh, alright. I just thought I'd tell you in person that Ethan and I hooked up last night."

Her two friends squealed, seeming genuinely excited for Freya. "No way!" Hannah exclaimed. "Tell us everything!"

"Yeah! I was hoping that was it when you messaged! What do you mean exactly by 'hooked up'?"

Freya laughed, suddenly feeling shy. "Well," she said, unwilling to just come right out and say it. "We were at the bar, and we were dancing... That's when you guys left..."

"That's *why* we left," Hannah interjected.

"Yeah, I know. Thanks, by the way," Freya said sheepishly. "After you guys left, Ethan was really staring at me and I asked him what was up. He said something about maybe being wrong, and I... I kissed him." Even retelling the story, Freya could hardly believe how daring she had been. After being so humiliated when Ethan rejected her, she was still willing to go in for a kiss just a few weeks later. That had to say something about her feelings for him.

"That's awesome!" Hannah squealed. "Go Freya! Then what?"

"Then we... went back to his place."

Hannah and Alex's jaws dropped open at the same time, almost comically. Freya knew it was out of the norm behaviour for her, but that was part of what she loved about it. It was nice to have a man make her drop all her inhibitions.

"You shagged him, you sly dog!" Hannah cried, and Freya laughed as she nodded her affirmation. "Four times," she said, holding up the fingers to match.

"Freya! Oh, I'm so happy for you!" That was Alex, nearly bouncing up and down on her seat. Freya tried to think of the last time she'd seen her sensible, intelligent friend look so girlishly excited. "I think you guys will just be so cute together."

At that, a knot of dread entered Freya's belly. As happy as Ethan made her, she couldn't help but worry that it was all too good to be true. "I hope he actually wants something long-term," she said.

"Didn't you guys talk about that?" Alex asked.

Freya shrugged. "Sort of. I asked if he was really into me, and he said the one thing I never have to worry about is how he feels about me."

Alex and Hannah groaned together, sounds filled with envy and longing. "Ugh, you're so lucky," Hannah sighed. "I wish I'd found that."

"So you definitely think it's a dead-end with Nick?"

"I mean, we have history... and we still have chemistry..."

"And biology... and a little French..." Freya intoned.

"Funny! But no, I think the kiss proved it, unfortunately. There's nothing there anymore, as much as I'd like there to be. It would be easy, wouldn't it? You know, falling back in with the high school boyfriend."

"This doesn't feel easy," Freya admitted. It had last night. Everything had seemed straightforward and simple. She'd been so happy in Ethan's arms, kissing him. But now, it all seemed like she was walking through a house made of cards, terrified it was all going to collapse around her. She'd thought talking to her friends about things with Ethan would make her feel good, and it had, momentarily. But it was only now she realised how much he actually meant to her. It was only day two of the relationship – if it even was a relationship – and she already didn't know if she could bear losing him.

"Stop that," Alex said firmly. "Don't be so... Freya."

"Did you just use my name as a verb?"

"Yes. You're Freya-ing everywhere."

"And what, precisely, does the verb 'to Freya' mean?"

"It means you're overthinking things instead of enjoying yourself."

"Yeah," Hannah said, sipping her hot chocolate. "And if *Alex* says you're overthinking things, you know you need to take a good look at your life choices."

Freya laughed despite herself. "Okay. I shall stop Freya-ing at once."

"That's a good girl," Hannah said. "So, tell us the important bits. How was the sex?"

FREYA TOOK HER FRIENDS' advice, deliberately stopping overthinking the situation with Ethan. She tried hard not to obsess. When her friends left she went for a run, blasting music in her ears to drown out her thoughts. The endorphins of a run always helped, and she soon found herself smiling.

When she got home, she saw she had a message from Ethan, which made her smile more.

"Hey, cutie. I had a great time last night (and this morning!) Just thinking about you x"

Freya practically swooned, wasting no time in copying the message to Hannah and Alex. She wasn't sure Ethan would love to know she was doing that, but she was just so happy, she needed to share it. Besides, she knew Sam probably knew all about the previous night by now, if not Nick as well.

"Me too," she wrote back, trying to sound cool. "We should definitely do it again sometime! xx"

His message came through faster than she'd expected. "Tomorrow night at 7? I can pick you up?"

"Sounds like a date," she wrote back, her heart beating fast in her chest.

Freya decided her friends were right. For now, she was happy. She would either stay that way or things would go pearshaped, but either way, stressing about it wouldn't help. She might as well enjoy the moment.

Chapter 24: 2019

Alex had been hesitant to contact Nick about getting his help with marketing. He'd said he was happy to offer mates' rates, but she still wasn't sure they would be low enough to fit her budget, and she didn't want to make things awkward if she had to turn him down. But she found herself perusing his website and sighed to herself. His work really was great quality, and it was perfect for what she needed. On a whim, she clicked on the "contact us" button on his site, which came up with his email.

"Hey, Nick. I just wanted to have a chat about what I need done for Teens in Turmoil. I don't think it would take too long, but let me know your thoughts! We're thinking mainly social media to get the word out, so I can handle that side of things, but I need a logo and a couple of ads to make things look professional. I'm also thinking some work on the website would be good, not sure if you handle that or if I'd get one of our in-house IT guys? Totally understand if you're too busy, just let me know."

She pressed send, wondering how she always managed to sound so passive in these things. She'd read online that it was the plague of the millennial woman, even though she was on the older end of that generational spectrum. There were even memes about it. "Oh I know I'm on fire, but only put it out if you have time! Don't let me trouble you!" She'd actually made it her New Year's Resolution a couple of years prior to make herself sound more assertive, but she clearly hadn't achieved that goal.

Fortunately, it only took about twenty minutes for Nick's reply to reach her inbox.

"Alex! Good to hear from you. What you're asking doesn't sound too time consuming, so I've attached a list of my current rates. Happy to offer a 30% discount since you know the boss! I can do the website, but you might find it better to work with your IT department to save some cash. Let me know your thoughts."

Alex opened the attached document, pleased to find that Nick's rates were fairly reasonable, particularly after she applied the discount. He was being more than generous with his time. She momentarily felt like she was taking advantage of their friendship, but dismissed the thought immediately. He'd offered, after all. It wasn't like she was holding a gun to his head. For the first time, Alex found herself wondering if he did still hold a torch for Hannah. Why else would he be so generous towards someone he'd only just recently got back in touch with after all these years?

HANNAH WOKE UP IN AN unfamiliar house, blinking as she looked around. She sighed as she remembered the night before. She'd had a little too much to drink and met a guy at the bar. They'd had some fun together, laughing and talking, and eventually things had progressed. She remembered the cab ride home with them, the two of them giggling and making out in the backseat. And now she had the awkward morning ritual ahead of her.

How often had she been through this before? The sex was always fun – well, usually fun, at least – but she so hated the morning after. The guys were either more into her than she was, or thought they had to pretend to be interested in something more than what they'd had the previous night.

She thought, suddenly, of Freya, of her story about waking up with Ethan after an unexpected night of passion. How he'd come in with breakfast for her and how they'd spent most of the morning rolling around in bed together, and she felt a strange stab of envy. She glanced over at the guy beside her, momentarily unable to remember his name. Craig, that was it. Well, Craig was still passed out, his mouth open in his sleep. He wouldn't be swooping in with a breakfast buffet any time soon. She wondered if she had to wait around for him to wake up. For all her one-night stands, and for how much she hated the morning after, she had never slipped away before the guy woke up before. It felt cheap and unfair to them, and she didn't like that feeling herself, so she hated doing it to someone else.

But today she decided it was the lesser of two evils. It wasn't as if Craig would care, anyway. On the off chance he did, he had her number, but she wasn't sure she wanted him to use it. She quietly sat up in bed, grabbing her discarded clothing and dressing as discreetly as she could. Craig stirred, but didn't wake up. Holding her breath, Hannah made for the door, letting herself out into the cool morning air.

Never again, she vowed as she walked around the corner to arrange an Uber out of sight of Craig's place. *Never again.*

HANNAH: I'm swearing off men.

Alex laughed to herself as she read it. "Whatever you say!" she wrote back.

Hannah: No, I'm serious. I just went back to this guy's place last night and all I could think about was Freya and Ethan.

Freya: Um... thanks?

Freya: I feel like that's a new level of kinky, Han.

Hannah: No! Not like that! I mean the morning after. He was all drooling in his sleep beside me and I thought about your romcom moment with Ethan bringing you breakfast and a little morning delight.

Freya: I never should have told you guys about that.

Hannah: I'm glad you did. It's got me rethinking my life choices. I'm becoming a nun.

Alex: Mmm-hmmm.

Hannah: Well, then I'm not having a one-night stand ever again.

Alex: Mmm-hmmm.

Hannah: Well, then I'm not having a one-night stand again this month.

Alex: You can do it!

Hannah: Exactly! I think I want to try to meet someone meaningful.

Freya: Awww! Our little Hannah's growing up.

Hannah: Shut up. Just because you're all blissfully coupled up.

Alex: Seriously, Hannah, that's awesome. I hope you do meet someone who's worthy of you.

Hannah: Thanks, Mum.

Chapter 25: 1999

Hannah had always envied how her friends seemed to know exactly where they were going in life, but at the same point, it wasn't a path she wanted for herself. She had never been much of a planner. On her days off she always refused to set an alarm or to make plans ahead of time – except for important things, of course, like parties. Sometimes she thought about getting a weekend job, but she always decided against it. The extra cash would definitely come in handy, but was it really worth losing her free time for? Hannah liked the excitement of waking up on her own time to a world of possibilities, rather than rolling over with a sense of dread at the alarm and a day of responsibilities. There was enough of that during the school week!

They were nearly adults. She could only imagine that life after high school would bring even more alarm clocks and a stomach full of dread. For now, she might as well have a little excitement in her life. It was her time to have fun. She wanted to spend as much time as possible with Nick and with her friends. Learn to make cocktails so she could have the cocktail party she'd always wanted for her eighteenth. Listen to Green Day as loudly – and as often – as possible. Annoy her brother by watching *Dawson's Creek* every week, religiously. Her friends could worry about the future as much as they wanted. She was worried about living her life now.

It wasn't as though she'd never thought of the future. She thought about being a hairdresser, or maybe working in a restaurant like her cousin, Sally. She could be a receptionist. Hell, she could work part-time somewhere and spend her free time learning to surf, or something really cool like that. It never really occurred to her to worry about the money she might earn in any of these jobs. She'd never had much of it, so it wasn't like she wasn't used to going without. The future would take care of itself. Her life stretched before her, wide open, and that was the beauty of it.

The one thing she was sure about was that she wanted Nick by her side. She might have only been in high school, but her feelings were real. She knew her love for Nick was never going to fade away. Her family friend Zane, who was twenty-five, had married his high school girlfriend just recently. It wasn't like it never happened. And if it could work for anyone, it would work for Hannah and Nick. They were simply meant to be. While he was in her life, nothing else really mattered.

Hannah knew her viewpoint wasn't really feminist, or anything, but she didn't really care. She felt how she felt.

Chapter 26: 2019

"So this is what I've done up for you," Nick said, pulling out his laptop.

Alex gasped as Nick showed her his designs. They were simple and stylish, but eye-catching. He'd designed a logo and a full-page ad for Teens in Turmoil, as well as a few social media posts he'd told her he'd "thrown in for her". Not being a creative person herself Alex had had no idea what she'd wanted, but somehow, he had delivered exactly the right thing.

"Nick! They're perfect!" she gasped, amazed.

Nick shrugged modestly. "I didn't have all your business details, so we'll need to add the web link and contact numbers in, but I wanted to show you a mock-up before I went too much further."

"This is amazing. Honestly. Thank you so much!"

Nick had told her he'd been planning to just send the proofs through to Alex for her approval, but when he'd found himself right near her office for a meeting with another company, he'd asked her to meet him for a coffee so he could show them to her personally. Alex was glad he did. Somehow this seemed more exciting than opening an email at her desk, like an official unveiling.

"You decided to go with the IT department for the website itself, right?"

Alex nodded, although having now seen his designs, she was starting to regret it. She knew he would have done a great job with the site. "So how does licensing work? We can use your logo for the website and everything, can't we?"

Nick nodded. "Sure, that's all part of what you're paying for. The logo and images are yours."

"Awesome. Thanks again, Nick. You've been so generous." She had paid for his coffee and muffin but seeing his work, she realised she would have to buy him something else. She made a mental note to ask Hannah what sort of alcohol he would like, or if there was another gift she could get him. Nick kept insisting the job wasn't time-consuming, but she was sure it had taken more time than the money was worth to him, especially if his business was as busy as it seemed.

"I think this is great, what you're doing," Nick added, taking a sip of his coffee. "It's really going to help."

"I hope so. I mean, part of me thinks it's all going to be a failure," she said. It was the first time she'd admitted it out loud. "The teenagers can already call our kids' line and they don't, so I'm not sure if it's really going to make a difference to throw the name 'teens' on there and let them text in rather than call. But I feel like if it even helps one teenager feel like they can reach out, then it's all worth it."

Nick smiled. "That's a great way to look at it," he said.

Alex nodded. She knew that was the part of it that she had to focus on. She wanted Teens in Turmoil to be a success because that was what she always strived for in her career, but more importantly than that, she really did want it to make a difference to some teenagers out there who felt like they had nowhere to turn. Wasn't that the whole purpose behind doing her job?

"I'd better be getting back to work," Nick said, swallowing the rest of his muffin in one bite. "Thanks for having a look over these. Send me all the business details and I'll send the ZIP files on when I've done the final versions."

"I'll send them on today," Alex promised. "Thanks again, Nick."

She was smiling as she walked back to her office.

THINGS WERE GOING WELL between Freya and Ethan.

They were going so well, in fact, that Freya started to wonder when the other shoe was going to drop. Things had never been this right before, not even in the early days with Jim, when she thought she'd found the one. She and Ethan fitted together like two puzzle pieces.

On their third date, she took him home to meet her family. Her parents, Lois and Roger, had Freya's best interests at heart and she knew they wouldn't want to see her hurt again so soon after Jim. Despite that, though, they were fairly easy-going people and she thought Ethan would charm them. Freya knew it was going to be Iris who was the hardest to win over.

It wasn't that Iris was difficult as a general rule, but she was always the protective big sister. Her own love story had gone so perfectly, it was hard for anyone else to live up to it. She had met Chris, her first boyfriend, at Uni. They'd dated for three years before Chris proposed. They'd married just over a year later and welcomed their twins, Cooper and Max, the following year. Cooper and Max were still little boys in Freya's mind, but in reality they towered over her at eighteen years old. She still called Cooper "baby" and Max "bear", the nicknames she'd given them as newborns. She still hugged them tightly every time she saw them and to their credit, the twins both allowed her to do so. They were two of her favourite people. Every so often it stung that her sister was the only one to give her parents grandchildren, but for the most part she was just happy to have the boys in her life.

"Hey, Freya," Cooper said, answering the door. The boys had never called her "Aunty Freya", even when they were little. Freya had never really wanted them to, even though Iris had tried to insist on it for a while.

"Hey, baby! Cooper, this is my friend Ethan." Calling him *friend* felt ridiculous, like she was some old lady, but she wasn't ready to call him *boyfriend* yet. He would have to make that move first. She noticed Cooper smirking just a little as he shook Ethan's hand.

"Nice to meet you, Cooper," Ethan said, slipping an arm around Freya's waist as they walked inside. She smiled, pleased that he was willing to be openly affectionate with her in front of her family.

The rest of her family was warm and welcoming, as she had known they would be. Her parents had met Ethan once or twice before when they were teenagers and needed lifts to the same parties, but she knew they wouldn't remember him. He'd never come over to Freya's as a teenager and she'd made deliberate efforts not to let her parents know about his crush on her. She had been so disinterested in the whole dating scene that even the idea of her parents knowing a boy was into her made her extremely uncomfortable. She was glad of that now. The new boyfriend meeting the family was awkward enough without her parents knowing that he'd spent his teenaged years pining after Freya!

Soon the group was seated around the dinner table. It gave Freya a warm feeling to have someone next to her when they were all seated, rather than being the odd man out. Even Cooper and Max often had their girlfriends of the month join them for family dinners. It had been one of the things she loved about being with Jim, at the beginning of the relationship. Towards the end, he had generally claimed to be too busy with work or other social engagements to come along to the Collins family dinners. Ugh, she thought; looking back on her relationship with Jim there had just been *so many* red flags. It made Freya doubt her own judgement, which was part of the reason why she was pleased to have her family meeting Ethan early on. They had always been accepting of Jim in support of Freya, but had never been his biggest fans. She decided to take their thoughts about Ethan more seriously. If they weren't enamoured with him, maybe there was something wrong.

"SO, WHAT DID YOU THINK?" Freya wasted little time in asking her family when Ethan left. They had arrived together, but she'd told him ahead of time she would be staying the night at her parents', and her dad could drive her home the next day. She said it was tradition to stay the night after dinner, which was true, but more importantly, she wanted to get her family's thoughts about Ethan as soon as possible.

Her mother laughed. "You don't want to wait until he's left the driveway?" she teased.

"Mum! Seriously. I need to know what you guys thought." The urgency of Freya's tone surprised her. She was only now realising exactly how much Ethan meant to her. Her family's approval was so important.

Her father looked stern for a moment, but then broke out into a smile. "I was going to give you a hard time, but I'll put you out of your misery. We both really like him," he assured her.

"You do?" Freya asked, relieved. "I'm so happy to hear it! You too, Mum?"

Lois nodded. "He's a good guy, angel. And he's completely besotted with you! It's so nice to see you with someone who deserves you." She didn't add *after the last guy,* but the meaning was clear.

Freya threw her arms around her mother and father in turn. "And you, Iris?" Her sister had just walked back in from the bathroom.

"Oh, he's great. I'm thinking I'll take him and you can take Chris."

"Seriously?"

"No, I don't seriously want to trade men with you, Freya."

Freya laughed, feeling a weight lifted off her shoulders. "No, I mean, you really liked him? You're not just saying that?"

"When have I ever just said something to spare your feelings?"

That was true. Hannah had once marvelled at how direct Iris and Freya were to each other. "You just don't have a sister," Freya had replied. "This is what it's like." She and Iris had always been close, but they fought like cats and dogs, even now they were older. Weirdly, it was part of what Freya liked about their relationship. As close as she was to Hannah and Alex, she and Freya had a shared history and a shorthand in the way they spoke to each other that no friendship could replicate.

"Do you think this could be something serious?" Lois asked a few minutes later, after they had made the unanimous decision to leave the dishes and go to the living room with cups of tea. Chris and the boys had stayed at the kitchen table, staring intently at their phones and clearly disinterested in the discussion.

Freya smiled, feeling colour rise to her cheeks. "I'm not sure. I think it could be. I really do like him."

It was an understatement but she wasn't ready to share her feelings just yet, even with the people closest to her. She had never felt this strongly for anyone before. Whatever she had with Ethan just felt right. She knew they needed to have a serious conversation about where this might be headed, before she got even more invested. She just wasn't sure how to broach the topic.

"I think it could be, too," Iris said decisively, looking at her sister.

"You do?"

"Yeah. There's just something... different about you. You seem head-over-heels for him but also really... I don't know, content or something. Like you've been in this relationship longer than you really have. In a good way," she added.

Freya smiled, feeling like she might be about to cry. Leave it to Iris to articulate what she was feeling better than she could herself.

Chapter 27: 2019

On a quiet Saturday night, Alex found herself snuggled up on the couch watching her favourite old romantic movie, *Fate*. It wasn't a classic by any stretch of the imagination, but it was about two lovers who had come together after several years apart. The main reason Alex loved it so much was because it had come out when she was sixteen, and just starting to become interested in boys. It had all seemed so romantic, the way they lost touch but were destined to come together again. The love-making scenes weren't graphic, but they were passionate and intense. The critics at the time had all raved about the actors' chemistry. Alex wasn't much of a film critic, but she knew what she liked, and this movie had quickly become a guilty pleasure. She had watched it at least once a year since and every time she did, she felt sixteen again.

When the movie was over Alex rolled over, sighing. It was still only 9pm. On a whim she typed "The Pact movie" into her search bar and laughed out loud when the film came up. It was the one that they had gone to back in Year 12, the one that started the marriage pact idea.

On a whim, Alex pressed the "rent now" button and settled back into her couch. She was going to message her friends to tell them what she was watching, but decided to wait.

The movie was cornier than she'd remembered, but still cute and sweet. The couple at the end was successful in their marriage pact, of course, just like Ethan and Freya might turn out to be.

Alex was entirely happy for her friend, but she couldn't deny there was a pang of jealousy involved. She had read something once about how a part of you died every time a friend had success. It was a cynical view, but there was some truth to it, at least as far as this was concerned. She wouldn't take away Freya's happiness with Ethan for the world. She just wished she could find the same thing for herself.

She thought back now to her own first serious relationship. She had had a boyfriend in Year 11 of high school, but it was nothing major, more companionship than anything else, with a bit of second base action that was more experimentation than passion. Her relationship with Ted, in her first year of Uni, was different. Her high school relationship with Josh had been a fleeting thing, and she'd always known it would be, even while she was with him. Her relationship with Ted was the first one she felt might have gone the distance.

It had also been *easy* in a way no relationship since had been. It had lulled her into a false sense of security. They had been friends first, then drifted into a relationship. They had stayed together for three years and at the end of university they had drifted just as easily out of the relationship. There were no huge fights or big, dramatic moments. They just hadn't been right for each other anymore, and they both knew it. They had stayed in touch sporadically over the years. Ted was married now, with a daughter. She had met his wife once when they had bumped into each other in the city. She was lovely. When their daughter was born, Alex sent them a gift. All relationships should be as easy as the one she'd had with Ted.

And yet...

She'd always thought of the comfort and familiarity they'd shared as a good thing, but had there ever really been passion?

Could you have both – the settled, easy relationship, and the passion that she'd always wanted?

Had she *ever* felt true passion with anybody?

After Ted had been Mike, and then Simon, and then James. They'd all been nice guys. They'd all been perfectly adequate relationships to fit in with her perfectly adequate life.

For the first time, Alex found herself wanting more. She always pretended to be interested only in non-fiction and crime novels, but she actually loved sappy romance novels, too, even though she hid them from the world. She wanted the kind of all-encompassing relationship you read about. She wanted a great romance, like you saw in the movies.

But maybe she just wasn't the 'great romance' type. Maybe she'd have to settle for something perfectly adequate.

Chapter 28: 2019

Alex had been messaging Freya and Hannah non-stop about her work with Teens in Turmoil, and Freya was thrilled for her. She really seemed to have found her niche with the new project. Freya herself was happily settled in her job, but sometimes it all felt a little too familiar. Every so often, she craved a new challenge. So when Vicky Chung, a Year 10 student, came to her one afternoon, Freya was only too happy to listen.

"Ms Collins?" Vicky asked hesitantly as she approached her. "Can I ask you something?"

"Of course, Vicky. Do you need help finding something?"

The school was too big for Freya to know all the students' names, especially since she didn't have classes with them, but Vicky was a regular in the library. She reminded Freya of herself as a teenager, with her love of reading and of learning.

"No, I... wanted some advice. I know I could go to Mrs Adamson," she said, naming the guidance counsellor, "but I know you better."

Freya nodded, smiling. This wasn't an unfamiliar event from her more studious students. She knew she herself as a teenager would have preferred to get advice from someone she knew. She just hoped it was something she was qualified to answer.

"It sounds so silly," Vicky said, "but it's my friend Sara. You know Sara?"

Freya nodded again. The two girls had always been inseparable.

"Well, she has a boyfriend now, and she seems to think she's so much more mature than me," Vicky burst out. Her normally calm demeanour started to slip as tears shone in her eyes. "She keeps making comments about how *jealous* I am, and I'm not jealous. I don't want a boyfriend. I just don't want him to come between us."

"Oh, honey." Freya was relieved and concerned at the same time. This was a problem she could definitely deal with, having had similar feelings herself in high school. She knew to a lot of people that Vicky's problem would seem laughably small, but she also knew that it was Vicky's entire world right now. Your friends were never more important than they were in high school, and it was also a time when you felt you had to keep up with them like you didn't have to any other time. In your adult years you could be childfree and have friends with multiple kids, or you could be single and go out with your married friends without a care in the world. In high school, you felt like you had to be in the same place in life at the same time, so you didn't get left behind. Everything was so... competitive.

"I know how you feel," she assured Vicky. "I actually had something similar in high school myself."

"Really? You did?"

"Really," Freya confirmed. "I'd say you'd be hard pushed to find a girl who hasn't had this kind of problem. I wasn't interested in boys at all during school, and one of my friends couldn't cope with that." She decided not to go into too much detail. She was still a staff member at this girl's school, after all. Vicky didn't need to know everything about Freya's life.

"So what happened?"

"Well, after a while I just started ignoring Hannah – that's my friend – when she carried on about it. I knew how I felt deep down, and I wasn't jealous of her relationship at all. I didn't want one for myself, either. I guess at the end of the day you have to do what's right for you. And the good news is, Hannah and I are still really good friends." She added that part because she knew Vicky was probably concerned about her future friendship with Sara. The path she and Hannah had taken wouldn't necessarily be mirrored by the younger girls, but Freya knew that anything could happen. They were still so young. Sara could end her relationship and cry on Vicky's shoulder, or they could adjust to the new normal, fitting Sara's boyfriend in around their own time together. Or maybe Vicky would get sick of Sara's attitude and find some new friends to devote her time to. Whatever happened, Vicky would be okay, and Freya knew that was what the girl needed to know the most.

"That's awesome," Vicky said, clearly relieved. "I guess I thought there was something wrong with me for not being more interested. I'm so glad to hear you were the same."

Another feeling Freya had been familiar with. She'd wondered the same thing about herself in high school. Would she ever start to show the interest in boys that seemed to completely absorb her classmates? When romance seemed like the only thing books, TV shows and movies – not to mention the people around you – could focus on, you couldn't help but feel like a freak for not being more interested in it.

"My advice to you is, take a step back. Give Sara some time to obsess over her new boyfriend for a while, because they all do, but in the end, she'll most likely come back to you. It's just a temporary thing, I promise. Girls don't lose their heads over boys forever."

"Yeah, it's just a matter of keeping sane while she's like this. She's my only real friend."

"Do you have a journal?"

Vicky looked at her like she was crazy. "No."

"I'd get one, if I were you. That's what helped me get my feelings out as a teenager without screaming or wanting to kill somebody. It could help you, too."

"Thanks, Ms Collins. You're really good at this," Vicky said, smiling as she stood up. "It's like you really remember what it's like to be a teenager. My parents don't."

Freya knew she should pack up the library and head home after Vicky left but instead she sat for a moment, smiling to herself. Vicky didn't realise what a huge compliment she'd paid her. Freya liked to think she could get inside the minds of her teenaged students, but she wasn't sure if she could anymore, with social media and the constant pressure to keep up changing what it was like to be at high school. Still, kids were kids, no matter what the world around them looked like.

Freya stood up to start gathering her things, then stopped, her jaw dropping open.

She had been wanting a challenge in her career, and she had just realised what that might be.

IT MADE HER FEEL A bit like Alex with her routines, but Freya and Ethan had started a few regular traditions of their own. Usually on a Tuesday they'd go to the cinema and watch a movie together, and on the weekends they would take day trips – to the coast, or up the mountain to have Devonshire tea or just admire the view. They weren't officially living together, but they might as well have been. She felt a little guilty that she wasn't spending more time with her girlfriends, but she knew they were nothing but excited for her. She was sure everyone could see how much happier she was now.

Friday nights brought takeaway, followed by cuddling on the couch in front of a movie, or playing a board game together. They always ate dinner together at the table, filling each other in on their day. It felt like something an old married couple might do, in the nicest possible way. She loved the way things felt when she was with Ethan. There was a cosy familiarity to their relationship, like she could just be entirely herself with him, in a way she never had been with anyone before. At the same time, though, she felt so *alive* with him. The sex was by far the best she'd ever had, and her stomach still did somersaults just at the sight of him. For the first time in her life, she found herself feeling bored by her work. She could spend hours just daydreaming about Ethan. Work felt like it was getting in the way of time spent thinking about her boyfriend. If anyone else told her they were feeling this way, she'd have thought they sounded insufferable. Now that it was happening to her, it was entirely different.

"I had an exciting day today," Freya told him now, as she piled spaghetti and garlic bread onto her plate.

"Oh, yeah? Start a new filing system?" Ethan teased.

"Funny boy. No, one of the Year 10 girls came to see me." She briefly filled him in on the conversation with Vicky and how much she'd enjoyed giving her advice.

"I told her to journal her feelings and it got me thinking about how much I used to love writing. I used to write short stories all the time. I actually thought about writing novels for a while there. And Vicky said how I was really good at remembering what it's like to be a teenager. So I thought... couldn't I maybe have a go at writing again? Like, writing for a teenaged audience?"

Freya had been excited when she'd started speaking, but now she just felt embarrassed, as though Ethan would laugh in her face. Who was she to think she could write?

She couldn't even remember being taught to read as a child; she was fairly good at it before she even started school. She could vividly remember when she was around seven years old, and her dad asked her what she wanted to be when she grew up.

Freya had frowned. It wasn't something she'd ever thought about before. "I want to read," she had said simply.

Her dad had laughed. "Good luck finding someone who'll pay you to do that."

"You could be an editor," her mother had suggested.

"What's that?"

"It's where you read people's writing and you make changes to improve it."

Freya had shrugged. She could do that, but it didn't sound like the *fun* kind of reading. She didn't want to have to worry about improving things all the time. She just wanted to read.

"Or you could be a teacher. They get to read a lot of stories aloud to their class. Or a librarian."

Freya had turned this over in her young mind. *A librarian.* She had always loved the library. She loved how the librarians could open up a world of imagination while at the same time, keeping everything in the library so neat and orderly and *quiet.*

"Yes," she said aloud. "I think I'll be a librarian."

From that moment on, she had never wavered.

When she was older she had started writing stories – both for school and for fun – and she'd always loved it, but she'd never taken it seriously. She enjoyed writing her stories the way some people dabbled in sketching; you never planned to really do anything with it, but it was nice to have a hobby. Now, though, the idea of writing – *really* writing – appealed to her. She didn't know if anything would come of it, but what was the harm in trying?

"I think that's a great idea, babe," Ethan said, and she was touched by his obvious sincerity.

"Really? You don't think I'm totally out of my depths?"

"I don't at all, but even if it turns out you are – which I doubt – who cares? It's a good creative outlet at the very least and best-case scenario, you might end up getting published!"

Freya could hardly even bring herself to think about that possibility. She focussed on the first part of Ethan's sentence. He was right, this would be a good creative outlet for her. If it led to something more down the track that would be amazing, but she wouldn't think about that for now. She would do it for enjoyment only. If it led to something else down the track, all the better.

She could hardly wait to start writing.

Chapter 29: 2019

"This guy," Alex said, pointing her fork at Nick, "is amazing. You should see what he created for us!"

"It was nothing," Nick replied modestly. "Any graphic designer could have done it."

"Maybe, but *you* did it, and you did it at 30% off!"

"We're old friends. Of course you get mates' rates!"

The six of them were sitting on the couches in Freya's apartment, plates of food from the local noodle place balanced on their legs. They had decided to gather for a casual lunch, and had barely sat down before Alex started exalting about Nick's work.

"Seriously, have a look," she said, pulling out her phone to show them the Zip files Nick had sent her.

Freya and Hannah had already seen the images but still made appropriate "ooh" noises over them now, so Nick didn't catch on that Alex had sent them screenshots ahead of time. She appreciated the effort.

"These are really good, mate," Sam said. "I might hire you myself. Spice up my sales."

"Sure, but you pay full price," Nick joked.

"So when does Teens in Turmoil officially launch, anyway?" Hannah asked.

"It's slated for two weeks from Monday, which feels ridiculously soon, but I think we're on track."

"Knowing you, Alex, you're well and truly ahead of schedule," Nick laughed. "You've started your social media campaign?"

"It starts this week," she said. "We didn't want to start it too early because it's a whole separate phone number to Kids in Crisis, so we wanted to make sure the number was up and running not too long after the advertising started, but we also wanted to get the information out there so it's not just dead air on our first day." Alex paused. "Which it might still be, of course."

"So you have a different call centre or something?" Hannah asked.

"No, it's all still in the same room and the same people can answer calls for both lines, but it's just important for us to know which service they're looking for. The whole idea is to distance the teen division from 'Kids in Crisis', so we want to know how to answer the phone. There's different on-hold messages and all of that as well, but we think a lot of our communication will be via text, anyway. And we do have some operators who will answer the teenaged line in the first instance." Alex herself was going to be one of them. It had seemed only logical, since Teens in Turmoil was her idea in the first place, but she was also looking forward to working with the older kids for a change of pace. She felt excited whenever she thought about her work project.

"Anyway, Nick, we're having a bit of a launch party the night before it starts and my boss said to invite you."

"Me? Really?"

"Yeah, it's nothing major and you can definitely beg off if you'd rather not go, but he thought it might be a good chance for you to network." Her boss was also looking for as many warm bodies as possible to fill the room and make the night look successful, but she didn't mention that now. "There'll be press there and all, so it could be a good opportunity to get your name out there." As soon as she said it, she felt embarrassed. Nick's marketing business seemed to be going pretty well, and she didn't mean to imply that he would need her contacts to 'get his name out there'. Nick didn't seem bothered in the slightest, though. "I'd love to come," he said, to her relief.

"Great! It'll be nice to have someone to chat to," Alex said happily.

BUOYED ON BY THE TALK of Alex's success at work, Freya decided to talk about her writing. It was like baring a little part of her soul. It was one thing to say you'd already written a novel, but to say you were writing one, when you didn't even know if you'd see it through? It was putting yourself out there in a way she wasn't sure she was entirely comfortable with. It suddenly amazed her how readily she'd told Ethan about her writing, without overthinking it at all. It said a lot for how much she trusted him. She hadn't even told her female friends yet, which felt like a kind of betrayal. It was time to change that.

"Speaking of work," Freya said, "I've started a little side project, too. You kind of inspired me, actually, Alex."

"Me?"

"Yeah, with your TIT work." The girls couldn't resist calling it that. Freya started filling them in on the basics of Vicky's visit and how it had led her to pursue her desire to write. She'd started a week earlier. To her surprise, she'd already written over ten thousand words. She'd read hundreds of young adult books over the years, vetting them before deciding whether to stock them in the library, so the writing style had come more naturally to her than she'd expected. She found herself excited, rather than shy, about sharing the news with her friends.

"I've had a peek over her shoulder, and it's brilliant," Ethan said warmly. "She's going to be a sensation."

"Not that you're biased."

"So the couple of the year thing is still going strong, then?" Sam laughed.

Ethan and Freya grinned at each other. "We can't help it if we're adorable," Ethan quipped.

Freya felt warmth spread through her body as Ethan wrapped his arm casually around her. Once again, she was floored by how lucky she was to be able to call this man her boyfriend. She thought of how she'd told Vicky about her disinterest in boys and dating while she was at high school, and wondered how the younger girl would react if she knew Freya was now happily loved up with the boy who'd had such a crush on her back then. They hadn't actually used the L word yet, but she felt like it was only a matter of time. She was absolutely in love with him, but she had already asked him out first, and then been the first to initiate a kiss. He could at least make the first move this time around!

"I guess the marriage pact had to work for someone," Sam said. "Actually, I've kind of had a marriage pact of my own." He held up his hand, which had a strong gold band on his ring finger.

They all gaped at him. "For real?" Alex cried.

He nodded, smiling. "For real."

They took it in turns to hug him. Freya smiled as she saw Alex embrace him excitedly as well. Her friend had been so angry at Sam when she was a teenager. It was nice to see how much they had grown up.

Chapter 30: 2019

The night of the Teens in Turmoil launch party, Alex changed her outfit three times. She'd decided what to wear a week before but suddenly, as she slipped into it, it didn't seem right. She ended up choosing a form-fitting gold dress which showed off her back, one of her favourite features. She had worn the dress to a wedding three years earlier and it had been hanging in her cupboard ever since. She didn't like to stand out the way she knew she did in it. Tonight, though, was her night, and she kind of wanted to make a splash for once. She knew she'd be overdressed for the launch party, but she didn't care. She did her hair simply, straightening it and leaving it down, figuring she would let the dress speak for itself.

She and Nick had agreed to meet at the convention centre where the launch party was being held. She was a few minutes early, so she was surprised to see Nick already standing outside, looking amazing in a navy suit. "Wow!" he said as he turned to see her approaching. "You look incredible! Great dress." To her surprise he leaned in and kissed her on the cheek, his hand holding onto her arm.

Alex smiled, feeling a shiver running down her spine that she tried not to think too hard about. "I'm so glad you could come."

"I'm happy to. You did all of this, you know."

She waved his comment away with her hand. "I didn't do much, really."

"You just had the entire idea."

"Yeah, but it was a team effort, and your work really helped. You're going to see your designs up there on giant posters," she told him.

"I guess we'd better go in, then."

The launch party was an elegant affair, with canapes and dancing and a live band. The crisis centre didn't often host things like this, so Alex couldn't remember the last time she'd been somewhere fancy. She momentarily wondered if the money couldn't have been better spent, but she waved it away. The whole purpose of the night was to draw attention to the Teens in Turmoil crisis line, after all, and you had to make a splash to do that. It seemed to be working, judging from the amount of press milling around. She just hoped they would be kind to the programme in their stories. Despite her words to Nick about the project being a team effort, Teens in Turmoil felt like her baby. She wasn't prepared to hear anything less than favourable about it.

"Alex!" Her boss came over to her. "Congratulations. This was all your vision."

Alex smiled modestly and introduced the two men. "Nick, this is Andrew, my boss. Andrew, this is Nick. He's my friend who did all the graphic designs for tonight."

"Oh, Nick. Good job, mate," Andrew said, pumping the other man's hand. "We might have some more graphic design tasks for you in the future, if you're interested."

"Absolutely," Nick smiled. "Alex can get you in touch with me if you've got something planned."

The three made small talk for a moment before Andrew excused himself and went to mill around the room. There was a momentary lull in the conversation and Alex felt suddenly, strangely nervous. Did she even know Nick well enough to spend an evening alone with him? Surely they wouldn't have enough to talk about to fill the whole night. Even as teenagers, they'd never really been alone together and since the six of them had reunited they'd always been a group. Sure, they'd exchanged emails, but they were all work-related.

It was Nick who broke the silence. "Are you still as busy as you were at high school?"

"Busy?"

Nick laughed. "Yeah. You know, you'd have debating, or band, or whatever else you needed to do. Then you'd help out your grandma at home."

"You remember that?" Alex was astonished. Sometimes she wondered if even Hannah and Freya remembered her grandma. Nellie had lived with them for three years while Alex was at school, before passing away in Alex's first year of uni. Looking after her had been a labour of love, but it had been exhausting. Alex had never talked to anyone about how much she'd struggled to balance everything. It was the Reynolds way to power through, to make everyone around you think you had everything together. Alex often pictured herself as resembling the old metaphor about the duck – calm on the surface while her legs were paddling frantically underneath, just trying to keep her head above water.

"Yeah. We'd put Grandad in a home around the same time, so I always wondered how different things would have been if he'd moved in with us the way your grandmother did. I guess..." He paused, trying to collect his thoughts. "I always thought it would be really hard in some ways, but a lot better in others. I barely saw my Grandad once he went into the home, so I thought it would be kind of nice to have him right there. You were a lot better at balancing things than I was, though. I could barely go to school and work a couple of shifts a week at Maccas."

Alex smiled. "I don't know if I was always as good at it as I seemed, but thanks. That's nice to hear. And yeah, I guess there's good and bad to both – grandparents moving in or going into a home, I mean. It *was* tough." She didn't want to go into any more detail. This was a time of her life she barely spoke to anyone, so to go into detail with her friend's ex-boyfriend would seem odd. She was surprised to find, though, that she wanted to.

"Well, enough of this heavy stuff," Nick laughed, perhaps sensing the mood was getting a little too serious. "Do you want to dance?"

"You dance?" she asked, surprised. She remembered the night Ethan and Freya had got together, and how she and Nick had just watched from the sidelines as they had hit the dance floor. She wasn't much of a dancer herself, but it seemed like the thing to do here. If you couldn't dance to celebrate the launch of your own new business venture, when could you?

"Not always, but I don't know. I feel like it tonight."

"Sure." She took the hand he was offering and the two of them went out to the dance floor. Nick surprised her by being a better dancer than she'd given him credit for. He wasn't go-ing to be winning any ballroom dancing awards anytime soon, but he moved with a confidence that made his every move look good. She smiled as they danced together to a few upbeat num-bers. When a slow song came on, Alex glanced up at him. It was his move whether they keep dancing or head back to the bar. Wordlessly, he held his arms open and she stepped into them.

Alex couldn't remember the last time she'd slow danced with anyone. She mainly only danced at weddings, and it had been years since she'd been at one with a romantic partner. She never slow danced with a friend.

Until tonight.

Right?

"HOW WAS LAST NIGHT?"

Alex's sister Katherine's text woke her. Alex groaned, rub-bing her face. She normally slept with her phone on silent, but she'd obviously been so tired she'd just passed out when her head hit the pillow. From the look of her phone she'd already slept through a few messages, but Katherine's message must have been the last straw. Alex groaned as she sat up. Her feet were sore from her heels and she was exhausted, and a little hungover. Everyone said life got better after thirty but *damn*, the hangovers hit you harder.

But she was happy.

A little *too* happy.

"It was good," she wrote back, aware that the lack of detail would be frustrating to her sister. Alex didn't go out anywhere fancy often, so Katherine would have wanted plenty of information about the night. She paused as she thought over the night, then sent another message. "Are you free to come over?"

Katherine left the baby with her husband and came over within the hour. Alex spent the time before her sister's arrival trying to make herself look halfway decent, scrubbing her face and brushing her teeth.

"What's up?" Katherine asked when the two of them were settled on the couch. "Don't get me wrong, I'm happy to have some kid-free time, but it's not like you to ask me over without advanced notice."

"It's about last night," Alex said hesitantly. Now that her sister was here, she felt ridiculous. Why was she dragging Katherine over to talk about the *nothing* that had happened? God, maybe she really was reverting back to seventeen. Although seventeen-year-old Alex had probably had more common sense than this. Scrap that – she definitely did.

"Did something happen? Is TIT okay?" Katherine was another one who couldn't resist calling Teens in Turmoil by its silly nickname. Alex had a sneaking suspicion most of the teens, in turmoil or not, would as well.

"Yeah, it's fine. I think it was a hit, actually. I haven't checked any of the news sites." Now that she thought about it, that seemed odd. Alex normally would have woken up and obsessively started Googling her business.

"So?"

"Well... you know I took Nick along."

"Nick?"

"Yeah, my old friend. Hannah's ex," Alex prompted her, and Katherine nodded.

"Oh, yeah. He's the one who did all the design work for you, yeah?"

"Yeah, so my boss suggested I bring him."

"And you fell madly in love with him and you're eloping," Katherine laughed. At the look on her sister's face, she stopped. "Alex...?"

"Well," Alex said with a shaky laugh. "We're not eloping."

"Oh my God. What happened?"

"Nothing! Nothing happened. I don't know why I'm making a big deal about this."

"But you caught feelings," Katherine said sagely. It was how she had always described getting a crush on someone. *Caught feelings,* like catching a cold. To be honest, it made a lot of sense. Catching a cold was also unstoppable and in Alex's view, crushes were almost as unwanted as getting sick. She hadn't had many crushes in her thirties. She either got into a relationship with someone or moved on. The thought of having feelings for Nick that wouldn't lead anywhere was enough to make her sicker than she already felt.

"Yes. I guess so. I don't know. Ugh! Katherine!" she cried, as if the whole predicament was her sister's fault. "We were dancing, and talking, and... I don't want to feel like this. Not about Hannah's ex! She'd never forgive me."

"If she'd never forgive you for having feelings for a guy she dated twenty years ago, then she's not a great friend," Katherine said practically.

Alex shook her head, frustrated. Sure, it sounded clearcut like that on paper, but this was reality. Even keeping Hannah's naturally highly-strung personality out of the equation, this was *Nick.* He wasn't just a boyfriend from twenty years ago for Hannah. Yes, she said there were no feelings between them now, and Alex believed her, but there was so much history. He was her first love. Her first time. The first guy she'd ever lost her head over. In some ways, the last guy she'd lost her head over. Adult Hannah was far more into flings than long-lasting romances. Looking back over her dating history, it was entirely possible to argue that Nick was the most significant relationship she'd ever had.

"It's different," she said finally. "Nick was her world for a long time there. She says there are no feelings there anymore, but he was the love of her life, basically."

"No one's high school boyfriend is the love of their life."

"I mean, our *parents* met in high school."

Katherine shrugged. "Things were different back then."

"Anyway, friends' exes are off limits, right? Isn't that the rule?"

"I'm not much for rules."

Alex knew that was true, but she also knew she herself was the poster girl for rules. And the rules on this one were simple. Hannah had been with Nick first, and that was that. He was off-limits to Alex.

"It's not like he's probably even interested, anyway," Alex grumbled, and Katherine raised an eyebrow.

"Really? Smart, successful, gorgeous women aren't his type?"

Alex smiled. Although she and her sister had become a lot closer over the years, she didn't often get a string of compliments like that from Katherine. "I'm just saying, he's probably not interested and I'll get over him, so there's really nothing to worry about. It was silly, me dragging you over here."

Katherine perused her for a moment before speaking. "Okay. But if you need to be silly again, call me over. That's what sisters are for."

Chapter 31: 1999

"Formal soon!" Hannah exalted. "Who are you taking?"

Freya bristled at the fact that her question was "*Who* are you taking?", rather than "Are you taking someone?" "I might go by myself," she said tartly.

"Ugh! Freya! You can't!"

"I can and I will," she said stubbornly. She hadn't really decided until that moment, but Hannah's shocked reaction made her all the more sure, in some childish way. It wasn't like she had a boyfriend or a secret crush on anyone, so why should she take anyone?

"And you, Alex? Don't tell me you're going alone too. Bunch of Nigels."

Alex grinned at the term. Hannah loved to call people Nigel No-Friends when she felt they were being the slightest bit antisocial. "I hadn't really thought about it, actually."

"You could take Sam?"

"Oh! Yeah... sure. I guess I could."

"Really?" Hannah squealed, looking like all her Christmases had come at once. She shot another quick look at Freya, just to make sure her disappointment at her friend was evident.

"Why not?" Alex shrugged. "He's single, I'm single. Just as friends, though," she added in a warning tone, as though

Hannah might have already started planning their wedding. Which, in fairness, she probably had.

"Yeah, yeah, friends." Hannah grinned. "But who knows what might happen on the night?"

ALTHOUGH THE FORMAL, and her date to it, ranked fairly low on Alex's list of priorities, she was surprisingly gratified when Sam said yes to her suggestion that they go together. It wasn't that she was interested in him – and she was very quick to make sure he knew it was just as friends – but she still would have been embarrassed if he'd turned her down.

The night of the formal, the three girls gathered together at Alex's place to get ready and have their photos taken together. Sam and Nick were going to come along there later on, while Ethan and Emily, who were still going strong, were meeting them at the formal. The three girls huddled together for photo after photo, giggling and chatting happily.

When the doorbell rang and Alex opened it to find Sam there, along with Nick, she was surprised to feel her heart skip a beat. Surely she didn't suddenly have feelings for Sam? She'd only ever seen him as a friend. No, she told herself firmly. It was just formal night. It had that kind of magic over you, even if you didn't want it to. Besides, Sam was cute, with his long, lean frame, his blonde hair and blue eyes. Now that he was all dressed up in his fancy suit, he looked even better than usual.

Fortitude High held their formal in August, to get it over and done with so it wouldn't cause too great a distraction before their final assessments. It was the last gasp of winter, but the night air was still relatively cool. Alex felt a warmth flood through her as Sam gave her a friendly hug in greeting.

"You look great!" she exclaimed, and he grinned back at her.

"You, too," he said, handing her a single rose. "I'm glad you asked me."

Alex was glad, too.

THE FORMAL NIGHT PASSED by in a giddy whirl of excitement. They sat at a table of ten, the seven of them plus their other friends Abed, Kim and John. Abed and Kim had been coupled up for as long as any of them could remember, but John had come alone. Hannah was less than subtle in nudging Freya to sit next to him. Freya obliged, smiling and shaking her head at her friend. With Ethan out of the picture, Hannah had obviously decided it was better to pair Freya up with *someone* than to have her be single. Freya wasn't interested in John, but he was a nice guy and she had to admit he was good-looking, too. There were worse people to sit next to, especially since she had Alex on her other side if the conversation lapsed.

In the end, it didn't matter. The ten of them chatted away together like old friends, laughing over their entrees and getting into a serious discussion about life after graduation over their main courses. Over dessert John got into a rambling discussion about the movie he'd just seen and had them all laughing and rolling their eyes at him good-naturedly. John wanted to be a filmmaker and getting into overly analytical discussions about movies was typical from him. Somehow, he managed to make it interesting, even as he went on too long.

When the meals were finished Hannah dragged Nick out onto the dance floor, against his better judgement. Ethan and Emily followed quickly behind them. Sam and Alex went off to chat with Sam's cousin, who was also in their grade. Abed and Kim went off without a reason – to find a dark corner to make out in, most likely – and soon Freya and John were left alone at the table.

Freya smiled awkwardly at him. Sitting next to him at a crowded, noisy table full of people was one thing, but it was entirely different to suddenly be sitting alone with him here, like they were on a date or something.

Perhaps sensing her discomfort, John said "I'm going to go outside for some fresh air. Do you want to come along?"

Freya paused, then nodded. She wasn't sure being outside with John would be any less awkward than being alone with him here, but she also didn't want to be stuck sitting by herself at an empty table until the others returned. *Nigel,* Hannah's voice said in her head.

She let John lead her outside. They were in the middle of the city, so there was plenty of noise and people walking by, but it somehow felt secluded at the same time. She shivered involuntarily.

"Cold?" John asked, and without her needing to say a word he took his jacket off and wrapped it around her. "There you go," he said with a friendly smile. She smiled back. What a gentleman.

"So you want to be a filmmaker," she said, for lack of anything else to say. She cringed as the words came out of her mouth. She sounded like one of those pamphlets they gave out in the career counsellor's office.

John grimaced. "I know I went on a little too long in there. But yeah, I love it. There's nothing better than going into a dark cinema for two hours and just forgetting everything but the movie in front of you. Nothing else compares."

Freya couldn't help but admire his passion. She had her love of reading, of course, but she wasn't sure she could articulate it the way he just had. She suspected his love of movies surpassed even her love of reading. She also suspected he would make it as a filmmaker one day.

"Do you want to go to Hollywood?"

John thought for a minute. "Not really. I'd love to make movies here, you know? There's not enough of a film industry here and the Aussie movies they do make are all like, lifestyle-drama type things."

"So what would you make?"

"Thrillers. Maybe some horrors as well, but thrillers are my favourite." That made sense – the movie he'd been going on about inside had been a thriller, something she'd already forgotten the name of. "And what about you?"

"I only like comedies."

"No, I mean, what do you want to do? Earlier in there you said you want to be a librarian. Do you want to be a librarian in a school, or the State Library, or what?"

"Oh. That. I guess a school," Freya said, although she hadn't really given the matter much thought. "I'd like to help kids love to read. So many don't."

John nodded. "That sounds cool."

There was a momentary lull in the conversation and before she knew it they were both leaning forward, tentatively. Freya's heart was racing. She'd never kissed anyone before, never even thought about doing it. But somehow, this felt right. She wanted to do this.

Freya never did anything she didn't want to do.

When their lips touched, her heart started doing somersaults.

If only she'd known then that this was the night everything would fall apart.

Chapter 32: 2019

Meeting the parents had never been Freya's favourite thing to do, but she was pleased to discover that Ethan's family was warm and welcoming. Ethan's parents had divorced back when Ethan was in high school, so she had to "meet the parents" not only once, but twice. She had gone to his dad Charles' place for dinner the week before. Charles and his new wife Claudia were lovely, and Freya felt like she'd made a good impression, which Ethan assured her she had. Now she was about to meet his mum, Bridget, who Freya remembered only vaguely from her high school days, and Ethan's brother Joe, who had been two years above them at school. Freya and Ethan had already been together for nearly two months, so it was well and truly time to meet the family. She knew from past experience how much more complicated relationships could be if you didn't get on with their family members, so she had to know, one way or another. She didn't need anything to complicate what she had with Ethan.

She greeted Bridget and Joe warmly with kisses on the cheek and a quick embrace, and then Joe's wife came in from the other room where she'd been looking after the kids.

The other woman stuck out her hand in greeting. "I'm Alicia," she said. "Everyone calls me Leish. It's nice to meet you, Freya."

Freya smiled warmly in response. "Nice to meet you, too, Leish."

"You're a school librarian, I hear?"

"Yeah, at the high school Ethan and I went to. I love it. I think it's the greatest job in the world," Freya gushed. It was true, but she was also babbling a little. Something about the directness of Alicia's gaze made her nervous.

"Yeah, it must be nice to get all those holidays."

Freya tried not to bristle at Alicia's words. They were something she'd heard time and time again from people who didn't realise how much unpaid work there was to do outside of school hours. "What do you do again, Alicia?" she asked politely.

"I work for the government."

"Oh." She bit back the urge to say, "It must be nice to have all that accrued time off!" She wanted to make a good impression on Ethan's family, after all; now wasn't the time to be snarky.

"Yeah, Leish works three days a week," Ethan added, a knowing twinkle in his eye. He knew exactly how Freya felt about 'harmless' comments about her work hours.

"Well, three days a week is like full-time when you have kids, of course."

"Of course!" Freya echoed, wondering what that made full-time work when you had kids. She tried not to look as annoyed as she felt. She would normally have been more understanding, but Alicia hadn't really enamoured herself to Freya so far.

"I mean, I used to work full-time but you just have *no idea* how much free time you had until you have kids and suddenly you don't get a moment to yourself! I know I'm working harder now than I ever have before," Alicia added pointedly, frowning at Ethan. "A lot of people who don't have kids just have no idea. Do you want children, Freya?"

Freya shrugged awkwardly. She and Ethan hadn't got as far as that conversation yet, and she had no idea what his thoughts were on having a family. Growing up, her mother had always told her that she should discuss future plans for marriage and children on the first date! Iris and Freya had always laughed it off as ludicrous, but now she was wishing she'd broached the topic earlier. "Ideally yes, but who knows? I'm no spring chicken," she said with a forced laugh. "I guess time will tell."

Alicia looked like she wanted to say more, but thankfully that was the moment when Ethan's mum called out that it was time to eat.

WHEN FREYA GOT HOME, she messaged her girlfriends immediately.

Freya: Met the parents! Ethan's mum is lovely, and his brother is great value (do you remember Joe from school?) Meanwhile, Joe's wife is... interesting.

Alex: Interesting is never good.

Freya: She's one of those who thinks you can't possibly understand hard work unless you have children.

Hannah: Ugh, yeah I'm sure someone held a gun to her head and forced her to procreate. EVERYTHING IN LIFE IS A CHOICE, BRENDA!

Freya: Her name is Alicia.

Hannah: I don't care what her name is. The point stands.

Freya grinned to herself. She had known that comment would get to Hannah. The truth was, Freya had nothing but empathy for working parents – male and female. She knew how exhausted she was at the end of a working week, and couldn't imagine what it must be like to add children to the mix. Besides, she wanted to be a parent herself someday; she could at least extend the understanding she hoped she would receive herself, if and when the time came. She just hated it when people acted like her life was a walk in the park simply because she didn't have children. She hadn't known Alicia before she was a mum, of course, but she had a sneaking suspicion that the woman could make herself a permanent victim. Before kids, she would have found something else to complain about.

The encounter with Ethan's sister-in-law had brought one thing to light, though. Sooner or later, Freya would have to have a serious talk with Ethan about what he pictured their future being like. She supposed there was no time like the present.

When Ethan came out of the shower, she greeted him with "Do you think they liked me?"

Ethan looked slightly startled by the question, probably because he was still half-naked. "I told you they did."

Freya shrugged, trying not to feel like a nagging wife already. "You said you thought I'd made a good impression, but we didn't really talk in *detail.*"

"Detail, huh? Okay, at 6:32 you smiled at Joe and he said he appreciated that."

She threw her pillow at him. "You know what I mean! Your mum is amazing, of course." That was entirely true. She could see where Ethan's kind, easy-going nature came from. Bridget couldn't have been nicer or more welcoming to Freya.

"Thanks. I think so."

"And your brother is lovely."

"And Leish?" Ethan was starting to grin now, clearly suspecting Freya's feelings about his sister-in-law.

"She seemed nice enough. Very... direct."

"Very," Ethan affirmed, hanging his towel up and climbing into bed beside her without bothering to put anything on.

"What did you think about her... well, you know, she asked about kids. What... I guess..." She was stammering like she'd never strung a sentence together before.

"Are you asking if I want kids?"

"Yeah. I know we haven't been going out for too long, so I don't want to scare you off or anything, but I thought it's something we should talk about before we get much further." Oh, God. He was going to run. Wasn't this kind of conversation a man's worst nightmare?

Ethan looked surprisingly laidback, though, as he thought about the question. "I always wanted kids," he said. "But as I got older, and I was still single, I started to wonder if it would ever happen. So I think... I still want them, but if it didn't happen it wouldn't break my heart, either."

Freya stared at him in surprise. His words could have come out of her own mouth. "Same," she stammered. "I do want them, but I'm in my late thirties now, so I don't know if I'll be able to have them when the time's right. So I guess..." She shrugged, unable to go on. What he'd said was perfect, basically. A steadfast refusal to consider children might have been a dealbreaker for her, but Ethan's secretly confessing to a long-held desire for ten kids would have scared her off just as much, simply because she didn't know if she'd be able to give them to him.

Ethan just smiled. "I do take issue with one thing you said, though," he added. "The bit about it being too soon."

"You don't think so?"

"No. Not when I've already fallen madly in love with you."

"You have?" It was more than she could have hoped for. She'd suspected that his feelings were there, but it was entirely different to hear him say it so unreservedly. She smiled. "That's good, because I love you, too."

Ethan grinned at her, looking happier than she could ever remember seeing him. As they kissed, it felt like everything was right with the world.

Part Two – Five Months Later

Chapter 33: 2020

"Remember when you were the sensible one of our group?" Hannah asked, looking at the sparkling ring on Freya's finger.

Freya grinned, still feeling exhilarated. "I thought that was always Alex."

"It was a tie," Hannah laughed, reaching over to hug her friend. "Congratulations! I'm so happy for you!"

Hannah wasn't wrong. Getting engaged after only seven months was a crazy notion for Freya. In the past she would have laughed at people who rushed to the altar so quickly. But everything with Ethan was just so *right* that when he got down on one knee, she'd barely let him get his sentence out. "Yes!" she cried, leaping up from her seat to throw her arms around him. The other patrons and servers in the restaurant applauded, but Freya and Ethan barely noticed. They were in their own world.

He had used her full name – *Freya Evangeline Collins, will you marry me?* She had always thought it was a silly tradition. "If you don't use their middle name, will the bride-to-be have no idea who he's talking to?" she had laughed to her friends, back in the day. It didn't seem silly now. It had seemed perfect, just like everything else Ethan did.

"You have to keep in mind, I've known him for twenty years," she told her friends now. "I mean, I might not have seen him for most of those, but I know he's not a scammer or something."

Alex and Hannah both laughed. "I don't think we were concerned about that," Alex assured her. "We're happy for you, really! I think it's amazing that you're so sure about him. I'm a little jealous," she added teasingly, "but it's nice. Good on you."

Freya smiled, knowing her friends' happiness for her was genuine. It was such a nice contrast to the grudging tolerance they'd always directed towards Jim. Her friends both thought so highly of Ethan. Her family loved him, too. All in all, he was the kind of guy she didn't think really existed anymore. She was so happy to have found him.

Every so often it occurred to her to wonder how different life might have been if she'd fallen for Ethan back in high school, the way he had for her. She couldn't really imagine it. Part of her thought they might have had this kind of happiness all along. Maybe they would have got married in their early twenties, rather than as they approached forty. Maybe they'd have kids, more financial security, and two decades of history between them.

But it was equally likely that they would have broken up, like most high school couples, and never spoken again.

She was so happy now, it didn't pay to second guess herself. She couldn't imagine any kind of alternative scenario where she was more blissful than she was right now.

"Anyway, I have a question for you both," Freya said now, dragging it out teasingly. There was no point; she knew her friends would know exactly what she was going to say. "Would you like to be my bridesmaids?"

The girls squealed as one, Hannah clapping her hands together happily. "Of course!" Alex exclaimed, grabbing her friend in a quick hug. "We'd love to! You're having Iris as well, I'm guessing?"

Freya nodded. "Yes, and she's going to be my Maid of Honour, so I already drew you guys out of a hat. Hannah, you're my second in command and Alex, you're my third. I hope that's okay." She had always been so close to both of the other women, she had decided that drawing the order out of a hat was the easiest way to figure out the order without hurting anyone's feelings.

"We're happy any which way," Alex assured her. "It's an honour. Thank you! Who's Ethan having?"

"I don't think he's asked them yet, but he was going to ask his brother Joe to be his Best Man and then Sam, of course. He's asking Nick, too."

"Awww, that's nice," Hannah cooed. "Considering they just got back in touch again after so long, I mean."

"Yeah, I think it's mainly because of our little friendship group. It works out kind of nicely, though. The six of us and the two siblings," Freya smiled. "Neither of us wants much of a fuss so it's going to be a pretty low-key day, but it should be good." She and Ethan had talked it over and they agreed that they didn't really care what the day brought; they just wanted to be married.

———— ⟋⟍ ————

ALEX SMILED TO HERSELF as she went home from her lunch with her friends. She was truly happy for Freya. She couldn't deny that there was a small tinge of envy there, but overall she was just pleased to see Freya so happy and settled with such a great guy. She shuddered as she thought about how close Freya had come to settling down with a loser like Jim instead. Thank God she had waited for the *right* guy.

She couldn't help but wonder if her own refusal to settle would lead her to a great guy as well, or if it would just mean she was alone forever. Statistically speaking, she knew the odds of finding a man were decreasing as she got older, but she also couldn't bring herself to take the first guy who came along, just because. She would rather be alone than with the wrong person.

Suddenly, an image of Nick came into her head. Alex caught her breath, taken off guard by her own mind. She had, of course, entertained a few overly romantic thoughts about Nick after the Teens in Turmoil launch party, but she had shut those thoughts down as quickly as they had come to her. After her chat to Katherine, she had decided it was all nonsense and had stopped thinking about him in that way – or tried to, at least. He had finished his social media work for her and things had become so busy with her new role at work that she hadn't seen much of him. Work had definitely made it easier to push Nick to the back of her mind. She was thrilled with how Teens in Turmoil was beginning to take off, and she felt a sense of drive and excitement about her work that she hadn't felt for a while. When everything else in life was going well, being single felt just fine.

When she and Nick did catch up, it was only in the group of six. Not having alone time together also made things easier. She just had to ignore the feeling of disappointment that seemed to hit her stomach every time she and Nick left without really talking to each other.

But now, there was this news from Freya and Ethan. She didn't know why, but it made her feel Nick's absence all the more. It was probably because Freya and Ethan had proven that love really could work out, two decades later.

Alex wondered what could happen if she saw Nick alone again, just one more time...

FREYA'S ANNOUNCEMENT left Hannah feeling... uncertain. She was happy for both Freya and Ethan, naturally, but she couldn't help but feel like she was being left behind. As the one who'd always been the first – first to date, first to kiss a boy, first to fall in love – she had always assumed she would be the first to get married as well. She wasn't entirely sure how she felt, watching her best friend get engaged. It was so surreal, especially considering it was Ethan she was marrying. Ethan! Hannah hated how conflicted she was feeling, but she couldn't deny it.

It wasn't that she'd ever thought the marriage pact was a real, viable solution for her love life. But it had worked for Freya and Ethan. Of course, things weren't meant to be for poor Alex with Sam, but was it too early to say things wouldn't work out for Hannah and Nick? True, their reunion had lacked the spark she expected, but that didn't mean they could never get it back, did it?

Maybe it was worth giving it one more try.

Buoyed on by her newfound thoughts about Nick, it was Hannah who organised their next outing. She suggested a pub in the city, thinking it might not be a bad thing to have a few drinks around if she was going to make her move. She still wasn't sure exactly how she felt about Nick anymore, but she was determined to find out, one way or another.

At the start of the night Nick sat beside Hannah, and she was filled with a sense of excitement. This was it. He had picked his spot for a reason, right? It had to mean something that with several seats still available, he had sat next to her. Across from them sat Alex and Sam, with Freya and Ethan sitting at opposite ends of the table from each other. "Are you two done with each other?" Sam joked when he noticed where they were sitting. Ethan just laughed. "We probably see more of each other than the rest of you do. I think we can handle one evening apart."

"Besides, we can gaze lovingly into each other's eyes this way," Freya joked, while the rest of the group made gagging noises.

"I thought of you today," Hannah said to Nick, once the group had settled into smaller conversations.

"Oh?"

"Yeah, I had this guy come into the gym for his first session who looked exactly like you."

"Oh, really? Maybe I have a brother I don't know about."

"Maybe! He was... fit, like you." Hannah smiled at him in the same flirtatious way that had won him over as a teenager, but this time around she didn't get much response. She decided to make her move, reaching out and putting her fingers gently on his arms. "I can see you've still got those guns I remember from back in the day."

She saw Alex looking across the table at them then, and nearly laughed out loud. She knew what Alex would be thinking. *That Hannah, such a shameless flirt. She never changes.* It was true, but this Hannah was thinking more seriously than the Hannah of the past ever had. If she needed to make things obvious for Nick, well, that wasn't *her* fault. This might be her last chance to make things happen between them.

Then she felt it. It was almost imperceptible, but Hannah had always been attuned to Nick's movements, and at the moment she was keeping a particularly close eye on him. For her, it was undeniable. As she moved closer to him, Nick moved away from her. He wasn't unfriendly, but as he shifted away he turned his attention to the game on TV. It was a pretty clear signal.

Hannah sighed a little to herself. It had been a long shot, but she'd given it her best try. Clearly, things were not happening with Nick.

She had to admit, she wasn't even that disappointed. She knew the spark was gone. It had just been nice to feel like she at least had some options. Now, she wasn't so sure she had any.

LATER THAT NIGHT, SAM and Nick went to the bar together. When they got back to the table, Sam said "Hey, I'll swap with you, if that's okay. I need to ask Hannah something."

"Sure. I'll sit there," Nick said, gesturing with his beer. Alex couldn't ignore the fact that her heart skipped a beat when she saw he was pointing to the now empty spot beside her. There was, of course, nowhere else for him to go, she reminded herself sternly. It didn't mean anything. Sam was the one who wanted to change spots, not Nick.

Nick climbed over her, putting one hand on her back to stabilise himself as he did so, then sat down beside her, giving her a quick smile.

"Hey," Alex said, trying to ignore the hammering of her chest. "How's your day been?"

"Oh, you know. Saving lives and all that," he said lightly. "Actually, I did use the work I did for you guys in a portfolio for a new job and they were pretty impressed. They said they want something similar – not too similar, I promise," he laughed. "How is TIT going, anyway?"

"Oh, it's great," Alex said, forgetting her nerves now as she started talking about her passion. "It was a little on the slow side at first, but it's really started to take off! I think word of mouth is getting out there. We're getting more calls and the bosses are starting to take notice." She smiled, proud of herself. Getting Teens in Turmoil off the ground had been a lot of work, and in the first week or so of its operation she had started to wonder if they were going to get a single call. She was pleased to see how well it had been received now, thanks to word of mouth. In addition to the expected calls from teenagers, they had also received some calls from parents who were asking for advice about how to deal with problems their adolescent children were having. It was more than she could have hoped for. Obviously the success of her venture was a personal victory, but it was more than that. For the first time in a long while, Alex felt like she was really making a difference.

"Good for you! I'm happy for you," he said, putting his hand gently on her shoulder as he spoke. She smiled, feeling the butterflies coming back again. It could have just been a friendly gesture, a "pat on the back" from someone she had known for a long time. It felt like more than that, but Alex knew all too well that that could just be her reading too much into it, rather than genuine feelings from Nick. She wished she could read his mind and know exactly what he thought of her.

Of course, even if she could read his mind, and even if he felt the same way about her that she was starting to realise she was feeling about him, there was still one small problem. And that small problem was sitting across the table from her right now.

Alex chanced a glance at Hannah. She was giggling with Sam and it looked like she hadn't even noticed Alex's interaction with Nick. It couldn't have been anything, then, Alex told herself, trying to slow her heart rate down. If there was any obvious chemistry between the two of them, Hannah would have caught on and would no doubt be giving them the evil eye right about now. Hannah hadn't exactly been subtle when she'd been flirting with him at the start of the night, so she obviously had more than friendship on her mind, despite what she'd told her female friends. No, Alex told herself, there was nothing going on with her and Nick. It was all in her imagination, and she needed to stop thinking that way. Alex had never been one for time wasting, and there was no way anything could happen between her and her old friend, so there was no point in even entertaining the possibility.

That was what she told herself, right up until it was time to leave at the end of the night.

She had hugged Nick before, but it had always been a quick, one-armed hug, the type you gave any friend in greeting. Now when she went to put her arms around him, he surprised her by pulling her in close, holding on to her tightly for longer than she'd expected. By the time she pulled back, she was speechless. They stared at each other awkwardly for a minute, then he smiled. "See you next time," he said casually, and she was once again left wondering if she'd imagined everything.

It was only a hug. But for the next week, Alex couldn't stop thinking about it. She would have been mortified if anyone knew. She was thirty-seven years old, for God's sake, not some swooning teenager! She didn't know anyone past their adolescent years who would get so starry-eyed over a simple hug between old friends.

But still, it had been a long time since she'd felt a strong male body pressed up against hers like that. It had been a long time since she'd felt so protected. So... seen.

It was a really bloody good hug.

Chapter 34: 1999

"That absolute scumbag," Alex yelled on the Monday following the formal.

Freya and Hannah stared at her in confusion. They had just got their lunch out of their lockers when Alex had come up and started yelling. About whom or what, they weren't entirely sure.

"Alex?" Freya asked hesitantly. "What's going on?"

"It's Sam," Alex said, now looking less enraged and more defeated. "He's going around telling everyone he *nailed* me Saturday night after the formal."

The other girls' jaw dropped. There was a moment of silence, and then Hannah asked, "Did you guys…?"

"No!" Alex looked indignant at the very suggestion. Freya was glad Hannah had been the one to ask because she'd been wondering, too. They'd all gone back to a post party at Ethan's place, but Freya had slipped out as early as she thought she could without attracting Hannah's ire. The last time she'd seen Alex and Sam, they were looking pretty friendly, sitting on the couch together and chatting away. It wasn't outside of the realms of possibility to think that they might have slept together, although Freya was relieved to hear that they hadn't. She wasn't ready to be the only virgin left in their group.

"Well, I have some issues, too," Freya sighed. She didn't want to put it into words, but she couldn't imagine not letting her friends know what was going on.

"What are your issues? The library didn't have the book you were after?" Alex's words stung, but Freya decided to let them go. She knew her friend was hurting.

"At the formal, I... I kissed John."

"No!" Hannah exclaimed, excitement gleaming in her eyes. "Your first kiss?" At Freya's nod, Hannah impulsively grabbed her in a quick hug. "I'm so proud of you!"

Freya laughed shortly. "I'm not sure it was anything to be proud of me about."

"You don't like him?"

"He's a nice guy and everything, but you know I don't want a boyfriend. But... that's not even it. Ethan saw us."

"Ethan? Really?"

Freya grimaced, remembering back to the formal. As she and John had pulled away from their kiss, her heart hammering in her chest, she had seen Ethan staring at them. He looked... crushed.

"So what? Ethan has a girlfriend."

Freya shrugged. "I don't know. I just felt bad, I guess. I mean, we're friends, and I've been telling him all along I don't want to date. It had to hurt to see me..."

"Sucking face with someone else?"

"Not how I would have put it, but sure, Han."

"He'll get over it," Alex said briskly. "It was just a kiss."

"And a rumour is just a rumour."

Alex's eyes flashed with fury. "I'll *kill* the bastard."

Hannah shrugged. "It might not be a bad thing, you know. I mean, it's 1999. It's not like people judge you for having sex."

"But I didn't have –"

"I know, I know," Hannah soothed her. "I just mean, if people *think* you had sex it's not really a big deal."

"The big deal is the lie, Hannah," Alex said, exasperated. "I don't appreciate people going around spreading lies about me. It doesn't really matter what the lie is."

Hannah nodded slowly. "I can understand that."

"Anyway, I think you're wrong about the lack of judgement," Alex frowned, looking over at a group of girls who were staring their way. The two groups of girls had never been particularly friendly towards each other, and now the other group was giggling, whispering to each other as they looked directly at Alex. They seemed to be doing their best to make it obvious that they were talking about her.

"What are you looking at?" Alex yelled over to them, her face twisted with frustration.

"Oh, nothing," Caroline, the leader of the group, called back. She turned to her friends and gave an exaggerated cough, badly masking the word "*Slut!*" The rest of her group fell apart laughing. Alex's face turned red and she turned away. Freya was surprised to see her hands were trembling slightly. For someone who never really worried what other people thought about her, Alex was clearly shaken by the other girls' reactions.

"Don't worry about them, Alex," Hannah said loudly, glaring at the other group. "They're just jealous that they can't get any."

"Hannah!"

"What? I'm helping."

"I'm not sure you are. I don't want to add fuel to the fire."

"Okay, okay. Let's go," Hannah said, putting her arm on Alex's back as they turned to go.

"Freya?"

They all turned back at the sound of the voice. It was John, looking hesitant. "Can I talk to you?"

Feeling like there was nothing she wanted less in the world, Freya walked away with him.

"I REALLY ENJOYED HANGING out with you Saturday night," John said sweetly to her when they were alone.

She smiled, trying to look more comfortable than she felt. "I did, too. But..."

"But?"

Freya paused, flustered. She had been about to tell him she wasn't interested in dating, but something about the way he was looking at her... She couldn't bring herself to say it. Instead, she shook her head wordlessly.

John looked down at the ground awkwardly. "Well, I was wondering if you'd like to go to a movie with me on Friday night."

Freya was going to say no. She was going to tell him all the reasons she wasn't interested in taking things further. After all, she wasn't going to date until Uni.

To her own surprise, she smiled at John. "I'd like that."

Chapter 35: 2020

There was only one thing for it. For the first time in her life, Alexandra Reynolds was going on an online dating site.

Hannah had always been a fixture on the online dating sites, and even Freya had given it a go – in fact it was where she had first met Jim, which wasn't exactly a ringing endorsement for the success of the apps, in Alex's view. But despite Hannah's best attempts, Alex had always resisted going on there. She wanted to meet someone organically, not with the help of some complicated algorithm. She knew she was being old-fashioned – so many people met their partners online now that it was considered mainstream. But it had never interested her.

Until now.

Well, she wouldn't go as far as to say it *interested* her now, either, but the fact that she had been unable to get Nick out of her head for over a week now was reason enough. If she was swooning so much over a simple hug from a friend, she was clearly hard up. She needed to find someone new; to remind herself that there were plenty of eligible men out there in the world. And like it or not, according to just about everybody, the dating apps were the way to do it.

In typical Alex style, she did her research first, looking at the different apps and the features they offered. She ended up settling for Aphrodite, a phone app which was designed to let the woman make the first move. She liked the concept as well as the name, given that she'd always been fond of Greek mythology. She signed up for Aphrodite and filled in the fairly basic questionnaire about herself – her likes and dislikes, religious and cultural backgrounds, and what was important to her in a partner. When she'd completed all the required information she put the phone down, taking a deep breath. It was crazy to put so much stock into just signing up to a dating site, but she was surprised to find that she really was hopeful about this whole experience. It was entirely unlike sensible, level-headed Alex. She was more surprised to find that she was quite happy about that. After all, she had done things "her" way for nearly thirty-eight years now and she hadn't had much luck in the romance department. Maybe changing things up was exactly what she needed.

AT THE SAME TIME THAT Alex was trying to sort her love life out, Hannah Nicholson was swearing off men entirely.

It wasn't that she was bitter, but she had had enough. If even her old flame couldn't bring himself to be bothered with her, what was the point?

It was true that she'd told her friends she was doing this months ago, after her uncomfortable morning-after sneak out from Craig's place. And she hadn't had any awkward one-night stands since then, which seemed to be progress, but she'd still gone on dates here and there. Actually, more often than "here and there", to be honest. She told herself it was because she enjoyed dating, and that she wanted to do it, so why should she deny herself pleasure? She tried to avoid the small voice in her head that kept insisting she was actually going on all these dates because she simply didn't know how to fill her weeks if she wasn't going out with guys.

Well, no more. It was time for her to take some time out for Hannah for a change. Now she just had to figure out what the single life – a truly single life – would look like for her.

She decided to start with something she'd always wanted to do. The year before, her friend Anastasia had started a power lifting routine and swore by it. Hannah had watched Anastasia get stronger every time she saw her. She'd even started entering some power lifting competitions. Hannah had been interested, but hadn't wanted to commit to anything.

On a whim she messaged Anastasia now, asking if her trainer was available to take on someone new. Within minutes Anastasia had replied with her trainer Travis' number, and Hannah had reached out to see if he could take her on.

She smiled as she sent the message, waiting to hear Travis' reply. She didn't know if it would lead to anything, but it felt good to take the first step.

"SO YOU'RE A THERAPIST?"

Alex smiled tightly at the man across the table, trying not to let her nerves show. She was on her first online date, with a guy named Mark. He'd seemed nice in their interactions online, and so far he seemed normal enough. She'd heard some internet dating horror stories, but she'd also heard of enough successes to propel her through her nerves and into meeting this guy in person.

"By trade, at least," she said, filling him in a little on her job. She didn't go into Teens in Turmoil, but filled him in on the Kids in Crisis line and how she helped callers out.

"Seems like you're selling yourself a little short, aren't you?"

Alex paused, sure she must have misheard him. "Sorry?"

"Well, you're a trained psychologist. Seems you could be making more money *and* making a bigger difference to people's lives if you went into private practice." Mark snorted. "You could be working with adults with real problems, not kids whose best friend has stopped speaking to them."

Alex tried to swallow down the anger that was rising inside of her. Who was this guy to judge what she did for a living? It was a fairly common viewpoint, to be honest – and it was true that she could be making a lot more money in private practice, but she disagreed on the "making a difference" point. They had kids – and, now, teenagers – calling up who were suicidal, or had eating disorders, and had nowhere else to turn. Alex was proud of the fact that their helplines were there for those kids. As for the so-called less important calls, the ones about best friend dramas and other squabbles – if they were important enough for a kid to make the phone call about, didn't that mean something? She knew a lot of people were quick to dismiss children and their problems as insignificant. She just didn't expect Mark, who was a father of three, to be one of them. Nor did she expect him to express that point of view on a first date. If this was how he acted when he was meant to be impressing her, how would he act further on in their relationship?

She already knew there wouldn't be a second date.

Chapter 36: 2020

"It's wedding planning time!" Freya exclaimed, throwing her arms up in excitement. "The moment you've all been waiting for!"

"I'm so excited," Hannah grumbled, stifling a yawn as she reached for her cup of coffee. "But why did we have to do this so early?"

"It's 10am."

"My point exactly."

Freya laughed. "We had to do this so early so we can go for a nice lunch afterwards. Quit your whining." The three girls, as well as Iris, had arrived in the city to try on dresses. Since Freya and Ethan were opting for a relatively simple wedding, they had decided to only have a six-month engagement. The wedding would be held in Ethan's family friend's sprawling backyard, with a catering company providing all the food. Simple, no-fuss, and then they would be married, which was all Freya and Ethan really cared about. Freya had discussed eloping, but Ethan had talked her out of it. "At the end of the day, we'll want all our loved ones there," he reminded her, and she knew he was right.

Although the wedding itself was simple, all the girls agreed they wanted the dresses to be as traditional as possible. "The whole point of a wedding is to have a nice dress," Hannah informed her, and Freya laughed. She agreed more than she let on, though. She'd never really dreamt of her wedding day, but she did have high hopes for emerging in a stunning gown, everyone holding their breath at the sight of her. It was a silly fantasy, especially as she approached forty, but she was entitled to it, and now she wanted it to come true.

They decided to tackle the bridesmaid dresses first and were only in their second dress shop when they found something that they all agreed was perfect. They were each trying on a different dress, but it was Iris who stepped out in a light lavender, off-the-shoulder gown. Iris had a tall, slim figure, but the way the dress skimmed over the lower half of the body seemed like it would flatter anyone. Hannah and Alex immediately went to get it in their sizes, hoping the dress would work for them as well. Alex was even taller and slimmer than Iris, and the dress made her look like a Greek goddess. Shorter, curvier Hannah shone in it as well, the dress hugging her figure in a flattering way. They were sold.

"Let's hope the wedding dress is this easy," Freya said as they paid the deposits for the dresses, Iris requesting a couple of minor alterations to hers.

"Only one way to find out."

In the end, the wedding dress was even easier. In the first shop they went to Freya tried on three dresses, which they all agreed were nice but not 'right'. When she came out of the dressing room in the fourth dress they all stopped speaking, staring at her.

"What?" Freya asked self-consciously. "Is it bad?" She had thought when looking in the mirror that the dress looked beautiful, but the way they were all staring now...

It was Iris who spoke first. "I don't know about the others, but I think it's *amazing!*"

Freya smiled at her image in the mirror behind her as the other girls agreed enthusiastically. The dress was champagne coloured, old-fashioned in a way, with delicate lace sleeves. In all her fantasies about blowing everyone away in her dress, she'd been in something more classically white, more modern and form-fitting. But this... she loved it. It was a little like her groom himself, she mused as the other girls urged her to *buy it, buy it now!* – nothing like she'd expected, but everything she'd needed.

Before long they were having their planned lunch together, talking animatedly over pasta. "I never thought we'd go lavender, but I love it," Alex enthused as they toasted their success. "It's just perfect."

"And your wedding dress, Freya! I'm so jealous," Hannah said, but there was excitement in her voice rather than true envy. "I can't wait for your wedding day."

"I wish our high school selves could fast forward and see this day," Alex laughed. "Little Freya, so uninterested in boys... so uninterested in *Ethan*... planning her wedding day to the boy himself!"

They laughed together, Freya shaking her head at the incredulity of it all. Ethan had become such a big part of her everyday life in a relatively short time that she sometimes forgot what a miracle this whole thing was, but Alex was right. If

Freya's high school self could see them today, she never would have believed it.

Chapter 37: 1999

"So, you and John are an item now?" Ethan asked, the hurt in his voice obvious. It was the Tuesday following the formal, and Freya had just run into Ethan for the first time. They didn't have any classes together so she'd been hoping to avoid him for longer, but she'd forgotten that their History classes were in adjacent rooms. It was probably better to get it over with sooner rather than later, anyway.

Freya paused, looking at her friend. She wasn't sure how to answer, but she decided to just be honest. "I don't know."

"You don't know?" He gave a short laugh. "How could you not know?"

"I guess... I mean, we're going out Friday night, so I'll see."

"Great. I hope you two are very happy together."

"What's the problem, Ethan? You have a girlfriend. It's not like I'm cheating on you." As soon as the words were out, she regretted them. Her tone was too harsh. Ethan was giving her attitude, sure, but it's not like he'd ever done anything bad to her. He was just hurt, and lashing out. She could be kinder.

"No. You didn't cheat on me, because you never gave me a chance. And yeah, I'm with Emily. But you know I'd rather be with you." He closed his eyes. "I didn't mean that. I really like Emily. But... I mean, I liked you for so long, and you kept telling me you weren't interested in dating anyone. And now I see that you just weren't interested in dating *me.*"

Freya stared at him, feeling dazed. She had always known Ethan was interested in her, but she didn't know he was *this* interested. She just assumed that when he met Emily he had moved on. But he had a point. Why was she willing to go out with John when she wasn't willing to go out with Ethan? All along, Freya would have sworn that her words to Ethan were true: that she wasn't interested in dating anyone. And yet, when John had asked her, she hadn't hesitated.

"I don't know," she said finally, taking a deep breath in. "I only know I'm sorry."

And she was. But what she was sorry for, she wasn't entirely sure.

"WHAT THE HELL IS WRONG with you?" Alex yelled at Sam the same afternoon. She knew Sam had been doing his best to avoid her, but he couldn't hide from her forever. They had Science together and she had made a point to get to class early, ready to ambush him.

Sam at least had the decency to look sheepish. "What have you heard?"

"I've heard your lies, you idiot! Did you really think it wouldn't get back to me?"

"I'm sorry, Alex. I really am. I didn't mean for it to get out of hand like that. But... Ethan asked me if anything happened, so I said it did. I mean, I'm the only one who hasn't..." He paused, a blush tinging his cheeks. "Anyway, I didn't realise that Mick overheard me, and he told Jack, and... anyway. It got out." He looked down at his feet as he said that last part.

"I'll say it got out! The whole school thinks I shagged you at the after party!"

"It's not that bad, though, is it? I mean... a bit of a reputation might not be the worst thing..."

"Ugh. Shut up. Now. You need to stop talking." Alex barely stopped short of putting her hands over her ears. "You're just going to make everything worse."

"I'm sorry, Alex, I really am. I'll tell everyone it was all a misunderstanding."

"That's like shutting the gate after the horse has bolted," she said, her voice flat. "No one's going to believe you now. They'll just think I don't want everyone to know."

A part of her knew she was overreacting. Most of the people in their grade had already said farewell to their virginity that year, if not before. She knew no one would really care that much about one rumour of her with a guy, even if Caroline and her band of bitches were delighting in the opportunity to have a go at her. But still, she was mortified. She'd always been a little shy when it came to sex, not even wanting to hear her sister Katherine talk about it. She certainly didn't want everyone talking about her so-called sex life, imagining her getting it on with Sam.

"I knew you'd be angry," he said in a quiet voice. "I really do like you, and I don't want to spoil our friendship. I don't know what I can do to make this right."

Alex shook her head wordlessly. The truth was, she was angry, but there was more to it than that. She was hurt. She thought she and Sam were friends, and he had betrayed her. It didn't matter that he hadn't meant it to go that far, or that he didn't think the lie was a big deal. The point was, he had told a lie about her, and he had done it deliberately. He hadn't considered her feelings at all.

"I know you're a really strong person," Sam went on, seemingly not knowing when to shut up. "I know you have great friends and a great family and all of that. So I know you'll be fine. But I don't want you to be angry at me."

Alex glared at him again, fury creeping back up inside. "I do have good friends," she said, her voice steely. "And I do have a good family. And yeah, I guess I'm a strong person. But that's not the point, Sam. Being strong... having support behind me..." She paused, her voice catching as she felt tears welling in her throat. "All of that doesn't give you the right to hurt me."

She turned and walked away.

Chapter 38: 2020

Alex's second foray into internet dating wasn't much more successful than the first.

She was getting better at rejecting men offhand, although whether that was a good thing, she wasn't sure. She had come up with an unofficial list of rules for online dating. Firstly, any guy holding his middle finger up in his profile picture had to go. That seemed like it would be a niche group, but she was quickly learning it wasn't. An astonishing amount of *grown men in their thirties* seemed to think that flipping the bird to the camera was an effective mating ritual. Did anyone find that appealing? *Look what a badass I am! I don't care about anything! I'll even give this phone the finger!*

Once she got past the profile stage, the first warning sign was the guys who tried to take the conversation sexual within the first three messages. Well, that one didn't take a detective to figure out. She supposed it worked for those who really didn't want any more than a fling, but she wasn't one of them. Someone who couldn't make witty conversation for five minutes before offering to lick peanut butter off her naked body wasn't the right person for her.

Then there was Peter, who seemed promising based on his profile and first few messages. After they'd been chatting for about half an hour, she received another message.

Peter: You seem to have such a good sense of humour. That's awesome! My wife doesn't at all.

Alex: Oh, you're separated?

Peter: No.

She blocked him after that.

At first Alex was wary of the guys who tried to initiate a date in the first few messages, but after a few weeks of online dating, she felt differently.

"He just won't ask me OUT!!!" she texted Freya and Hannah in frustration, talking about George, a guy she'd started messaging with weeks earlier.

Hannah: You can ask HIM out, you know.

Alex: I actually kind of already did. He didn't really reply. He said he wants to see the new Tom Cruise movie and I said I'd love to go with him sometime and he just said "cool".

Hannah: Mr Conversationalist right there.

Alex: I guess I could ask him more directly, but I thought that was kind of a pretty good hint.

Freya: Ask him more directly. Some guys need to be hit over the head with it.

Alex: You needed to be hit over the head with it...

Freya: Well, I guess I'm "some guys".

Alex dismissed her friends' advice at first but after another two weeks of talking to George with no suggestion of actually seeing each other, she gave in. "Would you like to go to dinner or something?" she asked, holding her breath as she sent it. It was ridiculous. She was a strong, powerful career woman. She was modern and forward-thinking. There was absolutely no reason why she should feel so nervous about asking a guy out. Hell, she wasn't even sure he meant all that much to her, but still, putting yourself out there was surprisingly difficult. She'd been lucky enough to always have men make the first move, and this shift wasn't something she was sure she was entirely ready for.

She was pleased when her phone beeped just a few minutes later, but her smile faded when she read the text. George had written "Oh, thanks for the suggestion! I think it would be really good to get to know each other a little more first, though? Maybe keep talking a few more weeks and then see?"

She growled in frustration as she threw her phone down. One thing she already knew for sure: George wouldn't be hearing back from her for another few weeks. He wouldn't be hearing back from her ever again.

AFTER THE GEORGE SITUATION, Alex decided it was time to start chatting to multiple guys at once. It was what everyone had told her to do from the beginning, but she'd felt a misguided sense of loyalty towards the guys she was speaking to. Now, she knew better. There was no way she was going to waste another five weeks talking to someone where it led nowhere. No, it made a lot more sense to talk to ten guys at once. It would maximise her efficiency while minimising the time she spent fooling around on this stupid app. If she was willing to play the numbers game then soon enough, surely, the right guy would come along.

She was in the middle of her face mask night when a man came along who actually seemed promising.

His name was Tom and he was a nurse, which Alex loved. Her grandmother had been a nurse, and he had to be caring to take on that job. He made her laugh and seemed relatively sane, which was more than she could say for most of the guys she'd met online. They chatted back and forth for about half an hour when he said he needed to go – his dog, the adorably-named Terrence, had been bugging him for a walk, and he couldn't hold him off any longer.

"No worries!" Alex wrote, surprised at the twinge of disappointment she felt. After all, it was just an online chat with a man she'd never even met. "Have a great night!"

The response she got back made her heart skip a beat. "I know it's soon, but I'd love to make a time to meet for coffee, if you're keen?"

Alex grinned as she typed her reply. "Sounds great. Go take Terrence for his walk and we'll make a plan later. Can't keep him waiting!"

THREE DAYS LATER ALEX stood at a local coffee shop, breathlessly waiting for Tom's arrival. She knew it was silly to get carried away, but this was the first date she'd felt had any real potential. For the first time in a long time, she had stopped thinking about Nick. It was a very welcome feeling.

A man approached – olive-skinned, good-looking, with dimples when he smiled. "Alex?"

Alex smiled back, relieved to see that he looked just like his picture. "Hey, Tom. Nice to meet you."

"You too!" he said, leaning in for a quick, friendly hug in greeting. "Shall we?" he added, gesturing at the coffee shop.

Once they'd found a table and placed their orders, Tom smiled at Alex across the table. "Have you been doing this online dating thing long?"

She sighed. "Only a couple of months, actually, but it feels like a lifetime." She laughed lightly, trying not to seem too serious about the whole thing.

"I know what you mean! You meet some... interesting people this way."

"Yeah, especially in our thirties." She knew from his profile that he was a year older than her.

"Yeah, it can be a bit of a minefield. I've been on there about six months," he said, "since I split from my wife."

"Oh. You're still married?" She thought back to the Peter situation. In fairness, at least Tom had said they'd split. She hoped that was the truth.

"Technically, but only technically. Divorce proceedings are *well* underway, but of course you can't file for a year. A year too long, if you ask me! The marriage was over a long time before we officially separated. I have no more than the average baggage, I promise."

She smiled, surprisingly not put off by the fact that he was technically still married. She'd never thought people had to be single until they had the divorce certificate clenched in their fist, but neither had she imagined ever dating someone who could talk about *my wife*. Still, Nick had been divorced, and if she'd met him when he was only separated, she wasn't sure it would have made any difference. Ugh! Nick! She shut her eyes, trying to force the thought of him from her mind.

"Are you okay?" Tom looked concerned, perhaps thinking that he'd encountered one of the "interesting" people he'd just been talking about.

"Oh, yeah, I'm fine. Just had a bit of a headache. I just need some water," she lied, picking up her water bottle, which she took everywhere with her.

"Anyway, enough about me," she said, taking a big sip and putting the bottle down. "What's the best part about being a nurse?"

"The patients," he said immediately. "I think my parents were a little disappointed that I didn't become a doctor, but I think you can just spend so much more time on patient care in nursing. It's much more personal."

She smiled, appreciating the answer. Tom seemed like a sensitive soul, which was definitely a tick on her list.

"What about your job?" he asked. "Is it just a way to make ends meet, or do you love it?"

Alex immediately thought back to her previous date and how scathing he had been about her career choice, so she felt a little defensive as she talked about her job and its benefits, but Tom just nodded and smiled. "That sounds great," he said.

They chatted about their hobbies, and then about their families. When she found out he was a voracious reader, they shared stories about their favourite books of the past few months, and Alex was pleased to discover they had one in common. She wasn't as big a reader as Freya, but she'd always thought you could tell a lot about someone from the books they enjoyed.

The date passed quickly and Alex was surprised to find herself feeling a little sad when they said goodbye to each other –

a nice contrast to the relief she'd felt at the end of the date with Mark. Maybe this "numbers game" idea really did work when it came to Internet dating, after all. She dated enough guys and suddenly, she found someone she could actually click with. It was a nice feeling.

She knew she was supposed to play it cool, but when she hadn't heard from Tom by the next day she sent him a message. *Just wanted to say it was great to meet you!* she wrote, hoping she sounded bubbly without being *too* excited. *I'd love to do it again sometime if you're interested.* She sent the message, feeling confident that he would feel the same. After all, the date had gone so smoothly.

Tom didn't reply for a few hours and when he did, Alex's heart sank. *It was so nice to meet you, Alex. Thank you! As for meeting up again, while I had a great time, I'm afraid I didn't feel any real chemistry. Sorry, and good luck with the hunt.*

She sighed, surprised by how disappointed she felt. She'd only wasted a couple of hours of her life, but she'd let herself get carried away by the thought that maybe, just maybe, she'd met someone she could have potential with. She wrote a quick message back thanking him for his honesty, and deleted his messages from the inbox of her online dating profile.

There was something worse than a bad date, after all, and it was a date that you thought had gone well... when apparently it hadn't.

Chapter 39: 2020

S am and Richie's wedding happened one Saturday afternoon in an inner-city park. It was a quiet, low-key affair,
with two groomsmen on either side and an enthusiastic female
celebrant who discussed stories of how the grooms had met
and fallen in love. It was Hannah's first time attending a same-
sex wedding, and she was surprised to find herself getting teary-
eyed, which she didn't normally do at weddings. All weddings
were special, and she couldn't wait for Freya and Ethan's, but
there was something about seeing gay people finally having the
right to marry that made it especially meaningful to her.

Instead of a traditional reception, Sam and Richie opted to
have canapes at a restaurant at Portside, overlooking the water.
The four friends not involved in the wedding stood together on
the balcony, chatting away.

"Who'd have thought our little Sam would be the first to
get married?" Alex asked.

Nick raised his hand. "Technically, I was the first." He
paused. "But Sam will be the first to be *happily* married."

Hannah looked at him curiously. Nick didn't talk about his
marriage much, which she knew was probably to be expected,
but it always sparked her interest when he dropped little hints
like that. It really was just the passing interest of friends and

exes, though. She knew the feelings she had once had for him were long gone, even though she'd given it her best effort to try to recapture them.

"And then Freya and Ethan! Our marital pact coming to life!" Hannah crowed. Even though the marital pact hadn't worked out the way she had planned, she felt she deserved at least a little bit of credit for the success of Freya and Ethan. After all, without her input the six friends never would have reconnected, and Freya would be single right now – or with another loser like Jim. True, the marriage pact was Alex's idea to start with, but Hannah was the one who had really kept the momentum going. Of course, if she'd had her way, Freya and Ethan would have got together twenty years sooner.

"Oh, speaking of which," Freya laughed, "I was going to wait until Ethan arrived, but I'm going to tell you all now."

"You're pregnant!" Hannah blurted out.

"Um, no. Now my announcement seems pretty anti-climactic."

"Go on," Alex urged her.

"Well, Ethan and I were talking about the Twenty-Year Pact and how we really wouldn't be here without it, and... we've decided to get matching tattoos!"

This announcement was met by a squeal from Hannah and Alex. "Seriously?!" Hannah exclaimed, staring at her. "I can't believe it! You always said you'd never get a tattoo."

Freya laughed, blushing slightly. "I know, but we were saying it would be really cute to get a '20' but with an engagement ring as the zero."

"Awwww," Hannah cooed. "That's *so* cute." She felt a slight twinge of envy. If things had worked out differently, she could be getting her own tattoo commemorating her engagement. Still, this moment wasn't about her. She was thrilled to think of her cautious friend doing something so fun and spontaneous.

"Ethan's getting an engagement ring tattooed on his body?" Nick asked sceptically, and Alex nudged him. He laughed. "I'm just saying, isn't that a bit... feminine?"

"It won't be anywhere most people will see," Freya said mysteriously, and Nick made a disgusted face.

"When is this happening, anyway?"

"Oh, next Sunday. I thought you guys might like to come along and watch."

"Not if I have to see Ethan's arse," Nick grumbled.

"We'll be there," Alex vowed.

"Wouldn't miss it!" Hannah added.

At that point Ethan came back to the group, his groomsman obligations temporarily fulfilled.

"I heard Freya is making her mark on you," Alex told him, and they all laughed.

Ethan looked confused for a moment, then he laughed, too. "Oh. She told you about the tat?"

"She sure did. We're all going to come and watch your triumphant moment."

"Oh, great," Ethan groaned.

"How nice was today?" Freya asked, in a seeming attempt to change the subject. "I'll be happy if our wedding is half as beautiful as that."

"It was a great day," Hannah agreed. "They both looked so handsome!"

"I liked the harp music. You should steal that," Alex said.

"We just might. I liked it, too."

Sam came up, then. "Hey, guys. Having fun?"

"We sure are," Hannah said, filling him in on Freya and Ethan's matching tattoo plan.

Sam laughed. "Thank God the honeymoon will be over by then. I wouldn't miss it."

"Are you having a good night?" Freya asked, looking around the room. "Everyone seems to be having fun."

"Yeah, it's great! I'm loving it! I have to keep making the rounds though, but just wanted to check in."

"We're fine. We're having a great time! And Richie is awesome," Hannah told him sincerely. It was Hannah and Alex's first time meeting Sam's partner. Freya had had brunch with him, Sam and Ethan a few weeks earlier.

"I'm glad you like him. He is pretty great, isn't he?" Sam said, smiling fondly over at his new husband. Hannah felt that strange twinge once more. It was starting to feel all too familiar. She didn't begrudge anyone their happiness – in fact, she couldn't have been happier for Sam and Richie, or for Ethan and Freya.

She just wished she could have some of that happiness for herself.

Chapter 40: 2020

The next morning, Hannah woke up as early as her partial hangover would allow and headed straight to the gym. Her power lifting routine was going well, and she could feel herself getting stronger by the day. She needed her personal trainer for her proper routine, but she could at least do some weights and some cardio, burn off some of this excess energy. She was disgusted by the way she'd felt last night at the wedding. It wasn't like Hannah to feel so sorry for herself. Swearing off men had been the best thing for her. She might go back to her casual flings in a month or a year, who knew? But for now, she was enjoying focusing on herself for a change. Once, years ago, Alex had told her that she needed time by herself *to really know who Hannah Nicholson is.* Hannah had laughed at her, accused her of putting her psychologist hat on. But Alex had a point. She had spent so long seeing herself through the eyes of men: desirable, flirty, fun. Finally being alone was giving her time to get to appreciate the deeper side to herself. It was a nice change.

THE FIRST MONDAY BACK at work after Sam and Richie's wedding was a long one for Alex. As much as she still enjoyed what she did, she couldn't stop thinking about Saturday night. She kept picturing the group of them laughing and chatting together. But it wasn't the whole group she was picturing. It was just one other person, as if no one else existed at all.

It was Monday night, which usually meant her cook up for the week ahead. Tonight Alex skipped her usual routine. Instead she made Mac and Cheese from a packet, had a quick shower and went to bed early. She tossed and turned, but it was no use. It didn't seem like she was getting to sleep anytime soon. Thoughts about Nick kept intruding. She pictured his beautiful, deep brown eyes. His dark hair, his dimples. He was the most insanely beautiful man she'd ever met, inside and out. She'd never realised it when they were teenagers. He'd always been a nice guy, and he'd obviously always been attractive, but he'd been... Hannah's.

Alex tried to picture herself with Nick, the boy Hannah had loved so much. The boy she sometimes thought Hannah had never got over, even twenty years later.

It was impossible. Nick wasn't for her. He never had been.

"I CAN'T *believe* we're doing this," Freya groaned.

It was the Sunday following the wedding and the six friends were crowded into the tattoo studio, giggling quietly and trying to stay out of the tattoo artist's way.

"It's going to be awesome," Talon, the tattoo artist, promised.

"Is your name really Talon?" Hannah couldn't resist asking. "Or is that some cool tattoo name you adopted when you started working here?"

"It's really Talon," he said, holding a hand up as if to swear his innocence. "My dad thought it was cool."

"Well, it's perfect."

"Who's going first?"

"I am," Freya said. "Otherwise I'll lose my nerve."

"Yeah, she needs to go first. I'm not getting it by myself because my fiancé chickened out."

"Where are you getting yours, anyway?"

Freya held up her arm and pointed to her inner wrist. "It's apparently quite painful, but it's where I always thought I'd get a tattoo if I ever got one."

"Ah, so you're not as worried about discretion as Ethan is?"

"Nope. If I'm suffering through getting it, I want everyone to see it. Ethan's only being discrete because it's a bit..."

"Girly?"

"I was going to say soft, but sure."

"Are you guys trying to talk me out of this?" Ethan demanded. "Because calling a tattoo 'girly' minutes before I put it on my arse should do the trick."

"No, we love the thought of you embracing your feminine side," Freya assured him. "Besides, I'm the only one who's going to have to see it."

"And doctors, who are going to be super impressed."

"Stop whinging," Freya laughed. "This was your idea in the first place!"

Four heads swivelled towards Ethan, who was looking appropriately sheepish.

"It was?" Nick laughed. "Mate, I just assumed Freya talked you into this."

"You designed it? That's adorable," Sam snickered.

"Yeah, yeah, you've all had your fun. Cheers, by the way, Freya, I was worried that would never come up."

"Sorry!" Freya giggled. "Talon here is going to make me suffer in a minute, don't worry."

"It'll all be worth it," Talon promised.

"IT ACTUALLY WAS WORTH it!" Freya exalted as the group of six left the tattoo shop.

"They look great," Alex said. The tattoos had come out really nicely – small and tasteful. The friends were also pleased that Ethan's wasn't as low down as they'd expected, so they didn't get as much of an eyeful as they'd been fearing. "We should get a photo of the two of you. I can make it so you can't tell, uh, *where* Ethan is marked."

"That would be great, but let's wait 'til we're at home, okay? We don't need me to get arrested for pulling my pants down in public."

"Your tattoo is higher than I expected, Ethan," Sam said.

"That's a good thing."

"Yeah, but I mean... it's only like a few centimetres shy of a tramp stamp."

They all laughed, even Ethan, who had become increasingly good-natured about the ribbing since actually getting his tattoo. "I guess I'm Freya's tramp, then," he said, grabbing his fiancé by the shoulders and pulling her in for a squeeze. She responded by giving him a quick kiss on the cheek.

"You two are truly nauseating, I hope you know," Nick said good-naturedly.

"Oh, we know," Ethan said, dipping Freya down in an exaggerated kiss, like something from an old movie. The four friends responded by making appropriate gagging noises, as if they were still their high school selves rather than people nearing forty.

"It's a bit of a lie now, though. I mean, it's 2020 now. It's twenty-one years since we made that pact," Alex mused. "You should probably update your tattoo."

Ethan laughed. "It was a twenty-year *pact*. I couldn't be expected to propose the day we first met up again."

"You could have. Slacker."

"Hey, at least I manned up! I don't see the rest of you fulfilling your end of the pact."

"Oh yes," Sam said in a monotone. "Allow me to leave my *husband* so I can fulfill the marital pact I made when I was seventeen and in the closet. That's clearly the much larger commitment here."

Hannah deliberately avoided making eye contact with Nick. Sam and Alex had a good reason for not working out, but she didn't need it pointed out that the only reason she and Nick hadn't made it work was a total lack of chemistry on the part of their adult selves. She was honestly over it now, but she still thought it was the strangest thing given how hot and heavy they had been in high school. Time really did change everything, after all.

"Lunch?" Freya suggested, and Ethan grimaced.

"Sure, if I can sit down," he said, and the six of them were soon laughing again.

Chapter 41: 1999

Hannah tried to keep the friendship going after the formal, but it was like constantly running into a brick wall. Ethan was angry at Freya. Freya, for reasons known only to herself, was angry at Ethan. And Alex's fury at Sam was all-encompassing. Sam, to his credit, was contrite and solemn, but it was too late for his apologies to do any good. Alex was clearly done with him.

"I just want everything to be the way it was," Hannah said plaintively to Nick one Friday night. They had gone to the video shop together after school and hired a movie, which they were now watching on the small TV she kept in her bedroom. She was lucky that her mum let Nick stay over. They weren't even doing anything tonight – well, not yet, anyway – but a lot of parents wouldn't have been cool with their daughter and her boyfriend locked away in her bedroom together, curled up on her bed, even if they were just watching a dumb action movie.

"I know, babe, but it can't be." Nick rubbed her back. "It's no one's fault. Maybe one day they'll get over it, but for now I think they're all too angry."

Hannah nodded, knowing it was true. If it was just one thing that had happened, they might have been able to work through it, but both 'couples' having problems at the same time meant they were completely out of luck. Alex was too damn stubborn to forgive Sam for what Hannah secretly thought was a pretty minor indiscretion, and she didn't know if there was any moving on for Freya and Ethan.

"Freya's not even *with* John, though," she grumbled to Nick now. "It's not like Ethan has to see them together. And he's with Emily, so why does he care, anyway?"

Following their first official date after the formal, Freya and John had agreed to remain friends. Not that they were really that, either. They didn't seem to have much to do with each other at all. Hannah couldn't see much chemistry between them, to be fair, but she also knew that Freya's famous reluctance to be in a relationship could have come into play, as well. She had been willing to at least consider the idea with John, which was more than she could say for any other guy, but she obviously wasn't willing to see it through. Maybe Freya had been right all along and she just wasn't ready to date. She was a lost cause, Hannah thought grimly. She should focus her efforts on Alex instead. Now that everyone thought Alex had banged someone, she might as well actually go and do it. There were still a few months of high school left. She could get her virginity well and truly out of the way before she graduated.

"So, what about us?" she asked Nick now, not stopping to think on how abrupt this change in topic would seem to him.

"What do you mean, us? We're happy, right?"

"Yeah, but can we keep being happy when our friends aren't even talking to each other?"

He shrugged. "The boys are still talking. The girls are still talking. We don't *have* to do everything together."

"Yeah, but I really had high hopes for this marriage pact thing. I thought we could make it work and we'd all live happily ever after."

Nick laughed. "Han, I love you, but you didn't really think it was going to work, did you? It was just a silly pact. It was never going to work out."

Hannah grumbled. "I suppose it doesn't matter, as long as it works out for us," she said, pulling him in for a kiss.

Their movie was soon forgotten.

Chapter 42: 2020

Ethan and Freya's wedding was approaching quickly, so the three women got together to go over their last-minute plans.

"We've got the engagement party next weekend – is everything sorted for that?"

"Oh, God, I hope so."

"Okay, then the hen's night... and you don't need to worry about that one," Hannah said mysteriously. "That's our problem."

"No penis straws. No penis hats. No strippers. Just... no penis," Freya sighed.

"Like I said, you don't need to worry about the hen's night."

"Don't worry, Frey, I'm keeping her under control," Alex promised.

"Okay, so then the actual wedding day itself. Flowers are sorted. Cake is sorted," Freya said, flipping through her notes. "The dresses are sorted – you're both still right to come along and pick them up next Friday?" Her two friends nodded. "Great, and Iris is in too. We can try them one more time and make sure everything's okay. The photographer and music are sorted... it's all looking good, honestly."

"It's going to be amazing," Alex assured her. "Anything that goes wrong will be such a tiny detail, it won't even matter."

"You think things will go wrong?"

Alex and Hannah both laughed. "Look at Miss Practicality over here, stressing about whether her flowers are cream instead of off-white," Alex teased. "It'll be fine. I just mean that there's always *something* that doesn't go quite according to plan. But who cares?! At the end of the day, you and Ethan will be married, and you said that's all you care about, anyway."

"It always has been," Freya said, a little frown appearing on her face. "But now I'm not so sure."

"You want the fairy tale?"

"Maybe. A little bit. I don't know! It's just... wedding planning is such a huge thing. It's hard not to get a little bit carried away by it all."

"It will be perfect," Hannah told her firmly. "To be honest, I'm a little jealous."

"Please. You're welcome to take over the planning," Freya joked, but she stopped when she saw the look on Hannah's face. "You're not *really* jealous, are you?"

Hannah shrugged, looking down. "I don't know. I mean, it's stupid. I know I have a full life, but I see you and Ethan so happy and coupled up and... I don't know," she repeated. "I guess there's a part of me that wishes things had worked out for me and Nick. It's such a romantic thing, this marriage pact actually working for you guys!"

Alex winced slightly. "I get how you feel," she said quietly. "It's not that we're not happy for you, Freya. We are, of course! It's just that we see you guys being so happy together and it's kind of a reminder of what we don't have."

Hannah nodded. Alex's words summed up her own thoughts perfectly. "Please don't be offended, though," she said to Freya. "Like Alex said, we're completely happy for you."

"No, I get it. I mean, I think if the situation was reversed, I'd feel exactly the same. It's only natural. But don't worry – I mean, try not to. Even though the pact didn't work out the way you guys wanted, that doesn't mean there's not someone out there for you."

"But what if there's not?" Hannah asked quietly.

"If there's not, then... you're fine. Aren't you? You have a job you love. You have the most *incredible* friends in the world," Freya added teasingly, coaxing a small smile out of Hannah. "You have your health and a great place to live. You don't need someone to complete you."

"I know, but..." Hannah sighed, hoping her words wouldn't sound too bitter. "But that's easy to say when you've actually got someone."

A momentary silence settled over the three friends.

"I've thought about that, too," Freya said slowly. "I keep thinking how happy I am with Ethan and wondering how different life would be if we hadn't met up again. And then I thought... hell, I have thirty-eight years of happy memories already. And the memories I cherish the most aren't really the big things. They're things like going out for drinks with you guys. Going to Melbourne with Mum and Dad when I finished high school. Watching Cooper and Max grow up. If I'd never reconnected with Ethan, then I'd still be happy, just like I always was."

"But not as happy."

"Well... no. He means the world to me – obviously! But Alex wouldn't be as happy if she hadn't started Teens in Turmoil. You wouldn't be as happy if you hadn't started your power lifting routine. We all have things we do that make us happier. I guess if you're feeling down now because you're single, then the key is to focus on those things that make you happier, and do them. Spend all your time on yourself and your own happiness. That's the beauty of being single, right? You can worry about yourself."

To Hannah's surprise, she felt herself beginning to tear up. "You're right," she sniffled. "I'm glad I've been doing this single thing for a while. I'd sort of forgotten what it was like to just be me."

"Do you think it's helped?"

"Yeah, I do. I mean, not at first. At first I think I was just trying to live the same life but taking guys out of the equation, which kind of made me feel a little... empty, I guess. But then I started actually focusing on me, and, I don't know. I'm actually enjoying myself without worrying about going on dates and getting laid."

Alex looked a little teary, too. "Wasn't this meant to be a fun wedding planning session?" she laughed, in an obvious attempt to lighten the mood. "And here we are having a therapy session instead."

Freya shrugged lightly. "What can I say? I'm wise. Maybe I need to start working for Teens in Turmoil." She paused. "Actually, I do have something to tell you guys."

"You're preg–"

"No! Stop doing that! Actually, it's about the book. Remember I said a while ago I was starting to write? Well, I've nearly finished it."

Freya had always been a little cagey about exactly what her writing involved, so her sudden willingness to talk about it was a big deal. "Are you going to tell us what this mysterious book is about?" Alex asked.

Freya laughed. "Well, mysterious is right. It's a young adult book, which I think I've told you already. It's about a group of girls at a boarding school, and one of their classmates goes missing and they discover a bit of a mystery going on. A bit like a Nancy Drew type thing, but darker. I've kind of based the girls on us, actually, although there's four of them. There's an Iris-type character in there as well. And I'm just under fifty-five thousand words in, so I'm really happy with how it's going."

"Wow!" Hannah paused. "How long is a book?"

"Oh, it depends, but a young adult book is usually about sixty to eighty thousand. So I'm doing pretty well!"

"That's awesome! You always did love writing," Alex said. "Back at school, I mean."

"Yeah, I did, but I'd really let it go. Anyway, I was thinking about it again recently and the whole reason I wanted to become a librarian in the first place was so I could encourage kids to read, and I thought, what better way to do that than to write a book they might *want* to read?" She shrugged, a self-conscious expression coming over her. "Not that I know for sure they'd want to read it, though."

"I'm sure they would. It sounds great! Everyone loves a good mystery. Can you tell us what happens?"

Freya shook her head. "You'll have to read it for that. Actually, I was hoping you guys would be my first proof-readers? I've shown some of it to Ethan, but I thought you guys could be my official first readers since my target audience is teenaged girls."

"I'd love to!" Alex said.

"Definitely," Hannah agreed. "I'll try to remember what it was like to be a teenaged girl. The memories are in there somewhere."

Freya laughed. "It's crazy, isn't it? Sometimes I still feel like a teenager, and sometimes I can't believe twenty years have passed."

Chapter 43: 1999

The week before graduation, everything fell apart.

Freya, Hannah and Alex had barely spoken to Sam and Ethan since the formal, way back in August. They were still friendly enough to them, but they knew their friendship would never be the same. Hannah still couldn't help but miss the days when it had been the six of them. Alex and Freya said they didn't mind Nick tagging along to their catch ups, but she knew they preferred it when it was just the three girls. Besides, Nick himself wasn't all that comfortable with it. He had started spending more time with the guys, and she wasn't entirely comfortable being the only girl in that group, either. Things were still great when she and Nick were alone together, but that was happening less and less often. Hannah sighed. More than anything, she wished she could go back in time and change the night of the formal. Freya's first kiss definitely wasn't worth the drama it had caused, and if she could do the night over again, she could somehow make Sam keep his big, stupid mouth shut.

Still, when Nick came to her house the Sunday before school finished, she had no idea anything was wrong at first. He was a little quiet, but she knew his parents were having some issues, so she assumed he was worried about that.

"Hannah, I don't think this is working," he finally mumbled. He'd been there for nearly an hour at that point, so Hannah was more than a little taken aback by his words. At first, she assumed she'd misunderstood him.

"What's not working? What are you talking about?"

"You. Me. Us. I don't think I want to be with you anymore."

She stared at him for a moment, wondering if he could possibly be joking. She'd just been talking triumphantly about how close they were to graduation, and suddenly he was breaking up with her? "What the hell, Nick? You don't mean that," she said, shaking her head as though she could will him to agree with her.

"I do. I'm sorry, Hannah."

"What... what did I do? Is there someone else?"

"No. No, there's no one else. Things just haven't felt... right the last couple of months. I'm going to Uni next year and I think we should have a fresh start. That's all."

Hannah glared at him, feeling fire behind her eyes. Her anger was keeping the tears at bay, but only just. "Oh, I see how it is. You want to ditch the high school girlfriend before graduation so you can go and sleep around at Schoolies, right?" Schoolies was the traditional post-high school escape, and Hannah and Nick were supposed to be going together. Neither Freya nor Alex had ever been interested in the party week at the Gold Coast, so Hannah was supposed to be staying with Nick and the guys.

"No, it's not like that, really. And I'll cover your Schoolies costs –"

"Oh, that's big of you. So, I take it I'm not invited to Schoolies anymore?"

Nick had the decency to look embarrassed. "I didn't think you'd want to go."

He was right, of course. She could think of nothing worse now than spending the week after graduation stuck awkwardly in a hotel room with Sam, Ethan and Nick. But that was beside the point.

"You couldn't have waited, oh, I don't know, another week or two? Seen out Schoolies? Seen out *high school?*" The tears were coming now. "Am I that unbearable that you couldn't stand to spend another couple of weeks with me?"

"I'm sorry, Hannah. I really am. But I knew I wanted to end things. Would it have really been fair to string you along?"

"Yes!" she cried. "It would have been fair. Fairer than *this,* anyway! Now... now I'll just look back on my last week of high school and all I'll think about is this." She knew it was true. Hannah had waited so long to be done with school, but even the thought of that paled into insignificance compared to the heartbreak of Nick leaving her.

It wasn't fair. It just wasn't fair.

There wasn't much left for Nick to say. He held her tight, a farewell hug, and then he left. Hannah broke down in proper sobs as he walked out the door.

She was glad she was finishing high school. There was nothing for her there anymore.

Chapter 44: 2020

Before they knew it, it was the night of the engagement party. They had opted for a dinner out, in a function room complete with a small dance floor and a stage for speeches. "This might be fancier than the wedding itself," Freya exclaimed when they arrived and looked around the function room. It was certainly more lavish than she'd expected – Ethan had done the booking, so she hadn't seen the room until tonight. She'd told him she didn't care what the function room looked like, and she'd meant it at the time, but she had to admit she was excited to see it.

"It just might be," Ethan agreed, wrapping his arm around her. "I did good, then?"

"You sure did," she said, rewarding his efforts with a kiss.

"Hey, lovebirds, break it up," Nick grumbled as he walked through the door with Sam and Richie. They were the first guests to arrive, which Freya put down to Sam's famous punctuality.

"Hey, guys. Good to see you," she said, kissing them each on the cheek in greeting. "Thanks for coming."

"Grab a drink," Ethan said. "I'm sure the others won't be too far away."

"We offered for them to share a maxi taxi, but they said they'd meet us here," Sam said. "Apparently there was *no earthly way* Hannah could be ready on time."

They laughed, Freya knowing from experience that that was true.

The party guests started filing in and Freya's night became a whirl of greeting familiar and less familiar faces. Thanks to their short pre-engagement romance, there were still a lot of Ethan's relatives and acquaintances she had yet to meet, so she was soon putting all of her energy into matching names and faces. She saw Joe and Leish and smiled at them, trying to convey a warmth towards her future sister-in-law that she didn't really feel. She hoped they would grow closer in time, but she wasn't sure that was on the cards for them. They were two very different people. She wondered, not for the first time, how Ethan's warm, kind brother had fallen in love with Alicia.

Freya was just meeting Ethan's aunt and uncle from Canberra when Hannah and Alex came in, both looking sensational in dresses they'd bought for the occasion. Freya smiled as they came up. "You guys look amazing!" she exclaimed. "Thanks for coming!"

"Yeah, I thought about spending the night washing my hair but you know, decided to stop by," Hannah said breezily. "You look pretty sharp yourself."

"Thanks." Freya smiled down at her new jumpsuit, white with a plunging neckline. It wasn't the sort of thing she'd normally wear – she'd never worn a jumpsuit in her life before – which was exactly why Iris had urged her to buy it. "It's your engagement party!" she'd said when Freya tried it on doubtfully.

"Throw caution to the wind! Ethan won't be able to keep his hands off you."

Now that the night itself was here, Freya was glad she'd listened to her big sister's advice. Everyone was full of compliments, and she wasn't half wrong about Ethan, who had already whispered in her ear about his post-party plans for her. It was nice to step out of her usual style, just for one night.

"So it's all official now, huh?"

"What's official?"

"Your engagement! It's not official until the party," Hannah informed her.

"Oh, is that so? Well, thank God we had a party, then," Freya laughed. "I'd hate to think Ethan could back out of this at any moment."

"Like he would!" Alex said. "He's besotted."

Freya smiled over at her fiancé, who was shaking her cousin's hand, knowing Alex was right. She had given Hannah the big speech about not needing a man to complete her, and it was true; but she had to admit, if only to herself, that she had never felt as happy as she did now, with Ethan in her life.

"Have you seen the guys yet?" Freya asked her friends.

"No, where are they?"

Freya pointed them out, and Hannah said "Cool, we'll go say hi. It looks like you're needed for wifey duties, anyway." Sure enough, Ethan was waving her over to meet yet another relative.

Freya smiled. "Catch up with you all later."

HANNAH AND ALEX MADE their way over to the three guys, who were munching canapes in silence. It always amazed Alex how even the best of male friends would just stand around in silence for long periods of time. She and the girls could hardly get a word in over each other when they were together.

"Hey, guys!" Hannah called out as they approached, and the men smiled over at them. Richie swooped in and hugged them both, which Alex appreciated, considering they'd still only met him a couple of times. Sam hugged them both next, and then it was Nick's turn. Alex's face turned crimson as he held her, even though the hug was relatively brief.

"What's good to eat?"

"Oh, these spring rolls are the best! I'll see if I can flag down the girl who has them," Sam said enthusiastically. "The samosas aren't bad, either."

"Mmmm. Just don't let me eat too much, I still need to fit into my dress."

"I don't think you're suddenly going to go bursting out of it," Alex laughed. Hannah looked amazing in a strappy pink number which hugged her curves and also showed off the new definition her powerlifting routine had given her. Alex had been pleased with her own royal blue dress, but next to Hannah, she suddenly felt self-conscious.

"You both look great," Sam said, causing both girls to smile.

"Oh, Alex, I have another one," Nick said suddenly. She glanced over, confused. "A flamboyance of flamingos."

Alex laughed out loud while the others looked on, confused. "It started when we were working together," she said. "I said we were 'a complex of psychologists' at work and he said 'no, no, it would be a shrink of psychologists', and it all went from there. We started sharing our most out-there collective nouns."

"Wow, that sounds really cool," Hannah said in a monotone.

Alex and Nick both laughed. "It kind of is, actually," Nick said. "There are some really strange ones around."

"Like a murder of crows?" Sam asked.

"Yeah, that's a pretty well-known one, thanks to the movie, but there are some others that are interesting. Like a conspiracy of ravens –"

"I thought it was an unkindness of ravens?" Alex interjected.

They both laughed again, and the others stared. "It's actually both," she clarified to the group. "We had an argument about it."

"You had an... argument... about the collective noun for ravens."

"It's more fun than it sounds," Alex assured Hannah, who merely shrugged in response.

"You're both geeks, so it shouldn't surprise me."

Alex smiled. Nick had been the popular jock when they were in school, so she'd never thought of him as a geek. She was delighted when she realised he was. She wondered if he always had been geeky and he'd hidden that side away during school, trying to fit in. Or maybe it was something he'd developed as he aged. Some kind of mid-life geek crisis. If that was the case, more people needed to have one. Older, geekier Nick was much more interesting to her than the perfect, good-looking teenager.

"What are some other ones?" Richie asked. "Could you tell me the collective noun for, say, bears?"

"I could," Nick said, pulling his phone out, "after I Google it." He typed into his phone for a minute, then grinned. "You'll never guess it."

"Herd."

"Pack."

"Fur."

"Sloth!" he said triumphantly.

"No way. Let me see." Sam grabbed the phone. "Well, he's right. A sloth of bears."

"So you're all finding this... pretty interesting, then? I'll go get a drink," Hannah said, walking off.

"Okay, what are the best ones you've found?"

"A rhumba of rattlesnakes," Alex said.

"A glaring of cats."

"A kindle of kittens is a good one."

"A shiver of sharks."

"A congregation of alligators."

"A flutter of butterflies."

"There are heaps, if you can't tell," Alex said, bursting into giggles again at the looks on Sam and Richie's faces.

"Obviously. Someone must have had fun coming up with them."

"Oh man, I would. I wonder if there's any need for a collective-noun-namer anymore? Is that a viable career path for me?"

"I'll join you," Nick said lightly. "We can start our own business."

Hannah came back with her drink then, passing one to Alex as well. "Sorry, I didn't have enough hands for the rest of you, so I had to look after the sisterhood here," she told the guys.

Nick grinned. "I can go up for us. What do you guys want?"

As he walked away to get their drinks, Alex wondered if Hannah's use of the term *look after the sisterhood* was as deliberate as it seemed.

Chapter 45: 2020

"You think everyone had fun?" Freya asked for about the hundredth time. It was two days after the engagement party and they had met up for a coffee and a debrief. Freya, in her boundless enthusiasm for all things wedding, had wanted to do it the day after the party, but the others had convinced her to give them a day to recover from their hangovers.

"It was great!" Hannah assured her. "Dancing, drinking, chatting... what more could you want from a party? Seriously, everyone loved it." Alex nodded her agreement.

"That's good. I had fun," Freya grinned. "If my wedding's half as good as that, I'm happy."

"And it'll be amazing, because you've got the best bridal party in the world!" Hannah said. "Oh, and you know, lifelong love and commitment and all that."

The three of them laughed. "Remind me not to get you to do my speech," Freya said.

"Hey, I've been meaning to ask you," Hannah said. "Why *weren't* you interested in Ethan back in high school?"

"How many times do I have to tell you? I wasn't interested in dating."

"Yeah, I get that, but I mean, you did end up kissing John. Not that you really dated him, but you wouldn't even kiss Ethan."

Freya looked thoughtful. "I've wondered about that, too," she said. "To be honest, I think it's because a part of me realised it could be something serious, and that scared me. I wasn't ready. John... I could kiss him and it didn't have to lead to anything major. Even when we decided not to date, I didn't really care about losing his friendship." She shrugged. "I guess my logic was flawed, because I ended up losing Ethan over it anyway."

"She says about the man she's marrying."

"True! I guess all that matters is the happily ever after."

Just then, Freya's phone rang, causing her to jump a little. "Oh! Sorry, guys, this is the caterer. I'd better get it." She ran off, phone in hand.

"Okay, I have something to ask you, and I want you to be totally honest," Hannah said to Alex as soon as they were alone.

Alex frowned. "Of course, but what's up? Are you okay?" She thought of Hannah's constant *you're pregnant!* proclamations whenever Freya had an announcement and she didn't want to do the same thing, but the serious look on Hannah's face made her wonder. True, Hannah kept insisting she was having a break from sex, but was her friend about to announce her own pregnancy? Ask for Alex's advice?

She never could have prepared herself for what Hannah was about to say.

"Do you have feelings for Nick?"

Alex sputtered. When she could finally speak, all she could manage was "What?" It wasn't her most genius retort, and it probably told Hannah all she needed to know.

"At the engagement party... I think seeing you two together in the smaller group made me realise. That, and your ridiculous collective nouns thing. There seemed to be a bit of a... spark there. Are you saying there isn't?"

Alex paused, torn. Part of her wanted to deny everything, but part of her knew this could be the opportunity she'd been waiting for. If she was basically forced into telling Hannah everything, she'd find out how Hannah felt about it. Still, there was no point. She already knew how Hannah would feel about it, and it wouldn't be good. Besides, it wasn't like there was anything to tell. Alex had a little crush on Nick. She had no idea how Nick felt about her.

"I'll take your stunned silence as a 'yes.'"

"No... I mean..."

Alex looked at her friend again, hard this time. Hannah still looked serious, but there was some kind of an almost playful twinkle in her eye. She looked strangely... amused?

"I mean, if I did, how would you feel about?" Alex finally managed. It was as good as an admission, but it gave her a tiny bit of wriggle room in case Hannah was completely opposed to the whole situation. They could at least pretend it was all a hypothetical situation, even if they both knew the truth.

"If you did..." The touch of playfulness was gone now. Hannah looked serious again, and almost a little emotional. "If you did, I guess I'd say that you're two of the best people I know, and you both deserve to be happy."

"Seriously?"

"Seriously. Alex! You should have told me! You know I think Nick is great, and there's a part of me that will always love him, but you know as well as I do that any romantic feelings are gone. We're just friends, so there's no reason you shouldn't be with him. He's a great guy. You're a great girl. Go be happy together."

"I don't know if he has any feelings for me, though."

"He does," Hannah said firmly. Hannah was known for being a little flighty and giggly, but when it came down to it, she could be more stubborn than any of them. Alex also knew her to be more observant and introspective than most people gave her credit for. "I saw the way you two were together. There's definite chemistry. I mean, at the end of the day, what do you have to lose?"

This, Alex could answer immediately. She'd thought long and hard about what there was to lose. "A six-person friendship, for starters."

"Pfft." Hannah waved her hand. "We survived without the boys for *twenty years*. If the worst happened, we'd survive without them again. Well, I guess we're stuck with Ethan, but we can do without the others. Besides, we're adults now. A breakup doesn't have to mean the end of our little group. I'm sure you guys could date and still be civil as friends. Hell, Nick and I are managing it," she said with a little snort. "And he's a good catch. He won't be single forever. If he meets some other girl who we don't even know he'd probably start to pull away from the group, anyway. I'd much rather see him with you than have that happen."

"That's true. But... what if we did get together and you actually couldn't stand to watch it? It's one thing to think you're okay with the idea in theory, but it's another to see it in practice." Alex knew that from experience. Watching Hannah flirt with Nick after she'd developed feelings for him herself hadn't been very enjoyable.

"Then I learn to live with it, or I force you guys to break up." Hannah laughed. "I'm joking! It'll be fine, honestly. Now, any other arguments?"

"He's too good for me." These words came out low, her voice hollow. Alex hadn't wanted to admit that part, even to herself, so she was surprised she was saying it to Hannah. It went against everything she believed about herself. She was strong and independent and here she was, saying she wasn't good enough for a man.

Hannah looked as shocked as Alex felt. "Alex! I never want to hear you say that again!" she exclaimed. "What do you think makes him too good for you?"

"Well, he's better looking than me, for a start." She knew it was true. Nick was gorgeous. He always had been. Wasn't that why Hannah had fallen for him in the first place? They were the It couple of Fortitude High and their mutual sex appeal was a big reason why.

"Please. You're stunning. *Stunning,*" Hannah said, the firmness back in her tone. "You're ten feet tall, skinny, blonde, blue-eyed... Hell, I'd give my right arm to look like you."

"You would not." Hannah was so gorgeous, with her petite figure and womanly curves. When Alex looked in the mirror, she saw someone who was straight up and down like a board, with a B-cup chest. It was nothing to write home about, that was for sure.

"I mean, hell, I'm gorgeous too," Hannah said flippantly. "But yeah, any woman would kill to look like you. So don't come at me with that. What else have you got?"

Even in her most doubtful mood, Hannah could always make her laugh. "Well," she said, "he's really intelligent, and kind and caring."

"Um, pot, kettle. Go on."

Alex shook her head. They were the main points, but she could see Hannah wasn't exactly going to turn around and agree. *Oh yes, you're right, he is too good for you. Go find someone you can slum it with.*

"Alex, seriously. I wish you could see yourself the way I do." Suddenly, Hannah's eyes lit up. "You need to spend the next week talking to yourself the way you would talk to a friend. If you mess up, don't be so hard on yourself. If I mess up you say, 'Don't worry about it', so do the same thing to yourself. I promise you'll see the world in a totally different way."

Alex smiled, knowing this was one of the tricks Hannah employed as a personal trainer, but liking the idea anyway. Hannah saw right through her. Alex had always been hard on herself. She never would speak to a friend the way she spoke to herself half the time. It was worth a shot, at any rate.

"You'd be a good therapist, you know that?"

Hannah shrugged. "I'd get bored." She hugged Alex. "I only want the best for you. You know that."

Alex nodded. She did.

Freya came back then, looking in confusion from one of her friends to the other. "Oh, you guys look... serious."

Hannah waved a dismissive hand. "Nah, nothing too serious here. Nothing as serious as spring rolls and party pies, anyway."

"You laugh, but wait 'til you hear the actual menu for the wedding. It's to die for." Freya sat down and pulled her wedding planning folder out, and the tone soon lightened again.

Chapter 46: 2020

"You look absolutely stunning," Alex breathed as she took in the sight of her best friend, wearing her wedding dress.

"Not bad, is it?" Freya grinned happily at her reflection. "I can't believe I'm a bride. On the wrong side of thirty, you kind of give up on all of that."

Alex wasn't sure she loved being referred to as being on the wrong side of thirty, but she wasn't about to call her friend on it on her wedding day. She knew what Freya meant, anyway. Whether or not marriage was a priority for you, after a certain age, you stopped imagining your wedding day. You stopped picturing yourself having a husband or a family. She was glad Freya was getting her happy ending.

"You're so lucky," Alex said, not for the first time. "You've found your prince and you're making it work. You're an inspiration to the rest of us!"

"I just wish the marriage pact had worked out for you guys," Freya sighed. "Who knew your prince would end up being gay, huh?"

Alex just smiled, not saying anything. Freya hadn't been privy to the conversation between Hannah and Alex about Nick, and she clearly hadn't caught on to any feelings Alex had for their friend's ex. Freya was too wrapped up in her own happiness, and that was entirely okay with Alex.

While she fixed Freya's veil, they could see Iris out the window. She was running around on Maid of Honour duties, barking orders and making sure everything was just right for her little sister's big day. Alex grinned, watching her.

"It doesn't matter how old you get," Alex said, "you never stop being the little sister. I feel that way with Katherine, anyway."

Freya thought about that. "I suppose," she said. "I like it, though. I know you don't always, with Katherine. I like knowing that even though I'm in my thirties now, I still have someone watching over me."

"That's a nice way to look at it." Alex couldn't help but feel slightly envious. She had always had a difficult relationship with Katherine, and had long wished she could have the natural closeness that Freya and Iris seemed to share. Even when Freya was at school and Iris at Uni, a time of life when sisters normally drove each other nuts, they had always seemed to just really like being around each other. It would have been annoying if Freya had taken it for granted, but she never seemed to.

"Alright, you're done. I suppose I should get myself dressed now," Alex said.

"You mean you're not going to walk down the aisle in your activewear?"

"Not today, thanks. And it's not activewear." Alex struck a pose. "It's an entirely new look that's sure to take off." Their hair and makeup had been done first thing that morning, so Freya had cautioned them to wear something they could unbutton rather than pulling over their head. For Alex, that meant a work shirt, leading to a rather strange ensemble of a businesslike button-up top, teamed with the most comfortable bottoms she owned – her activewear tights.

"Okay, you go get ready. It's nearly photo time."

Before long, the three bridesmaids were dressed and ready for their photo shoot. "Are the groomsmen suffering through this many photos?" Hannah grumbled half an hour in.

"Probably not as many, but they're getting some. No one cares about the groom or groomsmen on a wedding day," Freya joked. "It's all about us stunners. We'll get some group photos after the wedding. All of us and our partners."

She said the words innocently enough, but Alex's stomach flipped over. Thanks to Freya's system of drawing their order out of a hat, she was the third bridesmaid. Nick, of course, was the third groomsman, after Ethan's brother and Sam, who had stayed closer to Ethan all these years. She hadn't given much thought to being partnered with Nick on the day, but now it was all she could think about. She was going to walk back down the aisle with him, after the wedding. She was going to dance with him in the bridal party dance. She was going to get photos standing side-by-side with him, smiling at the camera like they were the couple.

It was the first time she'd seen him since Hannah had given them her blessing.

Not that that meant anything. For starters, Nick himself didn't know a thing about their conversation. Besides, Alex had no idea if he was even interested in her in return. And despite Hannah's words of reassurance, she still wasn't at all convinced that things would work out between them.

But she couldn't deny the way she felt when she saw him.

"WE ARE HERE TODAY TO celebrate the union of a special couple, Freya Evangeline Collins and Ethan Ryan Moore,"
the celebrant, a redhead appropriately named Ginger, began.
"Freya and Ethan were friends in high school, and in 1999 they
made a pact: if neither of them was married in twenty years,
they would marry each other." She held her arms out to in-
dicate the couple, as the guests laughed. "As you can see, it
worked out pretty well for them."

Freya felt a giggle bursting out inside her. It wasn't that
what Ginger had said was particularly funny, but she was so
happy she felt like she might get the giggles all day long. What
she'd said to Alex was true – she had long ago stopped imagining that she would have a wedding day – but now that the day
was finally here, it meant more to her than she had expected.
She felt girlish and younger than her years. The spotlight wasn't
often on Freya, so she was enjoying her moment now that it
was.

"After a whirlwind romance that somehow also lasted
twenty-one years –" More laughter – "It is my honour to marry
Freya and Ethan today."

The rest of the ceremony passed in a blur. Looking back,
Freya would always remember slipping the ring on Ethan's finger, and the kiss after they said their vows, but it all felt like
some kind of a dream. The happiest dream she'd ever had.

At the end of the ceremony, her loved ones rushed up to
kiss her – her parents, first, and then her brother-in-law and
nephews, and then the more distant relatives. Her bridesmaids
hung back a moment, letting the family greet her, and then

they rushed towards her as well. "Congratulations!" Hannah cried, jumping up and down as she hugged her friend. "I'm so, so happy for you. And you, too, Ethan," she added, throwing her arms around him as well. "You've got a good one here."

"Don't I know it," Ethan said, grinning over at Freya. He looked, suddenly, exactly like his seventeen-year-old self.

"Congratulations, Frey," Alex cried, hugging the bride and groom in turn. "You did it. You're married!"

Freya smiled. She couldn't believe they were actually married. The speed of their relationship still took her breath away, but it was true what everyone said: when you know, you know. She looked at Ethan and she'd never been surer of anything in her life.

Chapter 47: 2020

"Presenting, for the first time, Mr Ethan Moore and Ms Freya Collins-Moore!"

The crowd whooped and applauded as Freya and Ethan rounded the corner, raising their arms triumphantly. When they got to the bridal table Ethan paused, pulling the chair out for Freya. She smiled and thanked him as she sat down. As he sat beside her, she pulled him in for a kiss. The crowd continued to applaud.

"I'm Hudson, your MC for the night," Freya's cousin announced into the microphone. "We're keeping things fairly simple, but we'll have some speeches and of course, the traditional Bridal Waltz. So to start off the festivities, we're going to invite Freya's dad, Roger, up to say a few words."

The speeches were perfect. Freya, ever the control freak, had had to resist the urge to ask the people speaking – her dad, Iris, and Ethan's brother Joe – to show her the speeches ahead of time, but she was pleased to see that each of them had kept their speeches short, sweet and funny. Finally, it was Ethan's turn to speak. He cleared his throat as he went up.

"I want to start off by thanking everyone for coming," Ethan said into the microphone. "I know some of you have travelled a fair distance, and we really appreciate you being here to share in our special day.

"For the two people in the room who don't know, I've been in love with Freya Collins for as long as I can remember. We were friends at high school, but I always wanted more." He paused for effect. "Unfortunately, my dear bride here wanted absolutely nothing to do with me."

There was a sprinkling of laughter through the crowd of guests. Ethan and Freya's love story was nothing new to most of them, but Freya was still surprised to hear Ethan talking about it with such naked honesty. As extroverted as he'd always been, he was still fairly private about his personal feelings. She found herself getting goosebumps as he spoke.

"I'm actually glad, though, that Freya didn't go out with me when we were in high school, because... Well, because I was an idiot in high school, like most teenaged boys. I would have blown it, no doubt, and we wouldn't be sitting here tonight. So as many twists and turns as our story has taken, I'm so happy things worked out the way they did, because I have the most beautiful wife in the world."

Everyone cheered, and Freya felt herself blushing. She also felt dangerously close to tears at Ethan's heartfelt words.

"I'd like to thank you, Freya, for reaching out and reconnecting just a little over a year ago," Ethan went on. "Thank you for making the first move – this time around – and most of all, thank you for being wrong about us in high school, because it might be the last time I get to say, 'I told you so.'"

Everyone clapped and cheered as Ethan finished up his speech. When he got back to the table, Freya threw her arms around him.

"That was perfect," she told him, beaming. "Just like you."

"AND NOW, IT'S TIME for the bridal waltz! I'd like to invite Freya and Ethan up to kick-start the festivities," Hudson announced after the meal.

Alex and Hannah watched on from their spot at the bridal table as Ethan and Freya moved to the dance floor, which was usually Ethan's family friends' sprawling patio.

"They look so good together, don't they?" Hannah asked, staring dreamily at the bride and groom. She had always loved weddings.

"They do."

"Speaking of couples that look good together." Hannah looked slyly over at Alex. "I couldn't help but notice you getting pretty close to Nick during the photo shoot."

Alex flushed. "We were supposed to, Han. It was kind of the point of the photo shoot."

"Mmm, maybe, but you looked a little more comfortable together than Sam and I did. Or Iris and Joe, for that matter. I'm just saying."

Alex opened her mouth as if to argue, but just then Hudson made another announcement. "And now I'd like to invite the bridesmaids and groomsmen to the dance floor!"

Hannah smiled meaningfully at Alex as they stood up. "*Enjoy,*" she murmured, making her way to Sam and holding her arm out for him to take.

She saw Alex rolling her eyes as she went to join Nick, but Hannah didn't care.

"You may recall, I'm not much of a dancer," Nick said to Alex as they made their way to the makeshift dance floor.

"I recall you *saying* you're not much of a dancer, but I recall you *doing* a pretty good job of it."

"You're too kind. The good news is, tonight there's newlyweds on the dance floor, so absolutely no one is going to be looking at us."

Alex glanced over at Hannah, not as sure of that fact as Nick was.

They came together for the dance, a slow, romantic song that was much more suited to the bride and groom than to the rest of the bridal party. Was it her imagination, or did Nick hold her closer this time than he did during the slow dance at Teens in Turmoil's launch party? She thought about Hannah, and her insistence that Nick was interested in more than just friendship with Alex. She kept telling herself it wasn't possible, but every so often a voice in her head wondered if she was wrong. It was hard to imagine being with Nick, but it didn't seem impossible anymore, the way it used to.

The parents of the bride and groom joined them all on the dance floor, and Nick and Alex shuffled out of the way, to make more room. They were in semi-darkness at the edge of the dance floor now, and Alex felt her heartrate quicken. She wondered if they were close enough for Nick to feel her accelerated heartbeat. She wondered if he was as affected by their newfound privacy as she was.

"I don't think anyone would miss us," she said softly to Nick now, barely able to believe her own courage. "Do you want to slip away? I mean, I think our dancing requirements have been fulfilled," she added, trying to lighten the moment.

Nick nodded wordlessly and they slipped further away from the dance floor, finding a quiet corner of the garden. It was the sort of place that normally would have freaked Alex out; there was some lighting, but it was distinctly darker than the rest of the garden, and any kind of creatures could be lurking in the bushes. But tonight, that thought barely crossed her mind. Tonight, she felt safe.

Nick looked around. "God, this place is huge. Ethan's friends must be loaded."

"Yeah, it's really nice." Alex didn't want to talk about the backyard. She didn't know what she did want to talk about.

"Great night, hey?"

They normally had no problems making conversation. She wondered fleetingly if Nick just might be as nervous as she was.

"It's amazing. I'm so happy for Freya and Ethan." Maybe this was her chance. She risked taking a look at Nick. "It's nice the pact worked out for one couple, at least."

Nick gave a short laugh. "Yeah. I guess you were out of luck, being paired with Sam. At least we all got to reconnect, though. I missed seeing them. Well, seeing all of you."

"And you..." She didn't want to ask, but she had to know. Hannah might be through with Nick, but was he really through with her? "I mean, I thought if any couple stood a chance, it would be you and Hannah. You guys were such a great match in high school."

Nick shrugged, looking down. "We were, but high school feels like a lifetime ago. I thought of that during Ethan's speech, actually, when he said how dumb high school boys are."

"Oh?"

"Yeah. I was dumb, ending things with Hannah the way I did."

"Oh." Alex's heart sank. "So you wish you'd stayed with her?" She shouldn't have asked, after all. She didn't need to be here, standing in the garden with Nick, listening to how he felt about Hannah. Still, it was good to have all the information before she got even more carried away.

"No, no, nothing like that. I just... I mean, she said to me at the time that I should have kept things going just a few weeks more, and I probably should have. I thought I was doing the right thing, not stringing her along, but I shouldn't have ended it right before graduation. Or maybe I should have ended things sooner, I don't know. I just felt bad about it afterwards. I was checked out of the relationship before she was, so it was easy enough for me to end things, but I think I blindsided her."

Nick had never been so open with Alex before. She wondered if Hannah knew half of this.

"Well, for what it's worth," Alex told him, "I think she's done okay for herself."

Nick grinned. "Yeah, she seems pretty happy."

Now was her chance. Alex took a deep breath, unable to believe she was even thinking about saying it. Then, without giving herself a chance to second guess her words, she blurted out, "Actually, she really must have moved on. She even said she could see us as a couple."

Nick was completely still for a moment. "Us?"

"Yeah, you and me." She could laugh it off now and no harm would be done. "I don't know, she gets these ideas in her head, I guess. She said she thought there was a spark."

It was out there. Nick could laugh it off as well, and they could pretend the moment meant absolutely nothing, even if she would die of embarrassment a little every time she thought of it. Or...

"And what did you say to that?" Nick had moved a little closer now and he was facing her dead-on. She could feel his breath on her forehead. She shivered, even though it wasn't cold.

"I said..." Alex paused. "I asked her how she'd feel if that was the case."

"And she said..."

"She said she'd be happy for us."

"She's a good friend." He had moved even closer now. Alex's instinct was to take a step back, but she fought it. She didn't want to stop whatever was happening here.

"She is."

And then he was closer still, pulling her in tight, kissing her. She kissed him back, never wanting this moment to end.

When they finally drew back for breath, they were both smiling. "I guess she might have known what she was talking about, then," Alex said. "Felt like a spark to me."

"Let's check," Nick said, pulling her back in.

They kissed for what felt like forever, there in the quiet corner of the garden. Finally, Alex drew back. "We really should get back," she sighed. "They'll probably be looking for us."

"I guess." He looked at her. "You should fix your lipstick up."

Alex laughed, reaching up to rub his mouth. "You too."

They made their way back to the dance floor, where their friends were now doing a terrible approximation of the Zorba.

"You're back!" Freya exclaimed. "You disappeared in the middle of the bridal waltz!"

"Sorry, we were just... looking around the garden. Beautiful spot," Alex said to Ethan, trying not to sound breathless.

"Looking around the garden, eh?" Hannah looked like she was barely stopping short of wiggling her eyebrows up and down like a cartoon supervillain. "Do any... hoeing? Pull up any roots?"

Freya frowned, looking from Hannah to Alex and back again. "I'm missing something here."

Alex couldn't control the laugh that came out. Obviously sensing that they were busted, Nick moved closer and put his arm around her waist.

"Oh... *Oh!*" Freya exclaimed, staring at them. Ethan looked similarly mystified, and their reactions struck Alex like something out of a sitcom. Sam didn't look surprised at all, so either Hannah had filled him in during their dance, or he'd also caught on to something between Alex and Nick.

"Um, yeah," Alex laughed, blushing. "It was a good look around the garden."

"Obviously," Ethan muttered, still looking shell-shocked.

"Come here, girls. Bridesmaid conference." Freya grabbed Hannah and Alex by the wrists and dragged them off the dance floor. "When did this happen and why am I the last to know?"

"We just kissed for the first time," Alex said, holding her hands up in a gesture of innocence. "There's nothing really to tell yet."

"But.. you and *Nick?* Hannah's Nick?"

"He hasn't been my Nick for a while now," Hannah said. "I'm fine with it. Honestly!" she added when Freya looked at her sceptically.

"Well..." Freya was over her confusion now and onto excitement. "Did you talk about the future? Are you guys on the same page? Is our marriage pact going to claim another victim?"

"Slow down! No, we didn't talk about the future. Basically, I told him Hannah had given us her blessing, and..."

"And he didn't wait but a minute before sticking his tongue down your throat," Hannah said dramatically.

"Hannah! Were you watching us?"

"No! You mean that's actually how it happened? Jeez, I knew he was waiting to make a move, but..."

"I mean, I wouldn't put it the way you did –"

"Oh, honestly, Alex, it's fine. It's fine! I wouldn't have told you that if it wasn't. You know I'm not afraid of speaking my mind," Hannah said. "But since this whole thing is basically thanks to me, I do demand first bridesmaid privileges at your wedding, and if you ever have a baby girl with him, you can name it Hannah." She paused. "If it's a boy, you can name it Hannoh."

"What a lovely name."

"Indeed."

"I get some credit here," Freya protested. "It was my sad dumping that led to us even talking about the marriage pact at all."

"The fact that you chose a terrible boyfriend does not give you child-naming rights here."

"I mean, the twenty-year pact *was* my idea in the first place," Alex pointed out. "I guess some of the credit might go to me."

"You can't be your own first bridesmaid."

"I feel like this 'wedding and kids' argument could wait until we've, you know, gone on a date or something."

"I suppose it could," Hannah agreed.

"It could also wait until I'm not in a wedding dress. Isn't the attention supposed to be on me for one day?"

"Sorry, Freya," Alex laughed, knowing her friend didn't really mind.

"Aren't you curious about what the guys are talking about?" Hannah asked, peering over at the dance floor. "I can't imagine they're like 'whoa mate, did she use tongue?'"

"'Did the earth move?'" Freya giggled.

"'Can I be your Best Man?'" Alex intoned, and they all cracked up.

"Anyway, you said you just kissed for the first time, but you didn't," Hannah added.

"What?" Alex was confused. "I'm pretty sure we did, in fact, just kiss."

"Yeah, but not for the first time." When her friends continued to look confused, Hannah said, "Spin the bottle, remember?"

"Oh, God. God! I forgot about that!" Alex said, laughing. "You're right, Hannah. We actually had our first kiss twenty-one years ago, right in front of you. You and half the people at that party." She paused. "I don't know how I forgot. You looked like you were going to murder us both."

Hannah shook her head, mock-sadly. "I should have known then that it was all over for me."

Ethan came up to them then. "I hate to interrupt the gossip circle, but we're about to cut the cake, wifey."

"Oh, fine. My bridal duties will never end," Freya laughed, taking Ethan's hand as they walked off together.

Hannah and Alex trailed after. "Seriously, though, thank you," Alex said to Hannah. "If you hadn't given us your blessing, this never would have happened. I don't even know if it will lead anywhere, but it's nice to have a shot."

"Don't mention it," Hannah said, uncharacteristically seriously. "I'm happy for you guys, I really am. Just one favour."

"What's that?"

"I don't need to hear a *word* about your sex life. Not one word. It's too bloody weird."

"Done," Alex laughed, and the two friends shared a quick hug.

Chapter 48: 1999

"It's graduation day!"

Hannah groaned as her mum came in and started opening the blinds. "Mum," she complained. "I'm seventeen, not seven. I can open my own blinds."

"Humour me," her mother replied briskly. "I used to help you get ready for school every day when you first started. This is my last chance to do so."

Hannah laughed for the first time all week. Graduation aside, she knew her mother was making a special effort because Hannah had been moping ever since the break-up. It was nice to have a little extra attention. "Okay, okay. You can look after me."

"Good, because I made you a special breakfast, too."

"You really have gone all out!"

Her mother smiled as she bent down and kissed Hannah on the cheek. "Anything for my little graduate."

Hannah's only brother, Isaac, had never finished high school, leaving school to start an apprenticeship at the end of Year 10. Even if Hannah wasn't really in the right frame of mind for her graduation day, she knew how important it was to her mum. She would grin and bear it. After today she could sleep in for as long as she wanted – until her mum made her get a job, anyway.

Graduation day was different for Freya and Alex, Hannah knew. They both planned to go to Uni the following year, if they got the marks – which they would – so they were graduating with a purpose. Hannah's only purpose right now was to get away from school so she could stop seeing Nick every day.

Their school day was an abbreviated one. The Year 12s finished weeks before the rest of the school, so the day was really all about them. They would have morning 'classes', which would mostly be class parties and mass signings of each other's shirts and signature bears. They would then have a big school assembly to farewell the Year 12s before they finished school at midday. Half the kids were heading straight down the coast to Schoolies, and most others were having house parties to finish off the school year. Hannah would normally have been a part of all of that but with everything that was happening she, Freya and Alex had agreed to go for a lowkey lunch together, along with some of their other girlfriends. It wasn't the stellar celebration Hannah had always expected on her graduation day, but at least she was getting out of bed. After Nick had dumped her so unceremoniously, it was all she could do not to hide under her covers. He really had exceptionally shitty timing.

There was one bright spot. Since Schoolies was off, Freya and Alex had coaxed her into coming down to Sydney with them for a girls' week. She was looking forward to spending a week celebrating, eating and drinking her way around the city. She might even find a cute guy who would make her forget about Nick completely.

"Hey, Hannah."

Oh, speak of the devil. Hannah glared at Nick. "What are you doing, Nick?"

Her ex looked shy and awkward, two things that wouldn't normally describe Nick. "I was just coming up to say hi, and congratulations. You're graduating!"

"Yeah, it's a really special day," she snapped, not in the mood to be particularly friendly to him. "Congratulations to you, I guess. I'm sure you'll enjoy celebrating your way through Schoolies."

"Um, speaking of Schoolies, my dad gave your mum a cheque..."

"Yeah, she got it. Thanks."

"Look, Hannah, I'm sorry again. I know my timing wasn't good, but..."

"But you didn't want to be with me anymore and you couldn't possibly fake it," Hannah sighed. "I know, I know." She had tried to come to terms with Nick's way of thinking, but it was still too raw. She could kind of see his point – would she have really wanted him to string her along for an extra few weeks, just so he didn't ruin graduation? But that was no excuse for hurting her the way he had at what was supposed to be a special time in her life. She wasn't sure if she'd ever get over that.

"Well," Nick sighed. "All the best, I guess. Good luck next year."

"Yep. You too."

As he walked away, Hannah sighed with relief. Having to talk to Nick had been awkward, but at least it was over now.

———— ⟨∞⟩ ————

"CAN YOU BELIEVE WE'VE graduated?"

The three girls were at lunch and they'd spent most of their time so far making the same basic statement. No, none of them could believe they'd graduated. Yes, they all thought the concept of waking up without having to go to school every day was a strange one. Yes, they were all excited about the future. Yes, it was scary, too.

"I'm so done with school. I'm not reading or writing anything for at least six months," Hannah said.

"Reading's fun," Freya protested, and the other two laughed.

"Even you have to agree, we all deserve a brain break. We've just finished twelve years of schooling. *Twelve years!*"

"My dad said something interesting last night," Alex said. "He pointed out that we may never work in one job for as long as twelve years. This might be the longest thing we ever do."

"I bloody hope so!"

"I'm so excited about Sydney," Freya said. "I'm so glad we decided to do it."

"I'm just happy not to have to see Nick ever again," Hannah announced.

"And I'm happy not to have to see Sam again."

Freya laughed. "Well, I don't mind seeing any of them, but I'm sure Ethan's happy never to have to see *me* again."

"I guess that's the end of the Twenty-Year Pact," Hannah said, and they all laughed.

"I'd say that's a pretty safe bet," Alex agreed. "The Twenty-Year Pact that didn't even last one year. Honestly, it was the dumbest idea. What was I thinking?"

Chapter 49: 2020

"**I** have something to tell you guys, and no, I'm not pregnant," Freya said.

It was ten days since the wedding, and Freya was just back from her honeymoon. The three of them were having dinner at Alex's place, Baxter curled up on her lap. They had plenty to fill each other in on after over a week apart.

"You guys know about the book I wrote."

Hannah and Alex nodded. They had been her first two proof-readers, as promised, and they had both found the book genuinely well-written and engaging. They'd given a few edits and suggestions for improvements, but they both thought the book had potential to be a hit.

"I've found a publisher. A small one," Freya added hastily. "It's not going to be hitting the bestseller list or anything like that. But I'm going to be published!"

"That's amazing!" Alex cried. "Well done!"

"Seriously, Freya, congratulations. You're a star!"

Freya laughed. "I don't know about a star, but it was a nice email to get, that's for sure." She had received the affirmative email the day after coming back from their honeymoon, which was perfect timing. After a week away, reality had felt like something harsh to come back to, even if reality now involved being married to the man of her dreams. Getting the email offering her a contract had made everything better. She and Ethan had celebrated that night and she'd told her family the news the next day, but she had decided to wait until she saw her friends in person to tell them.

"Do you get an advance or something?"

"When does it come out?"

"No advance, but I get a percentage of sales. I honestly don't care about the money," Freya said, meaning it. She just wanted to see her name in print – and, hopefully, to encourage a kid or two to pick up a book when they otherwise might not have. "It's coming out next June."

"That's so exciting! Oh, I can't believe it! Everything's coming up Freya lately."

"And what about you?" Freya asked Alex. "I know I'm not the only one with stories to tell." Alex had told them over text that she and Nick were going out on their first official date three nights after the wedding, but she had insisted on waiting until they caught up before giving them any details.

Alex couldn't fight the smile that came over her face. "Oh, it was amazing," she said dreamily. "We played putt-putt and then went out to dinner."

"Putt-putt? That's cute."

"It was! I've never done anything like that on a first date before. It gave us a chance to talk but without the pressure of being across a table, you know? Plus, I won."

Freya and Hannah laughed. Leave it to Alex to zero in on the truly important details.

"So then we went to dinner and afterwards we just strolled along through the city and chatted. It was really nice. He's so easy to talk to."

Freya had the feeling that Alex was trying to hold back some of her enthusiasm. Her eyes were shining as she talked about the night, so "it was really nice" seemed like a bit of an understatement. She didn't push her friend, though. Even though Hannah seemed completely fine with Alex's developing relationship, it had to be a little awkward for both of them.

"Did you...?" Hannah asked, and Alex raised her eyebrows.

"I thought you didn't want to know anything about that?"

"I don't want any details whatsoever. I just want to know... *if*."

"Well, no. We haven't," Alex said, and Freya could tell she was telling the truth. "We've only been on one date, after all."

"Your point being?"

The three women laughed. "Speaking of which, Hannah," Freya said, "are you still swearing off men?"

Hannah shrugged. "Not really. I'm not desperately seeking one, either, but I'm open to the idea of meeting someone, now." She paused. "Why? Do you know someone?"

"That wasn't why I was asking, but actually, Ethan *does* have a single friend who I met at the wedding who's pretty nice. He's forty, works with Ethan and he's a fitness freak, too."

"So he's an accountant?"

"Don't look like that. My *husband* is an accountant, re-member."

"Yeah, but he's not... accountant-y."

"Well, maybe Scott won't be accountant-y, either."

"Sounds like he has potential. I may deign to break my vow of chastity for him," Hannah said, her voice filled with mock dignity.

Freya smiled. She knew it was possible that nothing whatsoever would come of Hannah's date with Scott, if it even happened, but she was glad Hannah was at least willing to put herself out there again. She had gone from sleeping with guys easily to completely closing herself off to the idea of love. It was promising to see her striking a healthy balance between the two.

"Actually, I wanted to thank you, Hannah," Alex said. "I've been doing what you told me to do."

"Like everyone always should! What did I tell you to do, anyway?"

"You told me to speak to myself the way I speak to my friends."

"That's good advice," Freya said, knowing Alex's tendency to be excessively hard on herself.

"It's really helped, honestly," Alex said. "It's taken some time, but I think I've got into the habit now. Is that what you do?"

"Please. My inner voice is much nicer to me than I ever am to the two of you."

ALEX HADN'T SHARED it with the girls, but her second date with Nick was happening the following night. She knew her friends would be nothing but encouraging about the whole thing, but the relationship – if you could call it that, and she figured you probably couldn't – was new enough that she wanted to keep it to herself for a little bit longer.

This date was dinner and a movie, and she hummed as she got ready. She took care to tidy up her bedroom a little more nicely than usual. It didn't mean anything, but it was good to be prepared, just in case.

Dinner went well, the two of them never running out of things to talk about. Going out with Nick was both fresh and familiar, a combination she loved. Alex had never been one for dating, always hating the awkward small talk and forced nature of a first meeting. After all, how many people did you meet and immediately sit down with for two hours to talk about yourself? It was like a job interview, but you were trying to convince someone that you were good enough to spend their entire life with. It was no wonder the online thing had never worked out for her.

With Nick, though, there was the steady familiarity of chatting to an old friend, mixed with the butterflies of excitement that came from falling for someone. And she was falling for him, she had to admit. She could see herself being deeply in love with this man, very quickly.

If she wasn't already.

It was so unlike Alex, she nearly laughed out loud.

After the movie they walked along the street, side by side, beside the Brisbane River. "It's so pretty here," Alex murmured.

"A perfect night," Nick agreed, and she could tell he wasn't just talking about the weather.

They walked along for a few minutes before, and then Alex gestured to a park bench under a tree. "Want to sit for a while?"

"Sure," he agreed, sitting on the bench and pulling her closer to him. They kissed, gently, and she felt her stomach flip upside down again. "You may just be the perfect guy," she whispered as she pulled away.

"And I may be falling in love with you."

"You what?" She pulled back, startled, searching his eyes. She'd never had a guy say those words to her so quickly before. It was only their second date!

"I'm sorry," he said, looking embarrassed. "I know that's really soon. I'm just... I've been interested for a while, and now that we're actually together, it feels..."

"Right," she agreed, nodding. "It feels really right."

"So... you're not going to run away?"

"No," Alex laughed. "Definitely not." She leaned in for another kiss, then looked down at her lap so she didn't have to face him as she said her next words. "Because I might be falling in love with you right back."

If his words had shocked her, her own floored her. She had only ever said "I love you" to two men before. True, "I'm falling in love with you" wasn't *exactly* the same thing, but it was basically there. And all on the second date. What would the third date bring, an elopement?

The atmosphere felt thicker, more serious, all of a sudden. She thought of ways to break the silence. "So," she finally said, "now that we've confessed our undying love to each other, do you think you might like to come back to my place?"

ALEX OPENED THE DOOR to her house, nearly getting knocked over by the dog as she walked in. "Meet Baxter," she laughed to Nick, who was walking in behind her. "He's a good guard dog."

"I can see that," said Nick, reaching down to pat the little dog, who was smothering him in kisses.

"Yep. No intruder can possibly walk in without getting licked to death."

"I love it. I'm a dog person myself," he said, which she already knew, "but I can't have one in my place. I'd love to, though."

Once the dog was finally settled, Alex got them each a cup of tea and sat down on her couch. "Come join me," she said, passing Nick his tea.

"Nice place."

"Yeah, it's not super fancy like yours, but I'm happy here. I've been here two years now."

"Rental?" he asked, and she nodded. It was so strange how you could go from telling someone you were falling in love with them to discussing your rental situation in just over an hour.

Nick took a sip of his tea, then put his cup down on the coffee table beside the couch. "I believe we were in the middle of something back at Southbank," he murmured, moving back in for a kiss.

Their kisses grew more urgent. Alex wrapped her arms tightly around him. She never wanted to let him go but at the same time, she was terrified. She had so much to lose. Aside from the alarming speed at which she was falling for Nick, there were friendships to consider. What would happen to the group of them if she and Nick didn't make it? Who was to say they even had the chemistry to make this work?

But then Nick started kissing his way down her body, moving his hands all over her, and she realised that their chemistry was the last thing she had to worry about.

Alex had been an overthinker for as long as she could remember, but right then, she decided it was time to stop thinking entirely, and to just let things happen.

WHEN THE GIRLS MESSAGED the next day, Alex mentioned that she and Nick had been out the night before. She didn't mention that he was still snoring in her bed, or that they had told each other they were falling in love. She would respect Hannah's wishes and tell her as little as possible about their sex life, but it was more than just that. For the first time, Alex found herself not wanting to share all the details of her personal life with her friends. She wanted to keep it a special secret, between herself and Nick. It was a nice feeling.

She laughed when she got Hannah's next message.

Hannah: Of course, you're missing the really important part of you two getting together.

Alex: Oh? And what's that?

Hannah: You're going to need to take a trip to the tattoo parlour.

2021: Epilogue

Three months after the wedding, the friends gathered for another of their long Sunday lunches. It was a beautiful day with sunshine and a light breeze, Freya's favourite kind of day. It was all the better because after lunch, they were going to the tattoo parlour. Nick and Alex had agreed – less reluctantly than they might have expected – to get their matching Twenty Year tattoos, as well. "That's a big commitment," Freya had said to Alex privately, once she heard the news. "It's basically saying you think you and Nick will be together forever."

Alex had just shrugged, uncharacteristically relaxed about the whole thing. "I think we will be," she said simply.

"Are you all excited about the big day?" Hannah asked Alex now. "Tattoo time! Breaking in your virgin skin."

"Stop," Alex laughed. "I'm nervous enough already." She poked Nick with her elbow. "This one's fine. He's got so much ink on him you won't even notice one more."

"Where are you getting them?" Sam asked.

"Well, we're thinking the same as Freya and Ethan," Nick replied. "We thought we might as well keep with the theme and I don't really want everyone seeing mine, either."

"Oh, good. It means we get to see your perfectly chiselled backside," Hannah teased. It was the sort of comment that could have been awkward, given their history, but somehow it worked. The past really was the past, after all.

"You two should get them, to complete the set," Freya said, gesturing at Sam and Hannah.

"Yes, to commemorate my marriage to Hannah," Sam said, deadpan.

"Yeah, you might not have noticed, Frey, but things didn't exactly work out for us with this whole marriage pact thing."

"Didn't it, though?" Freya asked, and the others fell silent, acknowledging the truth of her words.

"Maybe I should," Hannah said suddenly.

"What? Han, I was joking..."

"I know, but why not? After all, this whole twenty-year pact led to my two best friends finding the loves of their life. It led to me making this amazing group of friends again. Why can't I get a tattoo to celebrate that? It's not like it would be my first."

"Then I'd be the only one without one," Sam protested.

"You get one, too! Same reasons as me, and after all, you did get engaged twenty years after we made the pact. It just didn't happen to be to one of the girls you made the pact with." Hannah paused. "Or any girl."

Sam thought for a moment. "I mean, I guess I could."

"Sam! You can't!" Freya cried. "Don't you need to check with, you know, your *husband?*" Richie had been invited to lunch, as he was to all their get-togethers nowadays, but he had to work.

"Let me call him. If he's fine with it, I'll do it." Sam grabbed his phone and got up from the table.

"You guys are really nuts," Ethan said to Hannah, laughing. "There's no way in hell I'd be getting this tattoo if not for wifey here making me."

Freya nudged him. "They were your idea in the first place, you might recall."

Sam returned a moment later. "Okay, he's down with it. He thinks I'm weird, but he said I can do whatever I want. So... want to see if your man Claw can fit us in for two more people?"

"Talon."

"Whatever."

Hannah and Sam looked at each other for a long moment, seemingly both waiting for the other to blink first. Finally, Hannah shrugged. "Okay, screw it. I'm game. I'll call up now," she said, grabbing the phone.

She giggled on her end of the phone for a while, and when she hung up, she victoriously announced, "We're in! We have to go a bit later than the other two, but Talon said he can fit us in."

Her friends exchanged knowing looks around the table.

"What?" Hannah demanded.

"I knew I sensed a little spark between you and the tattoo guy last time," Alex said smugly. "Look at you. You're blushing!"

"I am not! I don't *blush!*"

Freya sighed heavily. "I guess that's it for Scott the Accountant. I had such high hopes. You'll have to break it to him, E. I can't bear to do it."

"That's not the worst of it," Ethan grumbled. "If she and this Talon guy really do get together, then for the rest of our lives the three of us will know that he's seen our arses."

Hannah ignored their jibes, instead looking over at Alex and Nick. "Should we give it to them now?"

"Nice way to change the subject, Han."

"Give us what?" Alex asked, looking suspicious.

Freya laughed, reaching into her bag. "We made you something." She pulled out a large photo frame, in which they'd made a certificate. "So, we got you this to commemorate your tattoo day, a day you'll never forget. We couldn't figure out what to get you..."

"Until we were making fun of you behind your backs one day," Hannah burst in.

Freya frowned at her. "I wouldn't word it exactly like that..."

"Well, I would. Anyway, I said 'I wonder what the collective noun for geeks is?'"

"So we had a look online, and we brainstormed some ideas... and..." Freya turned the frame around so Alex and Nick could see the certificate they'd made. The couple stared at the frame, then burst out laughing.

The certificate read "In honour of Tattoo Day for Alexandra and Nicholas – our own Gigabyte of Geeks!"

"Gigabyte of Geeks," Nick said, laughing. "I love it!"

"Me, too. But technically, being that there's only two of us, we wouldn't get a collective–"

Alex's voice was drowned out by the rest of them laughing and booing her. "We don't need to take this to a whole other level of geek," Nick said, patting her on the head. Alex just laughed and leaned closer to him.

"Here," Freya said, reaching into her bag for a second frame. "We made you two, so you can each display one proudly on your mantles."

She couldn't miss the look Alex and Nick exchanged.

"What?" Freya demanded. "What's going on?"

"Well..." Alex hesitated. "We weren't going to tell you until it was all finalised, but there's a chance we'll only have one mantle between us, actually. My lease is up at the end of next month, and Nick has an awfully big place for just one person..."

"Oh! Yay!" Hannah cried. "You're moving in together? Seriously?" She shook her head. "Freya getting engaged after five minutes, and Alex and Nick shacking up after three months together. Suddenly I'm the cautious, sensible one."

They all laughed, and Hannah frowned. "Not sure I love *that* reaction."

"You're very cautious and sensible," Freya assured her. She paused. "Actually, this is as good a time as any. I have an announcement."

A momentary silence followed her words.

Freya tried again. "I have an announcement."

Another pause.

"Hannah!" Freya said, laughing. "You missed your cue!"

Hannah looked around, confused. "What?"

"You missed your cue *twice*."

"I – what cue?"

"I said the magic words," Freya said, a smile forming across her face. Ethan had a big, goofy smile to match.

Alex caught on then, clapping her hands over her mouth. "You don't mean–?!"

"I'll try it again. *I have an announcement.*"

This time Hannah and Alex both launched in at the same time. "You're pregnant!" they cried, falling over themselves laughing.

"Yes!" Freya and Ethan responded, equally loudly. Ethan reached into his pocket and pulled out a sonogram image.

"Oh my God, you guys! How far along are you?"

"Three months. It's a honeymoon baby." It was also a boy, but she didn't share that just yet. They would, in time, but for now they would keep it to themselves. She and Ethan both would have been happy with a healthy baby regardless of the sex, but they were pretty delighted by the idea of a little boy running around their backyard. Freya hoped he would look just like his dad. She couldn't believe how much she loved him already, before he was even born.

"Forget honeymoon baby! We're going to have a little *Pact* baby!"

The six old friends all jumped up, sharing hugs and kisses of excitement and congratulations. Freya smiled over at Ethan, unable to believe their luck. They had been quietly trying for a baby since before the wedding, but she had kept telling him – and herself – that it wasn't going to lead anywhere. She was turning thirty-nine this year, after all. There were no guarantees. It didn't matter, anyway, she had said. If they had each other, they had the world. They didn't need a baby to complete their family.

But it was awfully nice that they were having one.

"Oh, I know! You should give it the middle name Pact, since none of this would have happened if not for the Pact," Hannah said triumphantly.

Ethan frowned. "Yes, or we could *not* do that."

"Oh, come on, Freya. You'll be fun, won't you? It's just a *middle* name."

"Well, never say never."

"Freya!" Ethan exclaimed.

Freya laughed. "I'm not saying we'll definitely do it. I'm just saying, stranger things have happened." She smiled at her husband, and then looked around the table at their group of friends. She looked at Sam, so loved up with his husband. At Alex and Nick, snuggling together in their seats. At Hannah, able to stand on her own two feet, but also finally open to the idea of love.

At the group of people she had thought would never be together again.

"Stranger things happen all the time."

ACKNOWLEDGEMENTS

I always start off by thanking my sister and fellow author, Gemma Johns, and this book is no exception. Gemma is my first reader and my biggest champion. It's also amazing to have someone close to share the highs and lows of writing with, and to help each other out with all our writing-related questions. Thank you, Gemma!

Thank you also to my other proof-readers, Kylie Smith and Rachael Young. As well as being a huge support to me all the time, they eagerly agreed to read the book and not only did they catch some mistakes, but they also provided their entire inner monologue over email. Thanks ladies, the book is definitely better for it!

I also owe a huge thank you to the rest of my family – my parents, Sandra and Noel, and my sister Melanie, as well as my extended family. They're always eager to hear about my writing adventures and they're the first in line to buy my books. Mum, I hope you enjoyed the reduced swearing in this one!

Thanks to the rest of my friends for your support, ideas and encouragement, and for letting me talk incessantly about my writing. Janelle, thanks for the collective nouns chat over the photocopier at work, which helped to inspire one of my favourite scenes in the book!

Thanks also goes to Kylie Sek of Cover Culture, for her amazing work on the cover. When I asked for a romantic cover with a nineties feel, I couldn't imagine how she'd pull it off, but she certainly delivered! Thanks Kylie, I love it!

Of course, the biggest thank you goes to my readers, especially those who have reached out after reading my books – it means so much to talk to people who have read my work! If you would like to let me know your thoughts about "The Twenty-Year Pact", I can be found @larissajohnsauthor on both Instagram and Facebook.

Did you love *The Twenty-Year Pact*? Then you should read *Without Warning* by Larissa Johns!

On an ordinary Tuesday morning a gunman bursts into a coffee shop at a busy shopping centre, changing the customers' lives forever.

Paula, a busy mum, was just stopping off for a milkshake with her 8-year-old son.

Fiona had decided to finally step out of the house after a personal tragedy, only to find herself once again in the wrong place at the wrong time.

University student Destiny was looking forward to finally having her first date with her friend Luke.

Rosie was meeting her twin sister, Betty, only to discover that they both had a life-changing secret to share.

In the aftermath of the tragedy, the four women rebuild their lives.

Without Warning is a story about finding yourself again, even after the darkest of days.

About the Author

Larissa Johns has been working as a primary school teacher for over ten years, but she has never forgotten her love of writing. Her lifelong dreams were realised when her first novel, *Having It All,* was published in 2020, followed six months later by *Without Warning. The Twenty-Year Pact* is her third novel.

When she's not writing - or teaching - Larissa spends her time reading, watching far too many movies, drinking tea and binge-watching sitcoms on repeat. She appreciates any sitcom recommendations you might have.

Larissa lives in Brisbane, Australia, with her spoilt cavoodle, Indiana Johns.